UNHAUNTED

A WHITE CROW MYSTERY

TRISHA SLAY

Published by Lost Hollow Press | Dahlonega, GA

www.losthollowpress.com

Library of Congress Cataloging-in-Publications Data is available upon request.

ISBN 978-1-947592-00-1

Book Cover | Design for Writers

For TY
Who made California dreaming my reality.

1
———

Now

Chaos. Everything around me is chaos.

Voices call out rapid-fire orders and questions, each voice getting louder and more insistent. Blue and red lights flash in erratic rotation, illuminating a line of redwood trees standing as silent witnesses along the side of the road. Boots crunch over broken glass close to my head. A stranger's face appears in my line of vision.

"Hey, there. Can you hear me? How are you doing?"

Stupid. How does he think I'm doing? Can't he see I'm broken and bleeding on a bed of asphalt?

"Can you hear me? What's your name? Tell me your name." His voice gets louder as he kneels next to me and shines a bright light in my face. I close my eyes.

"Her name is Asha," a calm, quiet voice says. "Stop yelling at her."

I know that voice. Relief washes over me. She's alive! I have not killed her. But when I try to turn my head, to search for her, to see if she's injured, terrible pain shoots through my body. An involuntary scream erupts from my core. The loud man grasps both sides of my head.

"No, Asha. Don't move." Over his shoulder he yells, "I need some help over here! Bring the board."

Again I close my eyes, the remnants of my scream still gurgling in my throat. The pain is so intense, it's ridiculous. Is it possible to survive this much pain?

Behind closed lids I search frantically for another light, a beautiful light that will end this nightmare. I listen to the night sounds, barely audible below the man's voice, straining to hear a chord of something beyond simple music. All I hear is the cacophony of the accident scene. I will myself to separate from this battered body as I've seen others break free. But nothing happens. None of the classic signs appear.

This is not my exit scene. The realization comes with mixed emotions.

The man is still shouting to someone, barking out orders, demanding faster assistance.

Don't worry, mister, I think. *I'm not dying.*

I'm trapped here. Trapped in this broken body. Trapped in this hideous pain. There isn't going to be any easy escape from this awful mess I've created.

How could I have been so stupid?

2

———

Before

I don't know when my mother lost her ability to communicate with the dead. But I remember the exact moment when I first suspected the great Xia Celeste had become a psychic fraud. It was not a happy revelation. Growing up as the daughter of a famous spirit medium didn't translate into anything remotely resembling a normal childhood. On the other hand, her gift for giving victims a voice paid the bills. Without her reputation as a dazzling psychic detective, we'd be homeless and hungry within a few months.

That's why I had to do it. I had to protect her.

The first hint of the terrible events that would change everything came in the form of a police vehicle parked beside our front door. Dance practice was cancelled that day, so I was home from school earlier than usual. The black and white sedan stopped me in my tracks. Visits from the police were not an uncommon occurrence in our household, but my feet itched to backpedal toward the San Jose Municipal Rose Garden where I could finish my algebra homework wrapped in the bloom and scent of living things.

Puberty had swept in like a tsunami two years earlier, bringing with it a new and terrible sensitivity to my mother's private consultations with the police.

I'm used to ghosts; I was raised among spirits. But I'll never get used to victims.

Pressing my hand to the K-9 unit lettering on the fender of the Palo Alto police cruiser, I took three measured breaths and focused on calming my skittish heart. Then I counted backward from ten, slowly, as a commercial jet sliced through the perfect bowl of turquoise sky above my head. The afternoon sun painted everything with a buttery light. Blue scrub jays and a variety of mottled brown sparrows chittered and sang around the birdfeeders in our small community of townhomes. It was a picture perfect day. It was definitely not the sort of day for a Hollywood ghost story. Then again, Hollywood usually gets it wrong and every day of my life is a freaking ghost story.

I could have walked away. Mother didn't expect me home from school for another hour. Maybe I should have walked away. Instead, I forced my feet to shuffle closer to the front door. I knew this police vehicle. This wasn't just any officer; this was my mother's cousin, Detective LaShawna Simmons. And if LaShawna was here, it was a safe bet her partner Kota had also come to visit. I loved LaShawna; she was our only family in this part of the world, and Kota was my favorite police officer on the planet. I never missed an opportunity to visit with either of them, even if they were here on official business.

When I opened the gate and caught sight of our tiny front porch, I stopped again. The front door was slightly ajar, which should have made it easy to slip in quietly. But there was an unnatural shadow around the door—a roiling, boiling sort of gloom. I clenched my teeth. Nothing about this visit was going to be easy.

Another deep breath was required before I could force myself to move forward and ease the door back so I could slip through. Kota was five feet from the threshold, stretched out in his down position. His beautiful black face swiveled toward me, one ear twitching in recognition before he looked back at the far corner of our living room. Anyone unfamiliar with a K-9 police officer might think Kota was relaxing, but I could see the bunched muscles under his tan fur and the tension in his perfectly still tail.

This was not a happy dog.

This was not a happy visit.

Moving in triple slow motion, I knelt next to him and buried my fingers in the thick ruff of fur at his neck. Kota continued to monitor one corner of the living room. I watched the drama unfolding in the open kitchen. Both of us were on alert, still and tense, allies in a strange land.

LaShawna stood with one hip pressed against the kitchen counter clutching a glass of iced tea in both hands. Her eyes were ringed with dark circles, and her lips were pressed together in a tight line. Her posture indicated she was restraining herself from getting too close to the chair where my mother sat hunched over a glossy photograph. I focused on the turquoise running shoe in Mother's left hand and ignored the flickering shadow in the corner of the living room Kota was watching with fierce concentration.

Promise me, Asha. My father's voice echoed in my memory. *Stay out of your mother's crazy crusades. Promise you won't let her pull you in.*

The shadow in the living room throbbed with wild, desperate tension.

Mother heaved a tremendous sigh and pressed her bejeweled right hand to her heart.

"Nothing. I'm getting nothing." She twisted in her chair to look up at our visitor with a look of benign peace plastered on her face. LaShawna's eyes narrowed to slits and her nostrils flared, but she remained silent. "Don't look at me like that, Shaw. This is good news. I don't think this girl is dead. She's probably hiding out with a boyfriend or something."

A molten wave of foreign emotions flooded my senses – shock followed by white hot anger and sickening panic caused my gut to twist. Without thinking, I gasped and clutched my stomach.

LaShawna's topaz eyes flicked over me briefly before turning back toward my mother. "This girl has a name. Her name is Ivy Brennan." Jaw clenched, she was grinding out each word. "This girl is an honor student. A star athlete. A devoted sister. In the past year she has logged hundreds of volunteer hours with my youth league. She has no history of trouble. No red flags!" She turned and thumped her fist on our kitchen counter.

"She's the same age as Asha," she finished quietly.

"Ivy," my mother repeated the name with a bemused expression. "I used to go to school with a girl named Ivy. We called her Poison Ivy. Total wild child."

LaShawna pressed her lips back into a tight line and glared at my mother, frustration making her eyes unnaturally wide.

"No red flags?" Xia pressed on, blithely ignoring the warning signs in her cousin's expression. "This girl's mother was a junkie, wasn't she? Didn't Mommy die of a drug overdose when the kid was eight? I call that a big old red flag, Shaw."

My focus slipped toward the shadow. Images flickered rapidly at the center of the writhing darkness – feet jogging on wet asphalt, white roses draped over a closed casket, a toddler hugging a dirty yellow teddy bear. The living room wall behind the shadow seemed to grow transparent and, like a hologram projection inside tinted glass, a blonde girl around my age appeared. She was sitting on a window seat, knees tucked inside her Palo Alto Vikings sweatshirt while tears streamed down her pale, freckled cheeks. An electric current rippled through my body, causing me to flinch and suck in air.

In the projection, the girl looked up. Her pale blue eyes widened. "You see me?" she asked. The pulsing, shadowy version of her spirit suddenly appeared next to my right shoulder, surging with emotion. I shuddered again and leaned away from the chaotic apparition, touching my forehead to Kota's neck while my mother said something about the erratic nature of all teenage girls.

"You hear me!" Ivy exclaimed while LaShawna begged my mother to try again.

Promise me, Asha.

I'd made a promise to my father nearly a year ago, right before he disappeared from our lives. The only way to keep that promise was to run away now, run away into the sunlight and bird chatter outside and keep running.

Instead, I peeked up toward the kitchen, silently begging my mother to get control of this mess. Holding the running shoe in both hands, she took a deep breath, straightened her spine and closed her eyes. My hopes lifted.

"I get the sense of water," my mother said after several

tense seconds. Her upper body began to sway a few inches side to side. "A large body of water but not the ocean."

Ivy appeared in front of me, blocking my line of sight into the kitchen. Her image cracked and dissolved into dust before reappearing, blue eyes boring into mine. I gulped, fighting the acrid dryness crawling up my throat.

No. No water where she was buried. Her grave was bone dry.

Xia Celeste was getting it all wrong. If I didn't do something, my mother would send LaShawna searching down dead ends all over the Bay Area. The purplish shadows around LaShawna's eyes indicated her fierce determination was barely covering terrible exhaustion. How many false visions had she already investigated?

"Sorry, Daddy," I whispered.

Slowly, filled with dread, I unfolded my body and stood up. This wasn't a girl who died peacefully in bed. I had no idea what horrors I would have to experience in order to help her find peace. Still, I'd made my decision. The deal was probably sealed when I'd felt that electric sensation – recognition laced with something I couldn't quite name – ripple through my body at the sight of her tear-streaked face. Looking directly at the dead girl in my living room, I dipped my head slightly in her direction.

"Tell me," I whispered as quietly as possible.

A flood of foreign feelings swarmed in, making me dizzy and disoriented. So many impressions flickered by so quickly, my brain couldn't process anything but desperation and panic.

"Slow down!" I'm not sure if I actually pronounced the words or if I sent the thought to her. I could barely breathe. I blindly reached out to the wall on my left for support. The sensations pulled away for a moment, but I could still sense them hanging tentatively at the edge of my awareness. It was a stupid rookie mistake, inviting a recently departed victim to simply "tell me" anything or everything. This is exactly why my father wanted me to avoid these sessions. Dimly, I remembered my mother saying it was a matter of filtering, of leading with the right questions.

Start with the basics.

In the kitchen, my mother continued to sway in place, moaning and occasionally muttering about her visions while LaShawna hung on every syllable. Neither of them were paying any attention to me.

"Are you Ivy Brennan?" The words were a barely articulated breath, softer than a whisper.

Frustration rippled through the air.

Yes!

The word was a violent hiss at the back of my skull, making me cringe.

"Calm down," I said through clenched teeth, jaw tight. "Do you know what happened to you?"

Instead of answering the question with words, the sensations swarmed back in. The edge of frantic desperation was still there, but this time I was able to focus.

Gurgling laughter. A little girl sitting cross-legged on a merry-go-round grinning under a tangle of messy blonde hair.

"Faster. Go faster!"

The blur of green behind her melted into mottled darkness. The girl's laughter changed to a frantic string of guttural noises. She was spinning, spinning, spinning in a dingy kitchen shouting nonsense syllables. A woman sitting at a tiny dinette table with her head in her hands.

"I can't deal with this."

The same woman curled in a fetal position on a bare

white bathroom floor. An acrid stench, making me gag. Icy terror in my stomach.

"Mommy, wake up."

White flowers everywhere. A dark, glossy casket draped in waxy white roses. Huge sprays of Easter lilies. The sickening smell of dying carnations.

"But Mommy liked sunflowers."

The little girl looking up at me, hugging a raggedy yellow bear.

"What happens to us now, VeeVee?"

Fierce emotions making it impossible to speak. A pair of hands – my hands only they are lily-white and freckled – appear with thumbs and forefingers pressed together. Relief in her answering smile. Her warbling voice takes up the silly song as I twist and connect, twist and connect my fingers.

"Itsy bitsy spider ..."

A shadow looming over both of us, stopping my fingers. One meaty hand pawing the little girl's tangled hair. Her back turns ridged, her narrow shoulders hunched to her ears.

No! Stop touching. She doesn't like touching.

"Don't worry, girls. Uncle David's here. You'll live with me now."

No! This can't be happening. Don't touch her!

Heavy, wet breathing in my ear. Raw, burning shame.

"Ivy, my little princess."

I SHOOK MYSELF VIOLENTLY, BLINKING AWAY IVY'S WHIRL OF memories. Nausea threatened to dump my lunch all over the entryway.

Enough! That's enough, I thought. *I get it.*

Again she pulled back, though I could sense there was more.

I looked toward the kitchen, where the adults were back to arguing, their words an angry buzz of meaningless chatter. Their voices seemed very far away. Useless. No matter how much I wished one of them would turn, notice this dead girl with her terrible secrets and swoop in to take the burden away from me, it wasn't going to happen. My mouth tasted foul, as though I'd been sucking on charcoal. I took tiny breaths through my nose and tried to concentrate on the best way to get the information I needed without drowning in her pain.

Did you tell anyone?

More giggling drew my attention back to the living room wall. Another girl was sitting with Ivy on the same window seat playing with a thick, shiny dark braid draped over her left shoulder. Her eyes were warm and brown, filled with mischief. Both girls were sitting cross-legged, open textbooks on their laps, exchanging idiotic French phrases using exaggerated, comical Parisian accents.

My father eats beef and green beans in the garden.

Next week, I will go to the grocery and buy grapefruits.

Every time the dark-haired girl giggled, my stomach felt bubbly.

Outside the window, a car door slammed. A flutter of fear rippled over my body. Ivy whipped back the curtain to reveal a dark blue SUV parked by the front door. Her relief was followed by a touch of annoyance.

"What is it, Ivy?" Spoken in French, the silly accent gone. A gentle hand brushed the hair away from her ear. Warm and liquid sensations flowed into my chest.

"It's nothing," Ivy answered, also still in French. "It's only my aunt and my sister."

"Why do you always seem so frightened?"

Ivy focused on her open French book, unable to look into those pure, sweet brown eyes.

"Mon oncle ..." Ivy whispered, but the French words failed her. "My uncle is not a nice man."

The scene blurred and disappeared as the ghost of a kiss touched my left temple, bringing prickles of tears to my own eyes.

This wasn't getting us anywhere. I needed something solid, some definite piece of information to help LaShawna find this girl's remains.

"Ivy? Do you know ... where?" Ivy's image reappeared looking puzzled, her head tilted to one side. "Your ... body. Where is it?"

The ghostly girl grimaced and faded into another scene. A sunny day. Trees drenched in sunshine. Bird chatter. The sound of traffic in the distance. Sharp, repetitive metallic noises that hurt my ears. Machinery grinding and churning. Men's voices shouting. So much noise and commotion. My scalp felt sticky under a hard hat. A cement mixer churned close by. The sound was distracting, growing louder and louder, throbbing in my brain.

"Watch out," a rough male voice barked. A truck screeched to a halt. Someone opened the chute, dumping great globs of wet concrete into a large wooden rectangular form as men scurried around using shovels to spread and distribute it evenly. A leaden weight pressed into my chest, heavier and heavier. My heart pulsed in my throat.

What was happening? Why was she showing me this? I didn't understand.

Breathe, Asha. You're safe. Just breathe, Baby.

The voice was familiar. It was a voice from my own childhood, intimate and comforting.

Everything shifted yet again. I was back in Moonville, Ohio, in the sun-washed studio space above my grandfather's garage. The pain and terror relaxed. My breath came easier.

This is our dance space. You are absolutely safe here.

My own reflection looked back from the mirrored wall, fingers resting lightly on the ballet barre. My feet turned out into first position, and Aunt Nicole appeared in the mirror next to me. She was dressed in a traditional black leotard, gauzy short skirt, and pink tights. This was her dance space before it was mine. Her ribbons and trophies displayed on one wall greatly outnumbered the few ribbons with my name. Her music CDs were stacked and scattered around an old, battered boom box held together with silver duct tape. A haunting, lilting song started to play; a gothic ballad from the early nineties. One of our favorites for ballet warm-ups. We point and flex, point and flex. The familiar routine eased the lingering effects of Ivy's terrible visions.

Aunt Nicole died eight years before I was born, murdered along with her best friend in a bizarre series of events that no one has ever fully explained to me. The mere mention of her name can turn my father into a hollow shell for hours, but Nicole is everything good and clean and home to me. When I woke from nightmares, she would comfort me. When my parents screamed at each other, she would sing to me. Now she sang again, the words of the song sadly bidding goodbye to Wendy, who was going to die. The mirror behind her darkened to black. Red roses appeared, followed by a single white rose with blood drops on the petals.

I knew the image that appeared in the mirror perfectly. It's the image on the cover of the CD that was playing. *Concrete Blonde.* It was the name of the album and the name of the band. And as soon as I recognized it, I knew where Ivy's body would be found. Not the exact geographic location, but I knew enough to send LaShawna on the right trail.

With that realization, I snapped back to the living room of our California townhome. Kota was pressed against my leg; his wet nose nuzzled one of my clenched fists. I opened my hand and settled it on his head. Every inch of my skin felt itchy and uncomfortable. I was fighting hard just to keep myself upright.

Ivy's avid, hungry attention was on my every move.

"Concrete blonde." I mouthed the words without looking up from the dog. "You're buried in concrete."

A sudden rush of relief flooded my senses. It was all the confirmation I needed. I looked back toward the kitchen, where the adults continued to bicker, still oblivious.

"Wh-why ... why didn't you tell—?" I pushed my chin toward my mother.

Trying! Ivy's voice boomed inside my head, causing me to wince. *Fraud!*

"No, she isn't, she's ..."

Lying!

"Stop!" I said loudly. Both LaShawna and my mother looked at me, finally noticing I was in the room. The deep line between my mother's eyebrows indicated she was highly irritated with her cousin. Years of experience told me she would be quick to refocus her anger on me with any provocation.

"What's wrong with you?" my mother snapped at the same time LaShawna asked, "Are you okay, Baby Girl?"

"I just want you to stop fighting," I said, staring down at my shoes.

"Oh, Asha! Honey, we're not fighting. I'm just upset about this case, and your mother is trying to help me."

Tell her, the girl's echoing voice vibrated in the air. *Help me. Tell her.*

"Mom?" I said carefully. "Is this about that Palo Alto girl who went missing last Tuesday?"

"Yes, it is," LaShawna answered before my mother could respond.

"Mom? Don't you remember what happened that night?"

"What nonsense are you talking about, Asha?"

"We heard that Amber Alert on your phone," I said cautiously. LaShawna's reaction told me I was right on track. "You started saying weird things, stuff I didn't understand. I think you might have been in a trance."

"I never, ever fall into trances accidentally," my mother snapped. "I'm always in complete control."

Uh oh.

LaShawna interrupted before I could come up with a response. "What did she say, Asha?"

My mother pushed her lips together and spiked a glare at me that could cut through glass. Behind me, Kota moaned and shifted his weight. His partner pressed one hand outward impatiently.

"Easy. Stay," she commanded in a low, firm voice. In a much gentler tone, she said, "Tell me what your mother said when she heard the Amber Alert, Asha. It might be very, very important."

"Oh yes, Asha girl, do tell us what I said." Mother's tone dripped poison.

"Mom said something like 'Why is there Ivy in the concrete?' and ... I don't know. I think she said something about a mon ... uncluh?"

"That's ludicrous!" my mother exclaimed but spun around when a glass hit the sink, shattering.

"Mon oncle!" LaShawna exclaimed, scrambling to grab the photo and the tennis shoe. "It's French. Ivy was a French honors student. It was her favorite subject. She had pictures of Paris all over her bedroom. And concrete? Her mother's older brother! The bastard owns a construction company! Kota, come on!" She squeezed my arm as she rushed past me to clip a leash to Kota's collar. "Thanks, Asha!"

After shutting the door behind them, I sagged and turned around to say ... something. I'm not sure what I was going to say. The words were knocked clean out of my skull when my mother's knuckles slammed into the right side of my face. Every silver and amethyst ring decorating her fingers bit into my cheekbone causing an explosion of pain.

"If you ever embarrass me like that again, little girl, I will drop you on the side of the road like a stray dog. Do you hear me?"

I nodded, trying to ignore the look of pity in the murdered girl's eyes.

3

———

Before

Banished to my room, I curled up on the bed, hugging a pillow to my stomach. I stared at the shaggy unkempt palm tree outside my window. Even though my cheek was throbbing and my heart was hammering wildly, my eyes stayed stubbornly dry.

Around the edges of my vision, a shadowy version of the other girl lingered but I refused to focus on her. She kept a respectful distance, silent but watchful. Her accusations from earlier echoed in my chest.

Lying. Fraud. Lying. Fraud.

On the other side of the wall, I could hear my mother getting ready for a date with her latest boyfriend, Todd the Toad. Not for the first time, I wondered why she bothered with the full hair, makeup, and wardrobe routine. Toad was an ugly beast, with bulging eyes and long weedy hair that he always wore in a ratty ponytail that emphasized his receding hairline.

But he was a filthy rich toad, CEO of some tech company that went public last year. According to my mother, rich men could always afford to wear the prettiest, youngest things on their arm so she had to make sure he liked what he saw each and every time he looked at her.

Perhaps it will all pay off and he'll marry her, I thought with a grim twist in my gut. And maybe the third time will be the charm. Then it won't matter if she's a fraud. We'll have a rich toad to pay the bills, and Xia Celeste will retire to focus on her happily ever after. Maybe she won't screw this relationship up.

Right. And maybe rainbow monkeys will fly out of my butt and shower us with gold coins.

The snort that escaped my nose startled me, and I looked over toward my new shadowy roommate. She returned my look with a placid, peaceful expression that really pissed me off.

"You can go now," I told her. "There's a light. Why don't you walk into it and go away."

Her image didn't move or react, but I felt a gentle coolness pressed against my injured cheek.

"Stop that!" I waved a hand around my head as if to shoo away a fly, then flung myself toward the tiny bathroom connected to my room. "Go away," I said over my shoulder before closing the door and flipping the row of switches that turned on the bright overhead lights and rumbling bathroom fan.

With shaking hands, I turned on the cold water tap and splashed my face over and over until the sting in my cheek subsided. When I finally turned off the water and pressed a clean towel to my face, the temperature in the room started to drop, bringing up goose pimples on my arms.

"I said go away," I growled into the towel still pressed to

my face, muffling my words. "I helped you. Now leave me alone."

No response. The air in the bathroom returned to normal, so I removed the towel from my face. A small section of the bathroom mirror was frosted but rapidly melting. In the frost, two words were written.

Not yet.

As I stared at the message, drips started to roll away from the bottom of the letters.

"Please, just go away." My voice was pathetic. "Please."

I turned from the mirror, crossed to the closet on the other side of my bathroom, flipped on that light, then stepped inside and closed another door. Folding myself into a tight ball among my shoes and hanging clothes, I pressed my forehead to my knees. Still, the terrible words continued to echo in my chest.

Lying. Fraud. Lying. Fraud.

"No," I whispered to myself, "it can't be true."

But a brief memory of my parents screaming at each other replayed in my head.

My father yelling, "This has to stop. You can't keep lying."

My mother shrieking back, "I wouldn't have to lie if you would keep yourself out of the bottle for one day."

At the time, the argument had been confusing and terrifying. Now, in light of what I'd just witnessed, the words took on a new and terrible meaning.

Daddy.

My heart ached for him. The sharp pain of his absence entwined with sickening guilt. It was my fault he lost joint custody, my fault he'd gone away. I knew my father had a drinking problem; he was always brutally honest about his stints in rehab. But he never drank alcohol on the days I stayed with him. Never. Not one drop. Until the weekend I confronted him about Aunt Nicole's murder.

Before that terrible weekend, we had discussed his twin sister many times. Her pictures were plastered all over Grandpa Elton's house. We decorated her grave every Memorial Day. He knew Nicole visited me, told me stories, even danced with me in her old studio. I never kept any secrets from him. But a stupid game of Truth or Dare forced me to realize my father – my hero, my best friend in the whole world – kept plenty of nasty secrets from me.

It started at a slumber party with seven members of my competition dance team. The questions being asked to illicit truths were getting too gross and personal, so I picked dare. Eyes shining with glee, Amberly Wilson dared me to send a postcard to San Quinton Prison addressed to the man who murdered my aunt.

"His name is David Lee Jenkins, right?" Amberly asked.

I stared back at her, confused.

"My dad says they have to give inmates any mail sent to the prison with their name on it. So he will definitely see it." Amberly looked thrilled. I felt sick.

Murdered? My Aunt Nicole was murdered?

"What's she going to write?" Bethany Barrows asked. *"Glad you're not here?"*

"Hope you rot in Hell?" someone else chimed in.

Head spinning, I looked around at my dance team. They all looked back at me expectantly. None of them looked shocked or surprised.

"What are you talking about?" I asked them.

One by one, I saw surprise and realization register on their eager faces.

"Wait, you don't know?" Maya Johnson asked.

"Are you serious? You really don't know?" asked Bethany.

After several excruciating rounds of begging them to explain, Sierra Middleton, who was hosting the slumber party, finally took pity on me. She produced a tablet computer, fingers flying over the touchscreen, until she found what she needed. All seven girls huddled around me as Sierra set the tablet in my shaking hands and pressed the play arrow to start the video she had queued up. We all watched, mesmerized, as a ten-year-old episode of *Dateline* described my aunt's murder as "a bizarre footnote" in a series of serial killings that stretched back to the early 1980's. David Lee Jenkins, a sad looking creature with a bald head and a moon-shaped face, was believed to have murdered over twenty women before he was caught and convicted in 1998.

I was mortified and felt totally betrayed. I couldn't believe my own father had kept such a huge and terrible secret from me. For the next six days, I stewed in my own righteous outrage. By the time my dad picked me up from school the following Friday, I was ready to explode. We didn't even make it out of the school parking lot before I confronted him.

For his part, Nate Kidwell looked like someone had punched him in the gut, but he didn't try to lie or placate me. Instead, he promised to answer all my questions when we got home. In his studio apartment, we sat on the kitchen counter with mugs of hot chocolate while my father calmly answered all of my hurt, angry questions as best he could. And when I stomped off to bed, still feeling deeply offended, he must have opened the first bottle of Jim Beam. The next morning, I couldn't wake him up to take me to dance practice.

So I called my mother. Huge mistake.

Before my father could complete yet another stint in

rehab, Mother arranged for sole custody that allowed only four hours of supervised visitation with my father every other week. She didn't do it to protect me. That was another lie. She did it out of sheer spite because she will never forgive him for filing the divorce papers.

During our one and only supervised visitation session, I cried non-stop and begged for my father's forgiveness. He told me all the things a father should tell his daughter in that horrible situation. He told me it wasn't my fault; he insisted it was him who had let me down. And then he dropped the bomb. He was going away. He called it a spiritual mission to get his head straight. He wouldn't give me any details, but he promised he would return and fight for custody as soon as it was possible. That was over a year ago.

After Daddy made me promise to stay away from my mother's spirit sessions, he gave me a smart phone with a prepaid plan and a short list of emergency contacts.

"Don't tell your mother," he warned me. "It's our little secret. Just in case everything goes wrong." As if everything wasn't already all wrong.

The phone was hidden in a box of tampons under my bathroom sink. It was just a few feet away from the closet where I sat huddled and miserable.

A sudden clatter of clothes hangers being pushed aside told me my mother was in her own closet on the other side of my closet's back wall. The building's paper-thin walls made a private phone conversation impossible, so I forced myself to stay still and wait for her to leave.

After what seemed like hours, there was a knock at the front door. Mother's heels clicked down the stairs. The Toad complimented her appearance in a voice that made my skin crawl, then I heard the blissful sound of the front door being locked. Car doors slammed, and the happy couple drove away.

Moving slowly and cautiously, I stood up on jelly legs and wobbled into the brightly lit bathroom.

The mirror reflected an empty white space, no sign of the dead girl or her earlier message. Taking a deep gulp of air, I opened the door to my bedroom and switched on the lights. Nothing. No hint of unnatural shadow or chilly air greeted me.

Allowing myself a sigh of relief, I fished out my secret phone and opened the contacts. I quickly selected the contact number marked simply as *Daddy*.

As soon as I heard his deep rumbling voice say "Hello there," tears swamped my eyes. "You've reached Nate Kidwell's voice mail. Please stop and listen to this message. I'm going to be out of the country with no access to messages for quite a while. If this is an emergency, please call my father, Elton Kidwell. He's had the same phone number for over fifty years. It's listed. Look it up. If this isn't an emergency, don't bother to leave a message. I probably won't ever listen to it. If this is you, Asha, I love you. Don't you ever doubt that, baby girl. I love you and I will come back to you, one way or another. I promise."

Before the beep, I hung up and redialed. After listening to the message three more times, I finally stayed on the line through the beep and left a message.

"Daddy, it's me. I'm scared. Please come to California or call me. Please. I can't call Grandpa Elton about this. I need you." I gulped back the wretched sobs that were building in my chest and heaved a deep breath to steady my nerves. "Daddy, I broke my promise. I'm sorry, but I had to do it. I had to. It was horrible." Another deep breath. "Daddy, I think Mom has lost ... her gift." The last two words came out as a whisper. "Did you know about this? I don't know what to do. Please, come here or call me." I rattled off our full address before ending the call.

Then I sat still, staring at the phone, willing it to ring. Nothing happened. Time ticked away until ten minutes later I had to do something else or go crazy. So I scrolled through the other contacts programmed into my phone.

As I'd said on my message, I could not call Grandpa Elton back in Moonville. And definitely not my Grandmother Ona in Sweden. LaShawna's home and mobile numbers were listed, but she was probably digging up a dead body right now. I shuddered. There was a long list of dance friends and school friends in Ohio and California, but none of them would be able to talk to me about this. At the end of the list was Zack, my stepbrother from my mother's second attempt at marriage. He didn't understand the whole "ghost biz," but he knew my mother's crazy fury all too well.

I pressed his name. The phone rang twice before he answered.

"Hey, Kid. How is California treating you?"

There was a wild cacophony of dogs barking in the background. Despite the fact that it was past eleven o'clock in Ohio, he was working in the kennels.

Of course he was.

Zack's grandpa founded All Creatures Animal Clinic back in the 1970's, but old Doc Warner was getting close to his eightieth birthday. Zack was always the one who nursed the most needy patients through the night. Zack watched over whelping boxes and IV drips. The clinic earned five star ratings from its clients because of Zack, not his grandfather or the three veterinary techs the clinic employed. During our parents' disastrous eighteen-month marriage, Zack used to bring me to the clinic to work with him on weekends and holidays. I could almost smell the sharp tang of dog and disinfectant that would cling to his clothes.

Every inch of my skin ached with loneliness.

"Hi, Zack," I said, a tiny hitch in my voice the only sign of crushing homesickness threatening to stop my heart. "You're busy. I'll call later."

"Hey, what's wrong?" he asked in the same low voice he used to calm skittish kittens. There was a snick of a door closing, and the barking disappeared.

What could I tell him? Zack has never seen or heard a restless spirit in his life, but he never ridiculed anything I described. Still, I didn't know where to begin. Every word I longed to tell him – about LaShawna's missing person case, the ugly images Ivy unleashed on me, Xia Celeste's obvious failure – it was all wedged deep in my chest, choking my breath.

"Just ... the Momster."

"What did she do?" Zack asked, his voice loaded with anger. A memory from the previous spring washed over me. Something I'd said, I'm not even sure what it was, sent my mother into a scratching, screaming fury. She lunged at me, and all I could think to do was close my eyes and wait for the pain. Instead, Zack shoved his way between us, taking the initial force of her attack. He grabbed her wrists and calmly informed her she was "a pathetic excuse for a mother."

There was fear in her eyes when she tore her arms out of his grasp and stormed out of the kitchen. One month later, she filed for divorce and announced the two of us were moving to California.

My throat ached with the memory.

"You need me to come out there?" Zack asked. "I swear to God, I will come get you."

He would, too. He was my legal stepbrother for only eighteen months, but I had no doubt he would fly across the country and whisk me back to Ohio if I asked him to come rescue me. That was just Zack.

"No," I said, pushing myself up. "Quit that. You have to save every penny to pay for vet school. You can't be storming across country to get all caught up in our stupid drama. I don't know why I called you."

"Don't you dare hang up," he barked as my finger was headed toward the red button. "Tell me what's going on. Did Xia go after you again?"

"No," I lied. "It's not that. It's just ... I just—" Taking another huge gulp of air, I said, "Zack, have you ever heard about a medium losing what they have ... like losing the gift, I mean." I hunched my shoulders and waited for him to laugh at me. I should have known better.

"I'm a biology geek, Kid. I'm hardly an expert in spiritualism. Have you talked to your dad?"

"He's still not answering his phone."

"Oh." With that one syllable, Zack managed to convey a world of understanding and compassion. "Okay, so you called me to hash it out. Let's do this."

The sharp squeak and slap of another door opening and closing told me he had exited the veterinary clinic to sit on the screened porch that overlooked Main Street. All Creatures Animal Clinic was housed in a Queen Anne Victorian that looked like a storybook dream. It was Zack's home, his burden, his family legacy.

My family legacy was listening to dead people.

A fission of jealousy tickled my stomach followed by a wave of shame. Zack didn't have an easy life; he was scooping dog poop, trying to hold everything together, while other guys his age were out drinking beer and talking to pretty girls.

"Tell me what's eating you, Kid."

Choking and stuttering over the pain in my chest, I told him all about the scene that had played out in the living room, neglecting to tell him about my throbbing cheek and the way the blonde ghost's pity made my guts seethe with anger and shame.

"So you could see this girl, Ivy? Is that her name?"

"She hated her name," I mumbled. An image popped into my head – a woman with dark blonde dreadlocks wearing a loose tie-die dress and silver Celtic jewelry. "Her mother was a New Age California hippie type."

"How do you know that?" Zack asked.

I wiggled uncomfortably with the flood of feelings the image evoked – affection mixed with fear and anger. There was a flicker of shifting shadow at the corner of my vision. These were not my feelings; they belonged to the dead girl.

"Her mother just appeared in my head," I said, pressing a tight fist into the center of my breastbone to ease the ache. "Ivy showed her to me, I guess."

"So you could see Ivy in your living room. And you could see her mother? And you know Ivy hated her name because ... which one of them told you that?"

"No," I snapped, frustrated. "I mean, yes, Ivy was here in my living room." *She's still here in my bedroom*, I thought, but I didn't tell Zack. He'd freak. "She showed me an image of her mother. Like, in my head? I don't know how I know she hated her name. This is so impossible to explain!"

"Asha, try. Help me understand."

There was something in his voice, a gentle sort of sadness mingled with a breath of hope. Zack's mother died of cancer during his senior year of high school. Lingering guilt and grief nearly caused him to flunk out of college, until a friend brought him to Xia Celeste. It was Zack's consultations with my mother that resulted in our parents meeting, marrying and, eventually, probably inevitably, divorcing. A series of events I felt certain he would always regret. Yet, whenever I heard the hope in his voice, I had to try to help him understand.

"Okay, Zack," I said sighing deeply and rolling my eyes.

"Stop that," Zack scolded in a playful voice. "I can hear you rolling you eyes." I fought back the urge to giggle.

"Okay, listen. It's not like a movie. There's no glowing see-through person standing there in front of me having a conversation. It's not like 'Hey, you. I'm Jane Doe. Professor Plum killed me with the candlestick in the library. My body is buried in his cellar.' It's not like that at all."

"You always want to tell me what it isn't like. Try telling me what it *is* like?"

"It's never the same thing ... the same experience twice. Sometimes images flash in my mind and that's all I get. Other times, I might feel something, like a coolness on my skin." My fingers brushed the sore spot on my cheek. "Sometimes I hear a voice crystal clear, either the voice of the dead person or, sometimes, something somebody said to them. But usually, most of what I hear is garbled, like a radio that isn't fully tuned in to the right station. I think it depends on the type of person they were in life. Maybe how they died factors in, too."

"Tell me something new," he urged in that overly patient voice he used to calm angry pet owners. "Focus on this time. Focus on this girl. Focus on Ivy, not Jane Doe."

I closed my eyes and tried to remember the moment when I walked toward our townhouse and saw the disturbance around the front door. "This girl was a mass of ugly energy ... like a violent kaleidoscope swirling inside a black hole. At first she seemed like this shadowy, shifting, hot-boiled mess. It scared me in a weird way. It felt like if I looked directly into the darkness, I'd be ... I don't know. Sucked down the black hole, maybe? I didn't want to look, but Kota never took his eyes off of her."

"Kota?" Zack broke in. "That's LaShawna's K-9 partner, right? He could see this ghost mess?"

"I don't know what he saw, but I think he sensed something. When I put my hands on him, he was like stone covered in fur."

"And yet you stayed there with this ugly, scary ghost?"

"She was only ugly because she was so frustrated." My eyes snapped open, surprised. I didn't know that until the words came out of my mouth. "As soon as she realized I could see her and hear her, everything changed. I could hear her voice clearly. I could see her, first flashes of her in my living room, then flashes of her in her life before she died. I tried to redirect her toward my mother, but she said—"

Liar. Fraud. Liar. Fraud.

"She said Xia couldn't hear her."

"Wait, wait, wait. Hold on right there. Even the dog could feel this girl's presence, but your mother was totally oblivious?" There was a sly, ornery smirk in his voice, and I found myself getting irritated.

"I don't know for sure about Kota; he might have been upset because his partner was upset. And this isn't a good thing! I know you hate my mother and would love to see her humiliated, but she is my mother, Zack. She pays the bills with this so-called gift."

Zack snorted loudly. "Listen, there's something I need to tell you, Kid."

Downstairs, someone tapped on the front door. Not a full-hearted knock, but a gentle tip-tapping I recognized all too well.

"What is it?" I asked. I stood up to look down from my bedroom window. Mrs. Tsien, our landlady, looked up at me, waved and pointed at the door. I waved back and nodded, holding up one finger.

"I didn't want to tell you this, but now I think it might be important," Zack said.

"Our landlady is knocking on the door," I told him. "Can you tell me quickly?"

"Xia stole money from my dad."

"What?" My head started spinning. "What did you say?"

"She stole money from Dad. It was stupid. He'd have given her the money if she asked for it. The bastard won't cough up a single penny for me to go to vet school, but he'd have written Xia Celeste a check for ten times the amount she stole from him."

"Then why?" I asked, totally lost.

"Crazy thing was she was stealing it from him, then pretending it was income from her business. She paid tax on it like it was real income. I think that's what ticked Dad off the most. Not that she took the money, but that she paid tax on it a second time. I think she was trying to make herself look more profitable."

"Are you sure about this?"

"I'm the one that figured it out. Remember that little fight where I grabbed her to stop her from attacking you?"

"Of course I do," I told him as the tip-tapping started up again. "Crap, the landlady. I have to go. Can I call you tomorrow?"

"Wait, listen to this first. After that fight, I snooped in her private office. It doesn't matter why, but I had a good reason. I found a list of all her accounts and passwords on a small notepad in her desk drawer. All of her passwords. Asha, do you hear me? Her Apple password, her Gmail password, all her banking passwords. Everything. I'd bet my grandpa's stethoscope she still keeps a list of accounts and passwords in her desk. Do you understand what I'm saying?"

"Yes," I answered softly, my brain buzzing, "I hear you. Now go finish your work in the kennel. I'll call you tomorrow, okay?"

"Call me any time, Kid," he said. The deep ring of sincere affection warmed me a bit. "Don't let the evil witch get you down. I love you, and I will come get you if you need me."

"Love you, too," I said, feeling awkward. Until Zack came into my life, no one other than Daddy ever said that to me.

I disconnected the call and jogged downstairs, stuffing the phone under a decorative pillow before opening the door. Mrs. Tsien stood in the weak light from our porch lantern gripping a plush blanket around her shoulders despite the fact it was nearly seventy degrees outside.

"Mom gone?" she asked, not one for any kind of social greetings.

"Yeah, but she'll be here tomorrow seeing clients," I said, automatically walking over to the breakfast bar and picking up the appointment schedule next to Mom's business phone. Flipping the page to tomorrow, I stopped and blinked a few times. There were no names on the schedule.

"She leave a check with you?" Mrs. Tsien asked.

"Check?" I echoed the word, not understanding what I was hearing or seeing. Flipping forward, I saw there were only three appointments on her calendar for the entire week. Sick dread churned in my gut.

"Rent check," Mrs. Tsien said.

"It's the middle of April," I responded, feeling stupid. "Rent's not due until the first."

"No, honey. April check."

My expression must have reflected my horror because Mrs. Tsien chuckled; her heavily wrinkled face was kind as she patted my shoulder. "Don't worry, we'll work it out. Maybe publisher check late again. Maybe another psychic event at the bookstore will get us all straight. I'll talk to Mom tomorrow." She stood there looking around our living room, not making any move to leave.

"Okay. I'll make sure she knows you're going to stop by," I said, taking a few steps toward the front door.

Mrs. Tsien smiled at me again; this time it was a sad smile. "Saw LaShawna here earlier. Ran out quick."

"Yeah," I said, wishing desperately for her to leave.

"Big case?" Mrs. Tsien asked, eyes glistening. Her grandson died in a hiking accident two years ago. It was my mother who helped searchers recover the body. That's why Mrs. Tsien offered us the San Jose residence at far less than the market rate. An outrageously low rent for this area — rent my mother was apparently having trouble paying. *But Xia Celeste did help this woman*, I reminded myself. Xia did find her grandson's body so it could be buried among his ancestors. That wasn't a fraud or a lie. It couldn't be. Could it?

I smiled with my mouth, trying to make the expression spread over my whole face. "I'm sorry, Mrs. Tsien. I can't say anything about the police business. It's still an open investigation. You know how it is."

"Yes, I know." She patted my shoulder again, then

hitched the blanket up higher on her arms and lifted her chin. "Mom does good work," she declared. "I'm happy to help." Then she turned and shuffled out the door, waving her hand in the air and chanting, "Don't worry, don't worry."

But I was sick with worry.

As Mrs. Tsien made her way toward her own unit, a shadow slipped past me. Every inch of my skin turned ice cold. I opened my mouth, but the warning stuck in my throat. What was I going to say? *Watch out, there's a murdered ghost on the loose?*

The light spilling from Mrs. Tsien's open doorway illuminated her front porch. It was slightly larger than ours and featured a red rocking chair that Mrs. Tsien liked to occupy on warm, sunny afternoons. Ivy appeared in the chair, hugging her knees to her chest. As she watched the elderly woman approach, her eyes were so wistful my heart shuddered in sympathy.

When she finally reached her own front doorway, Mrs. Tsien stopped and looked over at the red rocking chair. It was moving back and forth in the still air. I held my breath as she carefully removed the blanket from her shoulders and draped it over the back of the chair. It almost looked like she was draping the blanket over Ivy's shoulders. But that had to be an illusion, didn't it? She mumbled something I couldn't hear, shaking her head. Then she looked back at me and waved.

"Wuan aan," she called back to me. *Good night.* It was one of the few Mandarin phrases I'd learned from her in the past year.

"Jiu hao mung," Ivy's voice whispered in my ear. *Sweet dreams.*

Ivy knew Mandarin?

I locked the door, shot both internal security bolts in

place, and pressed my back against the solid wood. To my left was the living room where I'd first encountered Ivy Brennan earlier. Straight ahead was the staircase leading up to the bedrooms. To my right was a short stairway that led down into my mother's consulting room and office suite.

Sweet dreams were impossible. We were behind in paying our rent. What other bills were past due?

If a list of accounts and passwords really existed, it would be near her computer in the inner sanctum down below. Xia always kept the door locked, but I knew where she kept a spare key.

Shaking with the audacity of what I was about to do, I retrieved the keychain that held all her spare keys from a hidden hook in the laundry area and went down to the room where she met with clients. I'd only entered this room a few times and never without my mother present. My heart pounded in my throat. As soon as I touched the knob, the door swung open.

An uneasy chill skittered over my skin. Either Xia forgot to lock the door the last time she was working, or Ivy was trying to help. I flicked the light switch inside the doorway, activating the harsh overhead light she never used during her sessions and scanned the room. No signs of ghostly activity.

"Is anyone here?" I asked the empty room, feeling silly and yet still anxious. No response.

I hurried to her desk and sat in her chair, which was set up so that her back would be toward the wall and she faced anyone who walked through the door. Again, I surveyed the brightly lit room and breathed a sigh of relief. Everything looked blissfully normal.

It took less than two minutes to find the list. It wasn't in a notebook as Zack described; it was a single printed page tucked in a file folder neatly labeled *Accounts*.

What an idiot, I thought.

First, I fired up the three-in-one printer and scanned a copy of the list. I wanted my own copy for reasons I couldn't quite admit, even to myself. After powering down the printer and replacing the original list where I'd found it, I sat and stared at the darkened monitor. Was I really going to do this? *Yes*, I decided, biting hard on my bottom lip. One wiggle of the mouse brought the computer screen to life. My mother's screensaver—her most recent publicity photo taken a few months ago—smiled back at me.

"That woman is the love of her own life." I muttered one of my father's favorite insults as I clicked the web browser icon, then froze as a ripple of laughter cut the silence.

"Hello?" My voice sounded unnaturally high. I swallowed. "Is that you, Ivy?"

In answer, the monitor in front of me started flashing through a series of screens. Websites devoted to finding missing persons, crime scene photos, and news sites flashed by in rapid succession before landing on a website called *Unhaunted*. The banner declared the website's mission to expose modern spiritualist frauds. The same picture Xia was using as a screensaver was displayed next to a link that read, "*Xia Celeste – Psychic Sleuth or Something Sinister?*"

Just as I was reaching forward to click on the link, the overhead light flickered off and on several times, yanking my attention away from the screen. In the doorway stood the black silhouette of a girl wearing a long flowing gown. Chills snaked up my spine. The figure loomed, ominous, making my gut churn with dread. This black shadow looked nothing like the cute blonde athlete from earlier. And yet something told me it was her.

"Ivy?"

The office door slammed shut with a violent crash. I jumped out of the chair clutching the stolen copy of my mother's private accounts and passwords in one hand. As the lights continued to blink on and off, I stumbled across the office and grabbed the icy doorknob. To my relief, the door opened easily. There was no figure waiting for me in the hallway. I turned to look back. The office was empty, well-lit, and serene. The only sound was my breath rasping in my chest.

Although I wanted to run back upstairs to my bedroom, I had to erase any signs I'd ever stepped inside the office. Shaking violently, I crossed the room again to close the search window I'd opened and reposition both the chair and mouse exactly as I'd found them. After sweeping the room one more time, I switched off the light and locked the door. Perhaps Xia had left it unlocked, but I guessed the open door had nothing to do with carelessness. After the spare keys were back in the laundry room, I retrieved my phone from where I'd hidden it before opening the door to Mrs. Tsien and checked the screen.

No missed calls. No new text messages.

The disappointment was intense. I'm not sure why the silence hurt so much. It's not like I really expected my Daddy to sweep in after so many months off the radar to rescue me.

Did I?

4

Now

Strangers talk to me in loud, urgent voices. They move parts of my body that scream in protest. They cut away my clothes, chilling my battered body to the core. They ask questions that are impossible to answer. When I try to speak, they tell me to calm down.

Is this really emergency care? It feels so wrong. Violent. Invasive.

Finally, I'm deposited in a curtained cell somewhere in the bowels of the hospital. Here the lights are low. A male nurse covers my battered and bandaged body with a thin blanket and whispers that my mother will be here soon. I'm sure he thinks it's a comfort.

"Daddy?" I croak with an aching throat.

He shakes his head, giving me a tragic look that makes my teeth ache. "I'm sorry. We were told he's out of the country doing mission work and can't be reached."

The disappointment is like a bowling ball dropped on my chest.

"Tired," I mumble. "Sleep."

"I'll be close by if you need anything." He presses a call button into my hand. "If you push this, I'll come running."

As soon as he exits, another nurse whisks in. Wearing formal white nurse's uniform common in the middle of the last century, she appears to be painted in shades of gray. Her starched cap is perched slightly askew on top of an impressive bouffant hairdo. The effect is a little off-kilter and endearing. I wonder if her cap was always crooked when she was alive.

"Oh, good grief. He shouldn't be leaving her all alone," she frets. Her voice is distant and slightly garbled, like a radio not quite tuned in to the station — exactly as I described to Zack. "She's so young. Someone should be sitting with her."

"I'm fine," I tell her, hoping to calm her agitation. Instead, my words have the opposite effect. She zooms in close to the bedside and looks down at me with wide, horrified eyes.

"Can you hear me?" Her words sound crisp now and slightly hysterical.

"Yes."

"Oh, no! Push the button, push the button, push the button!" She streaks out of the room screaming. "You! Get back here!"

I close my eyes and wonder how many more visitors I'm going to endure before I'll be able to sleep. I'm so tired, so desperately tired.

"You're not coding." The dead nurse is back at my bedside looking calmer but puzzled. "Usually the ones who see me are about to ... go south."

"I'm not dying tonight," I reassure her.

My mother's braying voice announces her arrival in the emergency room. My heart sinks.

"Who is that yelling like a lunatic?" The otherworldly nurse sounds stern. "This is a place of healing."

"My mother," I tell her. "Sometimes she hears spirits, too."

Sometimes.

Xia Celeste sweeps into the room minutes later making a great show of motherly concern for her injured daughter. She actually manages to produce tears when she sees me. It's quite a performance. The dead nurse makes clucking noises and asks Xia to turn down the volume. My mother shows no signs of hearing her.

All I feel is shame.

One brave doctor, a sour-faced Pakistani man who is clearly not dazzled by the presence of Xia Celeste, enters the curtained cell and gives a dispassionate list of my injuries to my mother. Xia flutters and makes dramatic gestures, as though the mere mention of my injuries is causing her physical pain. It's all an act. I know it's an act. So does the doctor. The only one who doesn't know is my mother, who manages to produce a fresh flood of tears when he asks if she has any questions.

Two orderlies dressed in matching maroon scrubs arrive and ask the doctor if I'm ready to be moved to my room. Directly behind them stands a tiny bird-like woman watching the scene unfurl. Although her hair is pure white, her face is smooth and unlined. A bright lavender streak accents a pronounced widow's peak. Thick, hipster-framed glasses magnify her pale grey eyes to such a degree that she looks like a Manga character. It's impossible to guess her age.

"Hello, Vera," my mother says in a prim, respectful voice at the same time the doctor asks, "May we help you?"

The strange new arrival steps forward. "Xia? Do you have any questions for Doctor ... ?" She leans in closer to look at the plastic badge pinned to the doctor's front pocket until her nose is only inches from his chest. "Doctor Bahmani!" she exclaims, then flashes a warm smile up at him. The doctor no longer looks like he's sucking on a lemon; he looks bemused. "Xia, do you have any questions for Doctor Bahmani regarding your daughter's injuries? Or her treatment? Or prognosis?"

"No, Vera," my mother answers timidly, dipping her head like a chastised school girl. "No questions."

Wow. Who is this Vera woman? And what is her superpower?

As if she's heard my thought, Vera focuses her large, luminous eyes on me.

"Hello, Asha," she says in a voice that reminds me of a gentle sea breeze. "My name is Vera Birch. I'm your advocate. Do you know what that means?"

"Yes," I croak, even though I don't. I just want everyone to go away so I can sleep.

"Good." Vera steps closer and touches my wrist. "I'm here to help you. You're safe now. I'm here to make sure you stay safe and protected. This is an excellent hospital, and you're going to receive the very best care. All you have to do right now is rest and recover. Do you understand?"

"Okay," I barely breathe the word as my eyelids grow heavy.

"Oh, I like this Vera," the dead nurse proclaims and fades away.

"Your mother and I are going to step out and speak to your doctor for a moment," Vera continues. To emphasize her point, she steps back and places a firm hand on Xia's elbow. "While we do that, these nice young men are going to take you to your room." She points to the men in maroon scrubs with her free hand. "I know them. They are wonderful guys. They will take very good care of you. You are safe with them. I promise."

One of the orderlies smiles at me while the other looks down and shuffles his feet, looking embarrassed.

"Come on, Xia," Vera says, pulling on her elbow.

Xia starts to follow, then stops suddenly. My stomach clenches as my mother turns, rushes back to my side, and leans in to press her lips to my temple.

"Don't say a word," she whispers into my ear. "Keep your mouth shut."

5

___

BEFORE

MY MOTHER'S ALARM STARTED CHIRPING AT SEVEN O'CLOCK the morning after Ivy's first appearance. I crawled out of bed and went to examine my reflection in the bathroom mirror. An angry purple lump on my left cheekbone perfectly complimented the dark circles and raw redness around my eyes. My mother's tantrums rarely resulted in such visible results, but I spent most of the night pinching and poking at the sore spot to be sure the point of impact was noticeable.

I'd also neglected to braid my hair the night before so it was a wild tangle of black coils. I grabbed a brush and started to force the unruly corkscrews into my usual hairstyle, a messy bun at the crown of my head, but stopped when the pain hit me.

Eyes watering, I dropped the brush and gripped the edge of my bathroom sink. It wasn't just the lump on my cheek. My head ached, my jaw ached, my neck ached and my stomach churned.

A voice – faint, low-pitched, and lovely – started singing. It was a sad song about roses, cowboys, darkest nights, and thorns. I knew the song. It was an old eighties pop ballad I'd heard over and over as a child. The voice was as familiar to me as my own heartbeat. Air swirled around me gently, bathing my face and neck in coolness. My stomach eased, and I looked up to find a familiar face next to mine in the mirror. My aunt Nicole smiled back at me. A fluttering lightness eased the tight knot in my chest, making it possible to smile back in response.

Nicole winked and started to fade.

"Wait!" I whispered, always mindful of the thin walls. "Come back. Please come back. I need help."

No, you don't. Her low melodious voice already sounded so far away. *You don't need help, Asha. You need to give help.*

"What?" I exclaimed, forgetting to keep my voice low.

A faint image of Ivy Brennan appeared in the same space where my aunt had winked at me. The image was static, like a projection of a school photograph. This wasn't Ivy's ghost intermingling with my aunt's spirit. My aunt was showing Ivy to me.

"I helped her. I did what I could. Look where it got me." I jabbed a finger at my own mottled face.

Three sharp knocks on my bedroom door caused me to whirl around. "Asha?" My mother walked into my bedroom without waiting for a response. I hurried out of the bathroom to face her. "Who are you talking to?"

"Aunt Nicole," I answered, surprising myself with the honesty.

"Really," she said in a bemused voice, crossing her arms. "She giving you beauty tips, nature girl?" She combed glittering gold nails through her own smooth, glossy locks.

Best hair money can buy, I thought.

Gritting my teeth, I stepped forward into a patch of bright sunlight and, with my eyes locked on hers, swept my own short, bitten nails over the ugly lump on my cheek. "I think I'll stay home from school today," I said, working hard to keep my voice flat and devoid of emotion. No one can win a battle of hysterics with Xia Celeste.

She had the good grace to look sad, even concerned. "Do you have any tests you'll miss?"

I shook my head.

She nodded. "Okay, I'll call the school."

When she turned and started to walk away, I allowed myself a small sigh of relief. But then she stopped and faced me, bracing both hands against the frame of my bedroom door. She scanned the room slowly before looking back at me.

"We're alone right now." It was a statement, but there was a hint, just a slight hint, of uncertainty.

"Are we ever really alone?"

"Touché," she said with a half-smile. Then her face grew serious. "I've known since you were a newborn that you had the Sight. It was so obvious. Your father desperately wanted to believe it might skip you. He wanted you to have a chance at being *normal*."

She said the word normal in the same way she would say stupid or diseased, with a curl of distaste on her lips. She paused, waiting for me to respond.

"Well, I'm not very good at normal," I said, again working to keep my voice neutral.

"No, you're not," she replied with another half-smile. She sat on the end of my bed and looked at me as though I were a bug pinned to a board. "Were you really talking to your aunt just now?"

"Yes."

"Does she talk back to you?"

"Sometimes."

Xia looked around the room again, appearing a bit uncomfortable. Interesting.

"Do you know how she died?"

This was a tricky question. I knew. Of course I knew. I'd seen the *Dateline* investigation. But I wanted to know more.

In all the years she'd sung to me, danced with me, and told bedtime stories, Aunt Nicole never shared any details about her death. No one in my family ever discussed her murder in direct terms. Her name used to come up frequently in my parents' screaming matches. It was easy to piece together enough of the accusations they hurled at each other to know something terrible had happened to Daddy's twin sister, something he was afraid could happen again. Even when I forced my father to give up his secrets last year, the explanation was frustratingly sparse. Hours of internet research at the library hadn't turn up any new details that weren't covered on the television show.

"I know she was killed," I said, my voice tentative.

"She was murdered," my mother corrected me. Her topaz eyes were locked with mine. "Your aunt Nicole was murdered in cold blood by a serial killer who thought his victims were communicating with her. It happened here in California, in fact. She died on a lonely stretch of the Pacific Coast Highway between Carmel and Big Sur."

An involuntary shudder passed through me, causing my arms to wrap around my body in a useless protective gesture. "Do you know exactly where she died? Could we go there?"

"I've already been there." Xia waved a hand at me, palm

outward, dismissing my request. "Five separate times. Twice with your father before you were born and three times since we moved here. I thought maybe, if I could get some answers, the man would stop drowning in liquor and regrets. But there's nothing out there. No trace of any spiritual activity."

"But maybe I could –"

Dangerous fire flared in my mother's eyes. "You think you can do better than me, little girl? Better than your Daddy Dearest? One dead girl gives you a little information that hasn't even been verified yet, and now you're a high and mighty psychic superstar?"

"No! That's not what I was saying, Mom."

"Then what *were* you saying?"

"I just thought ... Nicole has been visiting me my whole life." Her expression was getting more thunderous with each word. The smart thing to do would be to shut up, but I couldn't seem to stop talking. "They think this guy killed more than twenty women, right? But everyone treats Nicole like a footnote. Like a mistake. Like she's just collateral damage on his killing spree. I thought –"

Ivy's silhouette appeared behind my mother wearing the same long flowing shadowy gown I'd seen in the doorway the night before. Within the gown, floral images emerged – white lilies, carnations, and roses.

"Flowers," I said, grasping Ivy's suggestion with relief. "We could set up a memorial for Nicole where she died. Someone should treat her death like it matters."

My mother's fiery anger cooled to bitterness. "Poor Nicole doesn't fit the Malibu Barbie image like the rest of the girls."

"Like ... Helena Sloan?"

Xia spiked another hateful glare at me, making me flinch. It was a crazy gamble. There are many rules for living peacefully with Xia Celeste. One is never, ever mention anyone with the name Sloan.

"That's right," she agreed, her voice tight and harsh.

If I didn't change the course of this conversation, everything was going to blow up in my face. Again.

"Mom, you said the killer thought Nicole was communicating with his prior victims. Was it true? Was Nicole really receiving messages from the others? Was she ... like us?"

Every article I'd found treated the killer's idea that Nicole Kidwell and Helena Sloan – two Tarot card readers who co-owned a tiny metaphysical shop in Pacific Grove – were speaking to his prior victims as a tragic delusion. Despite the fact that Helena helped police discover the body of one victim, serious investigative reporters never regarded her claims of ghostly evidence as fact.

"I don't know," my mother admitted. "It's possible, but I can't say for certain. Nicole and I, we were never exactly friends." The bitterness was back in her voice. "I believe she had talent, but your father and his sister never truly embraced their own gifts. They were too busy worshiping at the throne of Helena Sloan. Even when she fell from grace and ran away to California, they were still her faithful little minions."

"Fall from grace? Was it really that big of a deal? Lots of women have babies without getting married."

"Yes, but Mommy and Daddy Sloan thought their pretty little Disney princess was perfectly perfect in every way."

My father still carries a picture of Helena in his wallet. Not a picture of Helena and Nicole together, but a candid shot of her on a picnic blanket smiling up into the camera with a look my grandpa would call *pure come and get it*. And Dad keeps a shoebox in his photography studio filled with more pictures of her … hundreds more. I have a strong suspicion about Helena's "fall from grace" as my mother referred to it. If true, my suspicion would explain my mother's unwavering hatred for Helena Sloan. But I had never dared to bring up my theory with either of my parents. And yet, Xia was opening the door, wasn't she?

"Is it true she refused to tell anyone who the father was?" I asked, watching her face for a reaction. *Do you know who the father was?*

"Never mind that," my mother said, waving her hand. "It's all ancient history."

A tang of venomous frustration clotted my throat.

"I'm trying to make a point here," she continued. "My point is, dealing with murder victims is a tricky business, little girl. And very dangerous." She pressed her right hand to her chest and made a flourish with her other arm. "I constantly work with my spirit guides and guardians to make sure I'm protected. Sometimes that means they block communications." She paused, taking a deep breath to let that last statement sink in.

So that's your excuse, I thought. But then I was instantly uncertain if it was my thought or some other entity speaking to me.

Movement caught my attention. Ivy's silhouette was changing, elongating, expanding. Her arms stretched out, transforming into bare black branches that covered the walls of my bedroom. Similarly, her hair grew and twisted into branches that stretched up and across the ceiling.

"I've been neglecting your abilities," Xia continued, oblivious to the shadowy phenomena manifesting behind her back. "It's your father's fault. He has always been dead set against either of us doing any training with you. But he's a sad, scared, little moron. Obviously, after what happened yesterday, you're going to need some training. I can't send you off to a summer camp for that, can I?"

All I could do was shake my head. Feelings of curiosity and dread warred with each other in my frazzled brain. What was Ivy trying to tell me now? My mother's mouth continued to move, but her words were garbled buzzing at the edge of my consciousness. All that mattered was the tableau unfolding behind her. Black leaves exploded from the branches until Ivy's tree resembled the massive sugar maples that lined the downtown business district of Moonville.

Two birds swooped across my bedroom walls – one black as the tree, the other pure white – and landed on the branch that used to be Ivy's left shoulder. Both birds turned their heads to regard each other. The distinctive, chunky outline of their beaks identified them as two crows. The black beak opened and cawed loudly, sending a shiver down my spine. Ivy's message was now crystal clear.

Lying. Fraud. Lying. Fraud.

"Good, then that's decided." My mother stood up, seeming quite relieved and satisfied with our little discussion. I was just confused.

"What happens now?" I asked, anxiety churning in my gut. If Ivy was right, if Xia Celeste was a psychic fraud, how was she going to train me?

"We'll talk more about it later. I have an important appointment in Palo Alto today. You rest and put some ice or something on that." She wiggled her fingers toward my face then whirled away and left my bedroom, swinging the door closed behind her.

She wasn't cruel. We didn't argue. In fact, this was the

closest thing to a decent mother-daughter heart-to-heart talk I'd experienced in years.

So why did I want to throw something at the door after she left?

6
———

BEFORE

A**NYONE WHO HAS EVER LIVED IN OR VISITED MY HOMETOWN** knows the importance of a white crow in Spiritualist circles.

The term was coined way back in the 1880's when a Harvard professor famously declared to the world, "In order to disprove the assertion that all crows are black, one white crow is sufficient." It sounds like solid, sober, scholarly advice. Except Professor James wasn't giving a lecture to students on the scientific method; he was giving an interview to the New York Herald in reference to a famous trance medium of his day named Leonora Piper. Mrs. Piper was the professor's white crow – his one shining example of a person with proven supernormal powers and a pure heart.

So, according to the James metaphor, a white crow is a truly gifted medium sharing communications from beyond the veil with absolutely no selfish or evil intent. Cue the trumpets and the angelic choir.

And a black crow is ... quite the opposite.

As a side note, Leonora Piper was not a white crow by any stretch of the imagination. She was a complete wackadoodle. Piper claimed to channel spirit guides, or *controls* as the Victorians used to call them. One of her controls was a French physician who couldn't speak French and another described monkeys living on the sun. When a well-known psychical researcher died, Leonora pretended to channel him in order to use his name to discredit another medium. Mrs. Piper was total nutburger with a side of psycho sauce.

But the symbolism of a white crow lives on untarnished, except in Moonville where we celebrate shades of gray.

Granville Quinn, beloved founder of the Moonville Sanitarium and Spa that put my hometown on the map, wrote a letter to the editor of The Herald in response to the original article that quoted Professor James. In his letter, Granville declared that he did not simply believe in the afterlife; he knew it existed beyond a shadow of a doubt based on his own experiences. He also observed that pure black crows were common while pure white crows were rare, but there were many examples of crows with a mix of white and black feathers. Likewise, spiritualist mediums could not be easily sorted into two categories. The most gifted medium placed on a stage or under a magnifying glass would, invariably, resort to performing tricks when the spirits were silent. So he abhorred Professor James's purist metaphor and urged the readers to consider a more holistic view of spiritualism.

In Moonville, we love all our crows. Crow sculptures in stone and metal adorn our parks and public buildings all year long. There is an actual city ordinance on the books that forbids the display of scarecrows inside the city limits. Our All Crows Festival is like a spiritualist Mardi Gras – two weeks of costumes, outdoor art exhibits, parades, public séances, gothic concerts, plays that depict Spiritualist themes and a little dose of gentile debauchery – where plenty of revelers wear black feathers proudly.

My mother dismisses the entire debate over black and white crows as racially biased. I don't disagree. She also grumbles over the festival, calling it the Spook and Spectre Spectacular. But that doesn't stop her from donning a white feather gown every year and waving to all the wannabes on the parade route. White feathers. White crow.

Lying. Fraud. Lying. Fraud.

Yes, I understood Ivy's message.

What I didn't understand was how Ivy had tapped into that knowledge. White crows and black crows and Victorian spiritualist debates were not something the average modern teenager would know about. Was it possible Ivy could read my mind and drag up my memories the same way I'd lived through hers?

Suddenly, I felt itchy and restless. Sitting still was impossible.

The earlier mention of Helena Sloan, the dead psychic medium my mother still regarded as her archrival, brought another Sloan to mind. Helena's daughter, Lucy Sloan, published paranormal illustrated novels and maintained a gorgeous website that featured her haunting art. I'd lost many hours tumbling down the rabbit hole of Lucy's online art portfolio. But I wasn't in search of artistic escape today. The website included a blog where Lucy discussed her history with spirits. Sometimes she even answered questions from followers who contacted her for advice in dealing with haunted encounters. Perhaps she would answer my questions. Lucy is only eight years older than me, but she's lived an incredible life. She was the closest thing to consulting an older mentor for advice that was open to me.

Once again closed away in my bathroom, I retrieved the phone from its hiding place. As soon as I opened the web browser, a message appeared warning me only 10% battery power was left. I'd forgotten to charge it the previous night. Impatient, I dismissed the warning and opened Lucy's website, telling myself I'd just take a quick look then let the phone recharge while I ran through my ballet barre routine and took a shower.

Lucy's main blog posts tended to be brief and lyrical with rough sketches hinting at ghostly themes. However, it was in the comment sections where things really got interesting. On a whim, I typed "fraud" in the blog's search box and got a long list of results. Several of the results also featured *Xia Celeste*. With shaking hands, I opened the most recent section that included my mother's name in the preview.

It was a comment from someone called GhoulGrl99.

You're a Moonville native, right? What do you think about the new Xia Celeste controversy?

The comment ended with a link to the article I'd seen last night on the *Unhaunted* website. *Psychic Fraud or Something Sinister?* My stomach gave a queasy lurch. There was no way around it. I was going to have to read that article, but I dreaded it. First, I wanted to see what Lucy had to say. Several people had posted hostile comments. Then I found Lucy's response.

I'm not sure what to say about that article. I promise you Xia Celeste – or Shirley Simmons as she used to be known back in Moonville – was a very gifted psychic medium once upon a time. She's done great things. Unfortunately, she also suffers from an insatiable hunger for so many things that lead to bad decisions ... fame, fortune, glory, and a magic mirror to proclaim she's the fairest of them all. If Xia has sinned against anyone, it was in pursuit of one of those insatiable desires that the Buddhists call Tanha. I'm not Buddhist, not by a long shot, but I have a little experience in dealing with hungry ghosts. I feel sorry for anyone Xia might have hurt, but I also feel sorry for her. She's a hungry ghost walking around in a living body.

If my mother ever read that comment, she'd want to claw Lucy's eyes out. But it didn't sound to me like Lucy hated my mother nearly as much as Xia despised Helena Sloan's daughter. Feeling bold, I clicked on the contact link and started typing.

Hello Lucy,

I've been a huge fan of your art for years. I follow your Instagram and I'm always amazed at the way you capture

Delete.

Hi Lucy,

Sorry to bother you, but I'm freaking out.

Delete.

Dear Miss Sloan,

We've never met, but I'm like you. I see dead people too.

Delete.

Lucy,

The ghost of a murdered girl is following me around and telling me horrible secrets. Now I think maybe she's reading my mind. Has this ever happened to you? Do you know how I can make her go away?

With a sigh of frustration, I gave up on composing a message and hit the back button. Once again, I landed on the comment that displayed the *Unhaunted* link. Time to suck it up and find out what was so sinister. I clicked the link quickly, then held my breath waiting for the article to load. My mother's smiling face filled the screen.

· · ·

XIA CELESTE – PSYCHIC SLEUTH OR SOMETHING SINISTER?

It's been nearly two decades since Xia Celeste assisted the FBI in gathering evidence against evangelical preacher Anthony Harris. No one disputes that Celeste's efforts and courtroom testimony were crucial in convicting Harris of the murder of his wife Abigail Harris. Harris himself refers to Celeste as the "godless harlot who bewitched the jury into an unjust conviction."

Most people either love Xia Celeste, or they love to hate her.

From the beginning, Celeste was a controversial figure. Her brash personality and flamboyant appearance fed the media frenzy around the trial. One reporter following the trial commented that Celeste "looked like she dropped into the courtroom to testify on her way to a Spice Girls concert."

Despite her unorthodox appearance, the jurors believed her testimony. During a group interview, one juror stated, "She was clear, concise, and convincing. She didn't ask us to believe in ghosts. She explained how she used a ghost story to get a guilty man to hang himself. Even if you didn't like her, even if you didn't want to believe her, the prosecution had hours of tapes to back up her story."

Those tapes were the result of legal wiretaps recording conversations between Celeste and Preacher Harris in the weeks following the discovery of his wife's remains. Celeste ostensibly contacted Harris claiming she was in communication with his wife's spirit and urged him to confess his crimes. She purposefully laced her accusations with incorrect details. In his zeal to prove the psychic medium was lying, Harris incriminated himself numerous times by correcting her intentional misstatements.

To this day, there is still a great deal of confusion and misinformation regarding Celeste's role in the case. Skeptics are quick to claim that Celeste publicly admitted to being a false and fraudulent medium in her sworn testimony. But most pundits agree that her testimony clearly stated she intentionally wove a web of accusations using mostly truth and just enough misinformation to ensure Harris would take the bait and correct her apparent missteps.

It was a brilliant psychological strategy and it worked. Yet, the controversy may never be fully resolved.

Despite the controversy, or perhaps as a direct result of it, Xia Celeste's career as a psychic medium skyrocketed after the Harris conviction. She's written five books, starred in three seasons of her own reality television show, and boasts her client list would put Heidi Fleiss to shame. It's an unfortunate comparison ... or is it a little too close to the truth?

Click here to read more...

I sat on the bathroom counter, confused. Most of what I'd read so far was well-known ancient history. There was nothing sinister there ... unless you count Anthony Harris, and my mother helped lock that monster away. But those last two paragraphs puzzled me.

Heidi Fleiss?

The name was highlighted in blue and underlined, so I clicked the hyperlink — then quickly hit the back button, my face burning. Why in the name of all that is sane and decent and normal would my mother compare herself to a disgusting woman convicted of running a prostitution ring?

I really, really, really did not want to read any further. And yet, I clicked through to the rest of the article. Of course I did.

Xia Celeste has been on our radar since we started this website. Eight years ago we launched a focused effort to uncover any credible evidence that would indicate Xia Celeste is a psychic *fraud. We found plenty of people who wanted to discredit her, including three violent offenders serving terms in prison, but we did not find one shred of solid proof to discredit the woman's talents as a spirit medium. Quite the opposite, in fact.*

Still, we continued to receive requests to take action. Most of those requests seemed more concerned with Celeste's abrasive nature and lifestyle choices rather than any real deceit.

We didn't start this website to dictate taste or good manners. We have no interest in shaking our finger at someone who uses poor judgement in presenting herself and her abilities to the public. It is our mission to expose unscrupulous frauds who prey on innocent clients. To learn more about our mission, please read our About Us page.

Our mission? What was all this "we" crap? Was there an army of paranormal debunkers out there somewhere painting a target on my mother's back? Again, I clicked away from the article to learn more.

On the About Us page I found a drawing of three people – a man and two women – styled sort of like a comic book cover but without all the spandex, square jaws, and hulking muscles. The man stood front and center with his heavily tattooed arms crossed over his chest. He was wearing a black cape and an old-timey magician's top hat with modern blue jeans and a plain white t-shirt. Beneath his high-top tennis shoes were the words *The Illusionist*. On his right stood a middle-aged woman dressed like a stereotypical librarian – sweater set, dowdy plaid skirt, half-moon reading glasses on a chain. She was depicted with a large book tucked under one arm and a phone pressed to her right ear. Beneath her brown loafers it said *The Researcher*. To the left stood a dark-skinned woman wearing knee-high black boots, a short black dress, and a Burberry trench coat. Her face was mostly hidden behind a large digital camera. She was labeled as *The Investigator*.

A giggle bubbled out of me. They didn't look like angry paranormal debunkers. They looked like a quirky little group that didn't take themselves too seriously. In fact, they looked like people I'd like to meet.

Our mission, the page proclaimed in large, bold lettering, *is to expose con artists who pollute the ideals of healthy spiritualist belief with tricks and hoaxes aimed at exploitation and financial profit. We don't just believe in spirit communication; we know from first-hand experiences that some messages from beyond the grave are real. Unfortunately, fraudsters peddling false hope are poisonous to the ethical, enlightened work of most modern spiritualists.*

Wow. I set down my phone and rubbed my eyes, my mind racing. This wasn't what I'd expected at all. These people were true believers. And yet, they obviously had found out something that might be sinister about Xia Celeste. I sucked in a deep breath, picked up the phone again, and scrolled through the rest of the About Us page.

A longish blurb under the mission statement gave the full names of the people in the drawing and explained that their *Unhaunted* titles were directly related to real-world careers. The Illusionist really did perform on stage and, like Houdini before him, was annoyed whenever he saw carnival tricks masquerading as communications with the dead. The Researcher was a research librarian at an ivy-league university. And the fashionable Investigator was an investigative journalist with a long list of impressive awards to her credit. All three experienced real-life paranormal phenomena that sparked their interest in modern spiritualism. All three had run into fraudulent mediums selling lies to profit from innocent people's pain. And all three had been recruited to contribute their talents to the *Unhaunted* website by someone they called The Professor.

Below the group bio was another character labelled as *The Professor*. Unlike the previous illustration, The Professor was not depicted in human form. Instead, a drawing of a magnificent snowy owl wearing huge purple eyeglasses stared out from the screen. Long feminine lashes framed the magnified owlish eyes. This shorter bio explained that The Professor had to remain anonymous in order to protect her personal safety as well as the rights of her clients. She's a former prosecuting attorney who was gunned down on the courthouse steps by an unidentified assailant. After a near-death experience on the operating table, she awoke with a new and disconcerting awareness of the patients who didn't survive. At first she tried to ignore the voices of the dead. Eventually, she discovered a new career path. While operating a small private practice specializing in mundane estate law, she answers otherworldly pleas by doing pro bono work for victims' families. None of her clients have any idea she can communicate with their dearly departed, and she intends to keep it that way.

At the bottom of the page was a final statement that proclaimed *Unhaunted* was a non-profit, volunteer project. None of the contributors were paid any compensation for their work and frequently used their own personal funds in pursuit of the truth.

Crap. These people were practically saints of the Spiritualist variety. And they had something unpleasant to say about Xia – the least saintly person in the modern Spiritualist community. Heavy hearted, I clicked back over to the full article and resumed reading where I'd left off.

. . .

IN THE PAST FEW YEARS, XIA CELESTE'S STAR HAS BEEN FADING *rapidly. Although her first two books hit the best-seller lists, the next three suffered from lackluster sales causing her publisher to end the relationship last year. After watching three seasons of Celeste's onscreen tantrums and very little psychic sleuthing, her fan base stopped tuning in and the network cancelled her show. Both her website and Facebook page were plagued with vicious internet troll attacks fueled by Celeste's scathing replies. The insults and accusations became so vile, Celeste closed her website just a few months ago.*

We have no interest in joining in the crash and burn culture that has become Celeste's career. However, in the past six months we've received a new onslaught of emails with a fresh batch of accusations against Xia Celeste. The fear and loathing in these communications is palpable ... and also troubling.

And so, with much trepidation, we launched a second investigation.

A long list of anonymous sources spoke to us. Every single source we talked to seemed desperate, even frantic, for us to prove the messages Celeste is passing along from the dead are entirely false. And yet not one of these sources was able to produce a single example of Celeste committing a clear act of fraud. Not one.

The only accusers willing to go on record against Celeste were the three violent offenders who contacted us during the previous investigation. Although we declined speaking to them eight years ago, we decided to leave no stone unturned this time. All statements from the three men were variations on the same theme — they all started by claiming Celeste had framed them, stumbled through a creative re-telling of their cases in which they provided absolutely no evidence to support that claim, and ended with various versions of "Thou shalt not suffer a witch to live."

In other words, all three men had nothing of value to contribute — to our investigation or to society.

Other sources who were willing to go on the record were unified in their conviction that Celeste is a gifted psychic medium. Even people who claim to hate her admit she is talented. When asked why other sources, anonymous sources, might be desperate to prove Celeste is a fraud, we always heard a variation of the same answer.

Some people don't want anyone to hear what the dead have to say.

We have to agree. Look at Anthony Harris. His life might be very different today if Xia Celeste hadn't crossed his path.

Joseph Beauford, who retired from the FBI five years ago, was one of the lead investigators on the Harris case. He's still absolutely convinced Celeste's paranormal abilities are very real:

"Xia came to us when it was still a missing persons case. The information she provided was extraordinarily detailed and led us straight to the burial site. The forensic evidence confirmed Xia knew details of the crime no one should have known except the killer. In fact, that woman made herself our main suspect ... until we saw the video. Then we refocused on Harris and Xia was right there, eager to help."

[The video Beauford mentions is actually hundreds of hours of time-stamped digital footage shot by Celeste's first husband, Nathan Kidwell. The couple were filming amateur investigations of haunted properties around New England during the window of time when Abigail Harris was killed.]

BOOM! THERE IS WAS. I JUMPED OFF THE COUNTER, PUMPED my fists in the air a few times, and even did a little victory dance around my bathroom.

In the aftermath of the disaster I'd witnessed the day before, I'd somehow forgotten about Agent Joe Beauford.

Here was absolute proof that my mother was not a pure black crow.

I could see the man clearly in my memory. He always seemed like a giant with close-cropped salt and pepper hair, a weather-beaten face, and piercing blue eyes. Agent Beauford visited our home several times when I was a little girl growing up in Moonville, but I hadn't seen him since I was ten-years-old. It made perfect sense now that I knew he retired around that time.

Before he stopped coming over, Agent Beauford used to show up on the front porch wearing a black suit and clutching a thick folder in his beefy hands. His face was always grim. He'd speak to my mother for an hour or even longer, then he'd leave quietly looking a little less grim. As soon as he drove away, my mother would pack a suitcase and drop me off at my dad's or Grandpa Elton's house. When she returned, usually a week or two later, she'd be glowing with a deep sort of satisfaction. There would be no screaming matches, no angry insults, no painful punishments for weeks after those trips.

My mother consulted on more than just the Harris case. She helped the FBI solve multiple cases. I know she did. Why else would Agent Beauford keep coming back? Why else would three violent offenders doing time in prison want to badmouth her?

Feeling like a crushing weight had been lifted from my shoulders, I sat back down, this time on the closed toilet lid, and hastily scrolled down past an old picture of Joe arresting Harris.

After speaking with Beauford, we were ready to close down our second investigation into Xia Celeste.

Until we met Maisy Jacobs.

Maisy Jacobs. Seeing the name was like a bucket of cold water dumped over my head. I knew that name.

Maisy appeared on our doorstep back in Moonville on an icy January morning. It was Martin Luther King Day, so I was home from school and my mother's schedule was packed. Xia pressed me into service as an informal receptionist to meet and greet her clients. It wasn't a terrible chore, but I would have preferred helping Zack at the veterinary clinic or practicing dance in the studio over Grandpa's garage. Maisy's appointment was on the schedule for one-thirty in the afternoon, but she arrived three hours early clutching a large tapestry bag overflowing with yarn and knitting needles. There was a grim look on her face that melted into a grandmotherly smile when I opened the door. At first I was embarrassed, convinced Xia made some mistake in her scheduling. But Maisy assured me she knew the appointment time was in the early afternoon.

"Icy roads," she declared, as though that fully explained her early arrival. The old woman made herself comfortable in one of the two velvet-covered armchairs my mother positioned outside her consulting room and started knitting at a furious pace. In fact, there was something disconcerting about her knitting technique. Her fingers and knitting needles moved in jerky, harsh movements that seemed almost violent. Despite her grandmotherly appearance, Maisy made me nervous.

When the next client arrived, I felt a little relieved to have a third person in the room. Maisy stopped knitting and introduced herself.

"This is my first appointment with Miss Celeste," she declared. "Have you been here before?"

The other woman told her she came frequently. "Xia has been a blessing since I lost my little girl."

"Quite a price tag for a blessing," Maisy replied.

My hackles went up while the other client assured the old woman that Xia's talents were priceless. In fact, she would pay double or even triple the consulting fee.

Something was wrong here. I could feel this old lady's hostility looming like a dark shadow in the room. When the other client went in to see Xia and Maisy went back to her vicious act of knitting, I quietly consulted my mother's schedule book. In the block for Maisy's appointment, there were a few notes: *New client. Referred by HR? Something off …* *CIAGBF.*

CIAGBF translates to *Caution is a Girl's Best Friend*. It was my mother's personal code for new clients who might be troublesome. So my mother was already on alert. No need to jump in with my own unease.

When the next client arrived, Maisy started up a similar conversation where she again commented on the cost of Xia's appointments. This time, the client gave her a sour look and said, "If you have to check the price tag, you probably can't afford it."

The relief I felt when Maisy Jacobs finally disappeared into Xia's consulting room was short-lived. After only ten minutes, loud voices erupted. I sat up straight and snatched up the phone in case I needed to call 9-1-1. It wouldn't have been the first time one of Xia's sessions ended with police officers escorting someone off our property. But the call wasn't necessary. When Xia flung open her office door and ordered the woman out, Maisy left without argument. She marched out with her head held high and a smug look on her face. At the outer door she turned and pointed a crooked finger at my mother.

"I am going to prove what you did to that girl. If it's the last thing I do, I will make sure everyone knows what you did to her. Hanna was no angel, but you are much worse. You are a greedy, shameful, shallow slice of evil. Your day is coming."

With that threat, Maisy stomped out of our house slamming the door behind her. Before I could ask my mother what had happened, she slammed her own consulting room door. That was the last I heard of Maisy Jacobs. Until now.

MAISY JACOBS INVITED US TO HER HOME FOR TEA AND conversation. Jacobs lives in a modest duplex located in Cleveland's Waterloo Arts District and leads a quiet existence now, but that wasn't always the case. She looks like a stereotypical little old lady with a cap of iron gray curls and pale green eyes, but Jacobs led a wild and dangerous life in the sixties, seventies, and eighties. After a little success as a teen model and a few failed attempts at an art career, Jacobs became trapped in a web of pornography, prostitution, and narcotics addiction.

Today, she's the founder of Transcend, a non-profit organization that helps recovering addicts build a new life. It's a labor of love for a woman who openly admits she lost three decades to drug addiction.

We could not find any evidence that Jacobs ever crossed paths with Celeste. But her email stated she was very determined to share "the true nature of Xia Celeste's crimes."

In person, Jacobs started the conversation by declaring we were "barking up the wrong tree" with our investigation into Celeste.

"I've read your mission statement, you know," she said,

shaking one bent, arthritic finger. "You people seem to think the only harm one of these so-called spirit mediums can do is by giving false testimony, telling lies. I'm here to tell you Xia Celeste is a whole other kind of evil. You'll never prove she's a phony. Stop trying."

With that enigmatic statement, Jacobs produced a thick manila folder held together with a red rubber band.

"This is the story of Hanna Rybak," she said in a subdued whisper, caressing the folder. "At twenty-eight years of age, she battled her way out of opioid addiction and was building a reputation as a gifted metal sculptor. Two years ago, Hanna was one of my brightest success stories. Now she's dead. Hanna killed herself. Xia Celeste is to blame."

The phone vibrated and the screen went dark. A red icon appeared showing the battery was down to 1% power. It was all I could do stop myself from throwing the stupid thing across the room.

Hanna Rybak? The note next to Maisy Jacobs' appointment in Xia's schedule book mentioned an HR. *Referred by HR?*

From the other side of the bathroom wall, my mother started singing a Beyoncé song in the shower. Every off-key word was like a spike jabbed into my spine.

7

———

Now

Darkness surrounds me, pressing in. My eyes are wide open, staring into nothing but endless black. But it's not an empty void. It stinks of foul, rotting things. Something circles, moving closer, waiting for me to scream. Terror clots in my throat, strangling my breath. A bluish glow appears above my head. Relieved, I reach up both arms toward a tiny square of starry night sky but hot, sticky tendrils wrap around my limbs, pulling me back down, down, down into darkness.

Thrashing and struggling, I fight my way upward until I wake up in a dimly lit room gasping for air. Where am I? Bits and flashes of memory come back to me. Running. The scream of metal tearing. The sirens and flashing lights. The emergency room. My mother's voice whispering, "Keep your mouth shut."

Every part of my body throbs with pain and shame.

How could I have been so stupid?

As the nightmarish wave of memories ebbs, I become aware of another presence in the room. Slowly, gritting my teeth against the discomfort, I turn my head to the right. There's an IV in my arm. It's attached to some sort of medical monitor, beeping and flashing as my vital signs stare back at me. Beyond the display, there's a frosted glass wall. Vaguely humanish silhouettes surrounded by pale green light move to and fro in the corridor outside, like wraiths or aliens on a secret mission. To one side of the closed door, one solitary form stands still, feet braced wide apart and arms crossed. With a sinking sensation, I realize I'm looking at a guard, most likely a police officer, watching over the door to my room. And I know it is not LaShawna.

Turning my aching head to the left, I finally find my visitor.

Vera Birch is sitting in a comfortable upholstered chair watching me from behind her thick hipster glasses. A feeble nightlight positioned near her head makes her white and lavender hair glow. She is wrapped in a plush white knitted shawl flecked with pale gray and lavender. Something about her appearance jolts me. There is a feeling of recognition, but it has nothing to do with the earlier scene in the emergency room.

I blink a few times and she blinks back.

"Good morning, Asha," she greets me calmly.

Purple glasses. Round frames. Magnified owlish eyes. Oh wow. She looks exactly like a snowy owl wearing glasses.

"Are you ..." I falter, unsure of how to ask this question. It's ridiculous. Surely, my battered brain is playing tricks on me. And yet, I can't possibly leave it unasked.

"Am I what?" she prompts me gently.

"The Professor?" I ask, feeling my skin burn.

Her head twists and tilts to one side. Regarding me with

a quizzical, slightly amused expression she asks, "What do you know about The Professor?"

And I know. Right then I know all I need to know. I'm absolutely certain she's the owlish professor from the *Unhaunted* website. The same website that published Maisy Jacobs' accusations against Xia Celeste. And my mother, capable of tearing into her enemies with vicious zeal, acted like a tame little lap dog in this woman's presence. Until she whispered in my ear.

Don't say a word. Keep your mouth shut.

"I don't know anything," I mumble through stiff lips. "Never mind."

The machine clicks and whirrs softly. A warm, fuzzy feeling washes over my body. My muscles relax as my brain stops screaming. This time I embrace the rising darkness.

8

———

Before

Perched on my toilet lid, clutching a dead phone in one hand, I sat very still and waited for the howling in my head to subside. My skin felt scorched. My gut was on fire.

Hanna killed herself. Xia Celeste is to blame.

I knew I should move. I needed to stand up, to charge the stupid phone, to take a shower, to do something, anything that would quiet the noise in my head until I could finish reading the rest of the article.

Hanna killed herself. Xia Celeste is to blame.

Impossible. No one, not even my mother in the throes of her worst temper tantrums, could make someone kill themselves. It wasn't true. It couldn't possibly be true.

"To the left, to the left," Xia's voice sang loudly from the other side of my closet wall. Hangers clattered as she continued to sing about a cheating lover, instructing him to take a box of everything he owned and walk out the door. I pictured myself packing up my own box and escaping this nightmare. But where would I go? Zack would come get me if I called him, but what would be the cost? Could he be charged with kidnapping? Or worse?

A familiar ringtone erupted from my mother's side of the wall – Sister Sledge's "We Are Family." It was Xia's special ringtone for LaShawna. The closet noises stopped. A flurry of quick footsteps ended when the ringtone cut off.

"What's happening?" Xia snapped.

Her closet door slammed, quickly followed by her own bathroom door. I continued to sit perfectly still, every nerve ending on alert, but I didn't hear anything further. She had shut those doors deliberately, intending to keep me out of the conversation.

I needed to move. I needed to charge the damn phone. I needed to find out why LaShawna was calling my mother. Instead, I sat rigid and paralyzed by dread until my mother slammed back into my bedroom.

"Asha!?" Her voice sounded like a drill sergeant.

"Coming."

I dropped my secret phone into the wicker trash basket, covered it with a fat wad of toilet paper, and flushed the toilet. As soon as I emerged from the bathroom, my mother threw a white and green plastic object at my head. I managed to catch it before it hit me in the face ... barely. It was a bag of frozen peas.

"Congratulations, rookie. Welcome to the major leagues." Xia's eyes sparkled with a dangerous fire.

"I'm sorry, what?"

"LaShawna called. Nothing has been officially announced yet, but it looks like you were right." Xia pressed one hand to her chest and widened her eyes dramatically. "Oh, I'm sorry! I mean I was right. I mean, thank goodness you were there to witness those precious pearls of wisdom dripping from my insensible lips during my trance episode last week." The gleam in her eyes was getting downright venomous. "Damn it, Asha. Of all the stupid, paper-thin lies you could have come up with it had to be me falling into a trance and speaking in tongues? Seriously?"

Put that way, it was rather stupid.

"I'm sorry," I said, staring at the floor.

"You should be. I just endured a stern lecture from my dear cousin. She wants to make sure I'm never alone in case any more trances hit without warning. How could my only child be such a moron?"

"I'm sorry," I repeated.

"Sorry isn't good enough. Put sorry in one hand and cry your tears in the other. Which one fills up first?" She motioned toward the frozen peas. "Put that on your face. It's time for damage control."

She flounced out of my room slamming the door behind her. After counting to thirty, I crept back into my bathroom, rescued the phone from the wastebasket, and attached it to a charger hidden under my bathroom sink. Then I slunk back to bed and applied the peas to my swollen cheek as instructed. I knew from past experience it would take at least thirty minutes for the phone's battery to hold enough charge to allow me to use it. So I stared at the ceiling, sucked in deep breaths, and tried to patch together my shattered nerves.

The analog clock on my nightstand showed the time as 8:50. Pink with sweet little dancing ballerinas in place of numbers, the old-fashioned alarm clock was another relic from my aunt Nicole's childhood. I picked it up and pressed my ear to the back cover. Rhythmic tick, tick, ticking assured me the clock was still working. I'd been awake less than two hours. How could I feel so utterly exhausted, wrung out, and bordering on punch-drunk? Like I'd just finished dancing every role in the Nutcracker Suite at triple speed. No matter how much I wanted to curl up in a ball and sleep, my brain was racing. Jumbled thoughts ping-ponged inside my head.

Lying. Fraud. Lying. Fraud.

Her client list is more of a hit list.

Hanna killed herself. Xia Celeste is to blame.

You don't need help, Asha. You need to give help.

The bag of peas made an unsatisfying squishy sound when it hit my bedroom wall. Hot tears of frustration ran down my face unchecked. I was a fifteen-year-old kid with a black eye. What did they want from me?

XIA VISITED MY BEDROOM A THIRD TIME BEFORE SHE LEFT that morning to let me know she would not be back until early evening.

"You'll definitely have to get yourself breakfast and lunch," she said, as though I didn't make my own meals every single day. "Maybe even dinner."

Perfect, I thought.

"I'm fine. Take your time," I said.

"While I'm out, you've got an important reading assignment to complete."

Yes, I did. More than one. First, I needed to read the rest of that article. Then I intended to read everything I could find about Ivy Brennan. Maybe, just maybe, if I could figure out why Ivy was still haunting me I might be able to find resources that would help me convince her to move on and stop writing messages on my bathroom mirror. But I knew Xia wasn't referring to any of those pressing subjects.

She presented a copy of her first published book – *Let*

the Circle Be Broken: Autobiography of a Modern Medium – with a dramatic flourish.

"This is my origin story," she announced, placing the book reverently on my bed as though presenting a sacred text.

Origin story? Was she serious? Super heroes have origin stories. All the Spandex in my mother's underwear must be poisoning her brain.

"You think you know everything you need to know about this book and your own mother, but think again. Re-read the first eight chapters." She rapped her knuckles on the hardbound cover. "Pay special attention to how I handled visitations while I was still living in my parents' home. And make sure you read the chapter on Aunt Lettie very, very thoughtfully. Do you hear me?"

It was an easy promise to make. I've read and re-read those chapters in my mother's autobiography so many times they are tattooed in my memory. I could recite every word in my sleep. Xia's depiction of her childhood was like reading a Stephen King novel, more frightening than *Carrie*.

I've never met my maternal grandparents. Those chapters comprised all I knew about them. Like the murderer Anthony Harris, Abraham Simmons was an Evangelical Christian minister with Southern Baptist roots who ruled his household with an iron fist. Preacher Simmons wasn't just another one of those "spare the rod, spoil the child" idiots. If my mother's descriptions of his punishments were true, he was an evil, sadistic man. And Bessie Simmons was a sorry excuse of a mother. She baked pies while her husband tortured their children. Both of them believed communication with any spirits outside of the Holy Spirit was the devil's work. After a particularly horrific episode where the Simmons' and a select few devout members of their congregation tried to exorcise my mother's demons, Shirley Simmons finally found the courage to run away.

My mother was fifteen years old when she escaped her parents' abuse. Fifteen. My age. And she was dealing with worse injuries than a black eye. She had no car, no money, no phone, and no friends. Yet she managed to make it all the way from Hardaway, Alabama to Decatur, Georgia – over one hundred fifty miles – to her Aunt Letitia's doorstep. I focused on the book as a hefty dose of shame coursed through my veins.

"Earth to Asha? Do you hear me?"

"Yes."

"Yes, what?"

"Yes, Mother. I'll pay close attention to the early visitations. And I'll re-read Miss Lettie's lessons about the spirit world very thoughtfully."

"Good, girl. Rest up and get ready," she told me before hurrying down the stairs and out the front door.

Ready? Ready for what?

I waited a five full minutes, watching the time tick off on my pink alarm clock, before getting out of bed to wander the house. In the kitchen, I tracked down a granola bar and a cup of Greek yogurt. Chewing on the crunchy bar made my whole head ache, but I forced myself to sit there and finish my breakfast. Finally, I decided enough time had passed to check the phone. Like a condemned criminal headed for the gallows, I trudged up the stairs, sat cross-legged on the bathroom floor, and powered up. After navigating back to the same *Unhaunted* page I'd been reading when the battery died, Maisy Jacobs' accusation jumped out at me from the screen.

Hanna killed herself. Xia Celeste is to blame.

But before I could read any further, the lights in the

bathroom started flickering erratically. I scrambled to my feet as the temperature in the bathroom plummeted. Frost blossomed around the edges of the mirror.

"Ivy, quit it!" I screamed, furious.

Doors throughout the townhouse started slamming repeatedly, the staccato bursts sounded like gunshots going off. Books tumbled off the shelves in my room. For just a second, I thought this might be an actual California earthquake. Then I saw a new message written in the frost.

Help her!

I gripped the edge of the sink with one hand and pressed the phone to my chest with the other.

"Okay, you win," I said. "I just need a little time. Does time mean anything to you ... wherever you are?"

The alarm clock in my room started ringing. It was a harsh, grating sound that never failed to get me out of bed in the morning. But I wasn't the one who set it off this time. It gave me an idea. It was probably a stupid idea, but worth a try.

I rushed over and switched off the jangling alarm, then set it to ring again half an hour later.

"Thirty minutes," I announced to the empty room. "Do you hear me, Ivy? Just give me thirty minutes to get my head straight, okay?" I held the clock up facing outward and turned in a slow circle. "When the alarm goes off again, I'm all yours. I swear. I'll do whatever you ask, but I'm useless right now. Do you hear me?"

The doors stopped slamming. The lights in the bathroom stopped flashing and remained off. Finally, my bedroom door creaked open and all was still.

I scurried downstairs to find the front door wide open. As I'd done the night before, I secured the door with both bolts, grabbed the spare keys, and headed to my mother's inner sanctum. My stomach churned; my head pounded.

First I was going to finish reading that awful article. Then I was going to do my best to figure out why Zack thought I needed to look at my mother's financial records. If I tried to access the information on my phone, my mother would most likely receive an email notice that her account had been accessed from an unknown device. She would also be notified if I used a public computer at the library.

Not good.

If I was going to snoop around in her accounts, I needed her personal computer.

Everything in her office looked exactly as I left it. I perched on the edge of her desk chair juggling the phone, the clock, and the copied list of accounts in shaking hands. When I accidentally nudged the mouse, her screen came to life showing a Google Map to a spa in Palo Alto — probably the appointment she was rushing off to this morning. I clicked on the website link and did a double take when I noticed the list of treatments available. The cheapest one was nearly two hundred dollars. A bitter taste crept up my throat. Was my mother really out getting salt wrapped and hot rock massaged to the tune of hundreds of dollars while poor Mrs. Tsien waited on our rent check?

Shaking my head, I set the clock down on her desk, automatically noting the time. Twenty five minutes before I had to figure out what to do about Ivy ... if she honored our agreement. There was a jangling sensation at the base of my neck that made me suspect Ivy wasn't off in another place waiting for the alarm to pull her back, she was watching my every move. Once again, I navigated to the page with the full *Unhaunted* article and picked up reading where I'd left off.

. . .

"THIS IS THE STORY OF HANNA RYBAK," SHE SAID IN A SUBDUED whisper, caressing the folder. "At twenty-five years of age, she battled her way out of opioid addiction and was building a reputation as a gifted metal sculptor. Two years ago, Hanna was one of my brightest success stories. Now she's dead. Hanna killed herself. Xia Celeste is to blame."

It's an explosive accusation, but Maisy Jacobs believes she has the facts to back it up.

"Hanna was a trust fund kid. One of those spoiled young things with access to credit cards, fast cars, and too much freedom way too early in life. She didn't hit rock bottom because the money ran out. By all accounts, she was still flying high — reckless, rich, and carefree — right up until the day she walked into a rehab clinic and checked herself in."

Maisy Jacobs jabbed her finger at the folder. "I'm not talking about one of those exclusive, expensive, more-like-a-spa-than-a-rehab clinics. I'm talking about the kind of place where the unwashed masses are sent for court-ordered treatment. It wasn't prison, but it wasn't a Malibu resort center either."

According to Jacobs, Hanna's explanation for why she made such a drastic decision never rang true. "All she'd say was, 'I got so wasted one night, I lost my car in a poker game.' And she never looked anyone in the eye when she said it."

The mention of a car made Jacobs suspicious. DUI accidents are one of the main reasons she sees addicts voluntarily check into rehab.

"I told her she didn't have a snowball's chance in Hell of getting clean if she didn't come clean about all of her sins, but she proved me wrong. She did get clean. And she stayed clean for over five years. Not only did she turn her own life around, she helped others. She was an excellent sponsor for other addicts and volunteered with my group frequently. But I knew she had a terrible secret. There was a shadow behind her eyes, even when she smiled."

Two months before her death, Hanna Rybak took Jacobs aside after a group support meeting and asked for advice regarding a strange request. Her newest sponsee was a middle-aged woman struggling with unresolved guilt. The woman stole money and prescription drugs from her dying mother. The mother died before her grieving daughter could make amends. It was a sad, but not uncommon variation of the addiction stories that both Rybak and Jacobs had heard many times.

What they'd never heard before was this woman's proposed remedy. Hanna's sponsee made an appointment to visit a well-known psychic medium in the hopes of a connection with her deceased mother. She wanted to make amends beyond the grave, and she wanted Hanna to attend the session.

The medium was Xia Celeste.

"Hanna asked if I saw any harm in it. Step Nine is the most famous of the Twelve Steps. Everybody wants to make amends. What people frequently overlook or forget is there are qualifiers. We are supposed to make direct amends when possible, except when doing so would injure someone. In this case, I didn't think it was possible, but I also didn't see how it could injure anyone involved. I was wrong on both counts."

Jacobs said Hanna changed after the session with Xia Celeste. She frequently skipped support meetings. When she did attend, Hanna was a shadow of her former self — quiet, withdrawn, defensive, and frequently tearful. Fearing that the younger woman was using drugs again, Jacobs visited Hanna Rybak's studio apartment to confront her. What started as an intervention evolved into a confession.

"She finally admitted the story about losing her car in a poker game was rubbish. She killed someone. Hit and run. No witnesses. Just her and a dead man on a deserted stretch of road. Instead of *calling the police, she drove her expensive car to a high-crime neighborhood and left it unlocked, engine running, keys in the ignition. The next morning, she checked herself into rehab."*

Jacobs urged Hanna to go to the police and tell her story. But she was also curious. What had prompted this confession now after five years of silence and sobriety?

The answer was Xia Celeste.

"Sounds like Xia put on a cute little show for the client who scheduled the session, but then quickly zeroed in on Hanna as the bigger fish. She asked if Hanna knew a man who had died beside a road, then described the hit and run victim in precise and accurate detail. She never came out and accused Hanna of any crime, but she rattled off plenty of details that shocked that girl to the core. Then she suggested Hanna come back for a private session. Said she could help her clear the slate and break free. Xia kept pushing, needling her with details. Finally, Hanna agreed to another appointment just to escape. She never intended to go anywhere near Xia Celeste again."

A few days after the disturbing session, Hanna Rybak received two envelopes in the mail. Jacobs still has both envelopes in her manila folder. One contained a reminder of her upcoming appointment with Xia Celeste. A handwritten note at the bottom declared, "Standard consultation fee will be waived. Pay whatever amount you feel is fair." The second envelope contained a printout of an internet news article about the hit and run accident. There was no return address, but the post marks on the two envelopes matched.

"So what?" I snapped at the screen. "You have got to be kidding me."

Maisy Jacobs told my mother, "Hanna was no angel, but you are much worse."

In what kind of distorted, twisted, upside-down reality was that old woman living?

This Hanna person was a murderer. She was a spoiled rich girl who mowed down another human being with her car while driving intoxicated. It's called vehicular homicide. Then she covered up her crime and skipped off to rehab to build a new life ... until my mother let her know her secret wasn't going to be a secret any longer. And how did she react? Instead of facing the consequences and giving her victim any respect, she killed herself. And that's supposed to be my mother's fault?

Something sinister? Seriously?

I glanced at the clock. Twenty minutes left before the alarm would ring. Five precious minutes wasted on this idiotic accusation. Not to mention all the unnecessary stress and worry the article inflicted on me all morning. I was tempted to close the page without reading another word, but I knew leaving any part of the story unread would needle my nerves and distract me until I gave in and finished. Scanning the rest of the paragraphs quickly to see how much more of Maisy Jacobs I'd have to endure, one word jumped out at me.

Blackmail.

JACOBS CLAIMS XIA CELESTE'S MOTIVE FOR CONTINUING TO contact Hanna Ryback wasn't altruism. It was blackmail.

One week after her private confession, Hanna Rybak hung herself in the rented studio where she sculpted metal. A copy of her suicide note, which Rybak mailed to Maisy Jacobs instead leaving it to be discovered at the scene of her death, is in the manila file. Jacobs allowed us to read the letter, then pointed out one section.

"That woman won't leave me alone. Her eyes follow me everywhere, even when I sleep. She knows what I did. I don't understand how it's possible, but she knows. And she will never, ever let it rest. I thought I could pay her for her silence, but she will never go away. This is the only way I can escape."

The letter never mentions "that woman" by name. And Maisy Jacobs admits she does not have any solid proof that Xia Celeste blackmailed Hanna Rybak.

However, as the executor of Rybak's estate, Maisy Jacobs made a disturbing discovery in the dead woman's bank records. Hanna Rybak made several large cash withdrawals totaling fifty thousand dollars in the weeks leading up to her death. There's no record of any purchases or expenses that correspond to those withdrawals, and the money has never been found.

Could she have spent the money on drugs?

*"Fifty thousand dollars in five weeks? That's ridiculous,"
Jacobs argues. "Besides, the autopsy report says she was clean."*

Based on her suspicions, Jacobs made an appointment for a consultation with Xia Celeste in January of last year, saying she was referred by Hanna Rybak. Once they were alone, Jacobs confronted the celebrity medium with the suicide letter and the missing money.

"She didn't deny a thing. That witch looked me right in the eye and said, 'Sounds like little Hanna should have turned herself in to the police.' Her eyes were as dead and cold as a snake."

We attempted to contact Xia Celeste several times to give her the opportunity to tell her side of the story. We received back a short email from Celeste in reply:

"I only met Hanna Rybak one time. She was not my client. It was obvious that a terrible shadow of guilt was hanging over her, but she refused my help. Don't lose sight of the fact that an inno-cent life was cut short by Hanna's recklessness. She is not the victim here. I hope the proper authorities have been notified of her

confession and the family of the deceased man will be given some closure."

"THAT'S RIGHT, MOM," I WHISPERED, NODDING IN AGREEMENT as I closed the article. "Put the focus back on the real victim. Good for you."

But what about the fifty thousand dollars?

A stray memory popped into my mind.

My father wiping a hand over his tired face. "Let it rest, Shirl. You aren't judge and jury for the whole miserable world."

My mother glowing with fierce determination. "Rest? You mean hide my head in a bottle like you do? There's more than one way to make someone pay for crimes against humanity, Nate. "

No. It wasn't possible for me to imagine that woman accepting hush money from a murderer. But could the money have been part of some scheme my mother cooked up to punish Hanna Rybak?

There was one way to find out. The copied list of my mother's accounts and passwords suddenly felt heavy in my hand. This was no longer a wild goose chase assigned by Zack. Now I had another mission, not that I needed any more missions. But if this Hanna person paid my mother fifty thousand dollars in cash, there should be corresponding deposits in her bank account.

I bit my lower lip and pressed the icon on the favorites bar for Wells Fargo. The password on her list worked on the first try. Nervously, I started my research by clicking through the most recent transactions getting more and more confused.

There was money in the account. Not a huge sum, definitely not an extra fifty thousand dollars, but there was enough to pay the rent with a reasonable amount of money left over. And there were weekly payments from my father despite her repeated lamentations that his disappearing act left her high and dry without child support.

Liar.

She still had money in a savings account from her divorce settlement with Zack's father. That account was opened months after Maisy Jacobs confronted my mother about the suicide, but I checked the history anyway. It showed only one large deposit – from Robert J. Warner right before we moved to California – followed by a long list of withdrawals.

Looking back at the checking account, I located her publisher's most recent check. It wasn't late; it was tiny. Absolutely miniscule. I was surprised they even bothered to cut a check for that amount. I saw multiple deposits – mostly credit card payments with a few personal checks – that must have come from paying clients. But those deposits were much fewer and farther between than when we'd lived in Ohio. There were also multiple electronic deposits from something called the QFWC Fund. I'd never heard of it before. I spotted one five thousand dollar deposit marked cash in the last thirty days. The hairs on my neck stood up. Cash? It wasn't the missing fifty thousand dollars, but it was weird. Why would my mother have five thousand dollars in cash? Her busiest day with clients could only net around two or possibly three thousand and most clients paid with credit cards or checks. Factor in my mother's recent schedule was definitely not busy, and it didn't make sense.

Then I changed my focus to review charges on her account. Scrolling back in time, I scanned the list of debits since the last statement. There were a lot of negatives. Then

I reviewed the prior month, then one more month of transactions before stopping to open the calculator app on my phone.

After crunching the numbers, I sat back stunned. Beyond stunned. Totally disgusted.

My mother was burning through money at a horrifying rate, much faster than the money was coming in. Worse, she had three credit card accounts on her password list. When I opened separate tabs to view those accounts, I discovered two of the cards were maxed out. The third was getting close, and she was only paying the minimum payments each month.

Where was all this money going?

The lease payment on her Lexus nearly knocked me out of my chair. And who spends over a thousand dollars on a weave that has to be touched up every four weeks? Add to that all the charges from Bloomingdales and Nordstrom, personal training sessions, spa treatments, and expensive subscription services with words like Luxe or Posh or Opulent in the name. I could not believe my eyes.

We were headed for poverty at a dizzying rate.

Exiting her credit card accounts, I focused on the bank records. A search though sixteen months of extravagant spending turned up five separate cash deposits that totaled exactly fifty thousand dollars during the months of November and December just prior to Maisy Jacobs' appointment.

My heart dropped to my stomach. She did take the money. Xia Celeste accepted hush money from a murderer. Maybe it was part of an elaborate punishment she had planned, but my mother took Hanna Rybak's money.

And it was all gone.

There were no corresponding donations to a memorial

fund or victim's advocate group. She took the money and spent it on insane personal luxuries. And she was still spending at an obscene rate.

I scanned the notations on my copied list of accounts hoping to find something that would make this mess less horrible. A note at the bottom said, "*QFWC Fund*" followed by an email address. That was the source of several deposits in my mother's account. What was it?

I tried several Google searches with no definitive answer, just other people asking the same question I was asking in various forums. A few vague references to secret esoteric societies came up in my searches, but I wasn't sure they were truly related to QFWC Fund.

Finally, I did something I had not planned to do. I searched my mother's email account. It was mainly full of junk mail, advertisements, and newsletters from every store, boutique, and spa my mother had ever visited. But I found several short, business-like emails between my mother and someone who signed their name "*E. Quinn, Trustee.*"

Quinn? As in Granville Quinn and his daughter, Violet? The historic Quinn Estate was the crown jewel of Moonville, Ohio. The estate encompassed the Moonville Sanitorium, a gothic family mansion and ornate glass conservatory, along with numerous brightly colored Victorian cottages perched on a hill above the town. The property was part of a trust run by a Board of Trustees, but I'd never heard it referred to as QFWC. And no one named Quinn had lived in Moonville since Violet Quinn passed away over sixty years ago, leaving behind the Trust to manage her family fortune.

The content of the emails was more mystifying than enlightening. They referred to submissions received, pending committee reviews, and payment awards to be issued. Payment awards? It sort of sounded like she might be submitting new articles or manuscripts to this QFWC, but I couldn't find them listed as a publishing house.

Could they be giving her some type of grant money? None of it made sense, and my head ached.

Feeling totally defeated, I scrolled up and down through her inbox one last time, my eyes skimming over the long list of subject lines that announced sales and limited-time deals, until one subject line jumped out at me.

Definitely Sinister.

I clicked to read the body of the message. There was a link to the *Unhaunted* article followed by one sentence typed in all caps:

YOU WILL PAY FOR YOUR CRIMES.

I jerked back from the screen, shocked. The source address came from a free email provider synonymous with scammers, phishing, and trolls. It was probably just a troll.

The alarm clock sounded, surprising an involuntary scream from me. As if on cue, the lights started flickering.

"All right, Ivy," I said, my voice heavy with sickening shame and defeat. "I'm done here."

The lights stopped blinking long enough for me to close every window on the computer I'd opened but started flashing again in a frantic, erratic pattern before I could straighten up the office. The wild light show was making me dizzy.

"Ivy! I said all right!"

Upstairs, doors slammed in rapid succession. A series of loud bangs and thumps indicated my ghostly visitor was making an unholy mess. Something shattered.

Furious at this sudden assault, I ran upstairs yelling, "Quit, quit, quit!"

Then stopped, feeling foolish.

The living room and kitchen areas looked entirely

normal. I turned in a circle searching for any damage. Nothing. All that noise and ... nothing? Furniture was exactly where it belonged, no fallen items on the floor, no shards of broken glass in sight. Everything was quiet and still and in order.

"What the—?"

The television popped to life, then flipped through a series of channels, past weight loss programs and toothpaste smiles, until it landed on a local station showing a live newsflash. The camera panned over a white stucco mansion surrounded by milling police officers and yellow crime scene tape. A female voiceover explained the Palo Alto police department had made a grisly discovery earlier in the day at a construction site managed by David Brennan, uncle of Ivy Brennan, who has been missing for eight days.

"Oh, Ivy," I said, flopping down on the couch.

My phone started buzzing with alerts.

A missed call from Zack was quickly followed by two text messages.

The first text said *RU watching this?*

The second was a link to a live-streaming online news story on the local ABC station's website.

The voice on the television blathered on about human remains and said no official confirmation of the identity had been made, but I didn't hear a word she said. I knew.

They found her, I texted to Zack.

Thanks to U, he answered.

I looked around again, expecting to see or hear or feel something from Ivy, but the room felt totally empty. I climbed the stairs back to my bedroom. The books she'd dumped off my bookshelf earlier were still in a heap on the floor. My mother's book was in the trashcan beside my desk. That made me smile despite everything. I went into the bathroom without switching on the lights and gazed into the mirror.

"Ivy?" I asked. Nothing answered me, not even a tiny wisp of cool air. "Aunt Nicole? I helped her. They found Ivy's body. I helped her." Still no response. My voice sounded pathetic to my own ears, like a first grader begging for a gold star.

Using the phone, I watched more of the online news for a few minutes, searching the police officers at the scene for signs of a K-9 unit or LaShawna's face—something that connected what I'd done to the scene. After several minutes, I gave up watching the news and waiting for a message from the dead. For all I knew, the discovery of her body had sent Ivy into the light. But I'd made a promise earlier, and I intended to keep it.

After plugging the phone back into its charger, I switched on the lights to shower. Alternating between hot and cold water, a trick my Swedish grandmother swore was the secret to reviving body and spirit, I scrubbed every inch of my skin from shoulders to toes with a soft body brush and tried to figure out what to do next. There was no way I was going to revisit my mother's office. The walls were closing in on me. I needed to go somewhere and do something. But what? What could I do?

Just more research. But not here. Not on my phone. I needed more bandwidth. More power. And no temptation to sneak another look through my mother's emails or accounts.

With new resolve I hastily dried off, wrapped myself in a towel, and regarded my reflection in the mirror. This was going to require a special, unauthorized trip to my mother's closet.

Her bedroom looked like a tornado ravaged Saks Fifth

Avenue. This wasn't Ivy's handiwork; it was normal. Entering the bathroom, the first issue was my hair. The nature girl look wasn't working for me, especially with the bruise on my face. It made me look like a baby-faced thug. Any styling that involved a brush or comb still felt beyond endurance, so I tied the springy mess in a Burberry scarf my mother hadn't worn in years. So far, not so bad. Next, I had to tackle makeup then wardrobe. Surveying the array of brushes, powders, tubes, and jars covering every inch of her bathroom counter, I felt lost.

Behind me, the small television on my mother's dresser switched on. I twirled. What I saw on the screen took my breath away. Clutching the bath towel around my body with both hands, I look a few tentative steps toward the screen.

The breaking news story about the discovery of a body in Palo Alto was now a press conference. A solemn police chief with gray hair and hound dog eyes addressed a crowd of reporters, but he barely registered with me. Behind him, at the left side of the screen, stood Ivy's younger sister. Even though she was older now, just a year or two younger than me, I recognized her instantly from my brief glimpses into Ivy's life. Her eyes were dry, set in a fierce expression, and her mouth pressed into a grim line. Both of her thin pale arms were wrapped around her middle, as if to protect herself. She looked lost. Utterly miserable.

Jazz. Ivy's voice whispered my head. *Her name is Jasmine, but we call her Jazz.*

Beside Ivy's sister stood a woman who wasn't much taller than Jazz. Her posture looked stiff and straight. Her arms were at her sides with both hands clenched in fists. She was wearing a pair of huge black sunglasses that hid most of her face.

The sad-eyed police chief finished his statement, then

looked over at the two females standing behind him. The tiny woman gave a curt nod, then stepped forward and spoke into the microphone.

"We are very grateful to the Palo Alto police for finding Ivy." Her voice was crisp and formal with a pronounced Asian accent. "Ivy's body was found at a construction site managed by my family, but I beg everyone in this case not to rush to any judgment. We employ many workers and many others had access to that site. We will assist the police in every way possible to get to the bottom of this terrible crime. We offered a reward for information leading to Ivy's safe return. Now we offer the same reward for information leading to the arrest of whoever is responsible for this terrible outrage."

At a site managed by my family? The earlier news segment said it was a construction site for David Brennan's company. Who was this woman?

She stepped back, turned, and marched off the podium. Jazz turned to follow, but stopped to look back over her shoulder at the mass of reporters. Her eyes seemed to look directly through the camera at me. My breath caught in my chest.

You need to give help, Aunt Nicole had said.

This girl – this pale, wide-eyed, wild-haired, damaged girl – was living with a monster. Her sister protected her, but now her sister was dead. It was entirely possible I was the only living, breathing human being outside that household who understood the danger looming over Jasmine Brennan.

That's when it all got too real. I doubled over, feeling sick and panicked and overwhelmed. The bath towel was still wrapped tight around my body, but every inch of skin felt exposed, as though I'd been scorched. I couldn't even help myself; how was I supposed to help a girl I'd never met?

Breathe, Asha. Breathe.

Aunt Nicole's voice, low and soothing, eased some of the tightness in my chest. Once again, cool air caressed my face and neck. I focused on pulling air into my lungs and pushing it back out, detecting a faint scent of vanilla mingled with amber. The perfume was as familiar as her voice and her songs.

You've got this. You are not alone, Baby.

Tears welled up in my eyes. I'm not sure if they were from gratitude or fear. Probably a mixture of both.

"I don't know what I'm doing." I pushed the words out between little gasps, staring at the beige carpeting in front of my bare toes. "What am I supposed to do?"

Do whatever feels right. Pay attention. Witness. Speak up. Don't look away.

9

———

BEFORE

FOR MOST OF MY LIFE, THE PUBLIC LIBRARY HAS BEEN MY sanctuary and my refuge. When my parents screamed at each other, when Mother's clients filled the house with sorrow, when kitchen cabinets flapped open and closed violently while Xia Celeste chanted phrases about going toward the light, I would escape to the library.

My hometown library is a magical place. Located on Main Street, just two blocks away from Doc Warner's All Creatures Vet Clinic, it's a yellow brick Victorian with stained glass windows, octagonal turrets, wrought iron ornaments, dark paneling, and a sweeping mahogany stair-case leading up to a wonderland of books on the second floor.

Every librarian in Moonville, Ohio knew my name, and they also knew every member of my family. If I'd ever dared to walk into the Moonville Public Library at eleven o'clock on a school day, I had no doubt my grandfather would have stumped into the building within minutes to demand an explanation as to why I was not in class.

But I wasn't in Ohio anymore.

The Rose Garden Branch of the San Jose Public Library is all tile, glass, metal, and geometry. It looks corporate, like some billion-dollar software company ate a Starbucks and a Barnes and Noble then puked up a library. But it was still a library. No matter how cold and trendy the atmosphere, it was a safe place filled with books. Therefore, it was a better place to be than home alone with my ghosts and my nightmares.

Even though the librarians in San Jose did not know me and always seemed content to leave their patrons alone, it was still eleven o'clock on a school day. I didn't want to look like a school kid skipping classes. That's why I went shopping in my mother's closet instead of throwing on my standard school uniform – jeans, t-shirt, and pink high-tops – and heading out the door.

One of the good things about having a shopaholic mother was the plethora of abandoned designer items in every corner of her bedroom and closet. In addition to the Burberry scarf knotted over my hair, I close a Hermes silk shift dress that was relatively low-key and oversized Gucci sunglasses that did a pretty good job of hiding the lump on my cheek. A pair of chunky Prada shoes that looked like a cross between loafers and low pumps were the only shoes in my mother's entire inventory that looked like I could walk ten feet without falling on my face. A leather Coach satchel that had seen better days topped off my disguise.

When I caught my reflection in the mirror near our front door, I almost laughed out loud. I looked like a sad cartoon sketch of my mother, like I was trying out for a reality show that featured housewives in some pretentious rich place. Or maybe I looked like exactly what I was – a kid playing dress up. But I'd seen plenty of twenty-something women in the Silicon Valley who looked pretty close to this, so I shrugged at my awkward reflection and, feeling painfully self-conscious, headed out the door.

The walk to the library took less than ten minutes, but the stupid Prada shoes rubbed three blisters on my feet by the time I reached the front door. No wonder they'd been abandoned in the back of Mom's closet. But I'm a ballerina with seven years of practice dancing *en pointe*. Designer shoes weren't going to defeat me. Gritting my teeth to keep from limping, I breezed through the entrance doors and headed for the second floor without looking toward the circulation desk. There were computer stations in the teen room, but I wasn't going near that area. Aside from the fact it would call attention to my age, I hated the quarantine of teens from adults.

Instead, I swept into the tech room and settled into a chair in front of an available computer. One sour-faced old hag glared at me, as if the very fact I was breathing in the same space she was offended her. I tensed, waiting for her to say something, but I relaxed when she redirected her disapproval toward an elderly Latino man who shuffled into the room a few minutes after me.

Apparently, she was an equal opportunity hater.

Starting at the local news website where I'd seen the earlier live-streaming coverage of Ivy's body found in Palo Alto, my next hour was spent clicking through trending news stories. I read about the Ivy Brennan case in reverse chronological order, from the coverage of the news conference I'd watched earlier, following the links back through earlier related stories until I found the original missing girl bulletins. Then I followed that same backward process on every major news source website where the name Ivy Brennan returned results. They were all reporting the same facts; none of the stories varied in the important details

Jasmine Brennan initially called the police Tuesday evening when her older sister failed to show up for dinner after school and did not respond to multiple texts and calls to her cell phone. Jasmine called the police — not her uncle, who was the legal guardian for both girls, and not the aunt I'd heard her mention when she showed me flashes of her life. Weird, and yet none of the articles I read pointed out the strangeness.

When the police interviewed people who lived near Palo Alto High School where Ivy was a sophomore, someone claimed to have seen her get into a black SUV with a temporary license obscured by dirt. The tip prompted an Amber Alert; I'd been right about the alert and its timing. But no one ever identified the SUV or the driver, and the case had stretched on for eight days without any additional leads.

Two days after her sister's disappearance, Jazz was paraded in front of press cameras to make a public plea for information about her sister's whereabouts. Her red-rimmed eyes were dry, her expression stoic. The words she spoke were heart wrenching, but her voice was flat, wooden and well-rehearsed. Why on earth had her aunt and uncle allowed her to be put on display? Why weren't they making the plea? Four days after Ivy's disappearance, her uncle, who the stories referred to as a "successful local business-man," offered a fifty thousand dollar reward.

The large reward startled me. I sat back, amazed.

Both my mother and father had been involved in numerous missing persons cases throughout my life. I could not remember such a high reward offered so quickly in any of the missing cases they had worked. Didn't anyone working the case think that was strange?

Six days after her disappearance, there was a prayer vigil outside the high school. Alongside a Facebook photo of Ivy smiling widely, there was a slideshow that displayed pictures of flowers, candles, and crying teens. One picture made me gasp, drawing a hateful look from the hag who had glared at me earlier. I gave her an apologetic shrug and mouthed the word sorry in her direction before looking back at the picture that had caused my outburst.

There was cousin LaShawna, wearing street clothes instead of her police uniform, with one arm around Jazz Brennan. Before I could freeze the image, the next picture in the slide-show replaced it. This one showed Jazz looking down and away as though she was embarrassed while a man in a clerical collar and a tiny, well-dressed Asian woman clasped hands in prayer.

The caption read, "Local minister prays with Ying Brennan for the safe return of her niece #IvyBrennan."

Ivy's mysterious aunt. This must be the woman from the press conference. My breath caught in my throat as I zoomed in on the image. The first thing that struck me was that Ying Brennan looked terribly young, not much older than Ivy ... or me for that matter. Her long, shining black hair was gathered in a neat ponytail at the nape of her neck. She wore a simple white blouse embroidered with flowers, black pants, and pearl earrings. Even though the picture was not posed, she looked soft and tragic yet flawless.

This beautiful, delicate little person was Uncle David's wife?

The term China doll popped onto my head, and I closed my eyes. That was a racist thought, wasn't it? Or was it sexist? Or maybe it was both. Regardless, it was not the sort of term that would come to me without an outside influence. Where had I heard that term before?

Then I remembered.

Not long after we moved to San Jose, my mother stood in our kitchen with a glass of white wine in one hand complaining to LaShawna about a disastrous blind date the night before. Apparently, the man had looked my mother up and down carefully, then leaned in close to whisper she was probably too much woman for him — about fifty pounds too much woman.

"China dolls!" my mother exclaimed, waving her glass of wine around. "That's what all these flabby white geek boys are looking to find. Fresh off the boat China dolls!"

"You know," LaShawna replied in a dry voice, "Xia *is* a popular Chinese name. Maybe he was a little confused, Shirley."

Mother, who hated hearing her birth name, shot her cousin a nasty look. "Zia is an old Arabic name, LaShawna. I spelled it with the X for a little extra flair. And what kind of moron fails to Google someone before agreeing to a date?"

I shook away the memory and refocused my concentration on Ying Brennan's picture. Maybe it was a derogatory term, but Ying was definitely a China doll in every sense of the word. She looked almost too perfect to breathe. Definitely too perfect to marry David Brennan. Then I wondered if the images of Uncle David through Ivy's eyes were somehow exaggerated and monstrous. How could I be sure he really looked like the images that came to me from Ivy?

Mother was right. What kind of moron doesn't Google to know what someone looks like?

I opened a different tab on the internet browser, took three deep calming breaths, and started a new search. The wedding website was easy to locate, and the pictures were every bit as bizarre as I'd imagined. Ying and David Brennan had been married three years before Ivy's disappearance.

Delicate Ying, encased from chin to toe in red silk heavily embroidered with colorful thread, stood next to a hulking David Brennan. He wore a loose, untucked white linen shirt and black pants. Nothing else. Not even a tie. But the difference in their clothing was not what stood out to me.

David Brennan looked like he could eat Ying for breakfast and still be hungry before lunch. Worse, he looked old enough to be her father, no, her grandfather. And yet, beneath her elaborate gold headpiece dripping with gold chains and tassels, Ying smiled peacefully.

She looked confident, calm, and blissful.

Was it an act? It had to be an act.

I continued searching until I found recent pictures of Ying and David Brennan at several charity events around San Francisco and the South Bay area. In every single picture, Ying had the same peaceful, carefully composed smile on her face.

My heart ached for her. It was definitely an act.

She'd married the Incredibly Ugly Hulk, a man who liked his women tiny, young, and helpless.

Enough. I returned to the news websites and finished reviewing the timeline of Ivy's case.

Yesterday, the day LaShawna came to my mother for help, had been the eighth day of Ivy's disappearance. There was no mention of the visit in the news stories, but I didn't expect to find any. LaShawna left our condo gunning for David Brennan and the Palo Alto Police had found Ivy's body at one of his company's construction sites less than twenty-four hours later. How had she managed to solve the puzzle and point the investigation in the right direction so quickly?

I finally found my answer while reviewing the press conference where I'd first seen Jazz Brennan. There was a transcript of the droopy dog police chief's statement, most of which I had missed while showering and getting ready for this excursion. According to the transcript, police investigators received an anonymous tip that led them to interview many of David Brennan's employees. Many of the interviews indicated "something strange" had happened at a Palo Alto construction site around the time of Ivy's disappearance.

Construction workers arrived at the site to pour a concrete foundation for a new guesthouse only to find that the concrete had already been poured overnight. There was also a new padlock on the temporary fence around the foundation. When they called David Brennan, he told them there had been "a change of plans" and offered to pay his crew for the full day despite the fact they could not do any work.

"A senior investigating officer on this case obtained permission from the property owner to search the site with cadaver dogs," the police chief stated. "At nine o'clock this morning, police technicians found human remains encased in the cement foundation."

I sat back, rubbing my tired, aching eyes.

There was something wrong here. Something I couldn't quite figure out. The edges of my vision danced with shadows I couldn't identify, so I closed my eyes and rested my forehead against my palms. What was wrong?

Everything Ivy had shown me replayed in my head, bringing on a fresh wave of nausea. I'd very clearly seen early images of Jazz and their mother's death. I'd seen vile

Uncle David sneaking into Ivy's bedroom and whispering in her ear. I'd seen Ivy and her friend practicing French and sharing secrets, Ivy curled up on a window seat crying, and an oddly disturbing visit to a construction site in broad daylight.

I hadn't seen her death.

In fact, I had absolutely no idea how Ivy died.

And yet, I did know she was buried in concrete.

My eyes popped open in shock. I didn't know how Ivy died, but I knew she was buried in concrete. How was that possible?

Daddy didn't teach me much about living with the voices of the dead, but there was one lesson he did teach me. It was something he repeated many, many times.

"Contrary to popular belief," he assured me, "a cemetery is always the least haunted place in town."

Why? According to my father, it was because the pure spiritual essence of a deceased person doesn't follow their dead body around. Dead, decaying body parts hold no allure, no focus. The dead will haunt the places and the people they love. They may linger at the site of a tragic death. But, for the most part, they do not rattle around graveyards. That is why my father loved cemeteries. We would have picnics among the granite memorials and he would take pictures, his eyes bright and trouble free, because there were rarely any ghosts in graveyards screaming for our attention.

So how did Ivy Brennan know she was entombed in concrete?

Was she alive when her tomb was poured?

The thought was so sickening, I had to press one clenched fist to my lips to stop any sound that might pop out.

"Are you okay?" A finger tapped my shoulder lightly. The elderly Latino man who had shuffled into the tech room after me stood next to my chair. "You seem upset?"

I stared up at him through tears, unable to say a word. When he smiled, the deep lines around his eyes were more pronounced. A thick white scar cut through one dark eyebrow. He wore a stained yellow cardigan. From one drooping pocket, he withdrew a crumpled tissue and handed it to me. Then he noticed the image displayed on the computer screen.

"Dios mio! Was she a friend of yours?"

I nodded, scrambling to gather my things. The air in the library suddenly seemed impossible to breathe.

"Que descanse en paz," he said softly, crossing himself as he stepped back to give me room. *May she rest in peace.*

Unlike Ivy, I chose Spanish as my foreign language elective and I knew that phrase all too well.

I shook my head violently. "She doesn't," I gasped out, the tears flowing heavily. "She doesn't rest at all." Then I hurried out of the tech room, down the stairs, and out the main doors.

BACK ON NAGLEE AVENUE, I BLINKED IN THE BRIGHT SUNLIGHT for a few minutes and tried not to think about anything I'd read. I had nowhere to go and all day to get there.

Across the street to my left, the entrance to the San Jose Municipal Rose Garden bloomed with life. I loved the Rose Garden. And yet, I turned to the right, toward the Rosicrucian Egyptian Museum one block away.

If there was one culture in the history of all the world that understood living with the dead, it was the Egyptians.

Pausing to peel off my mother's overpriced, uncomfortable shoes and toss them into the leather satchel, I walked barefoot toward the distinctive white and blue columns that marked the front of the property.

I didn't have the money to visit the museum itself, but there was a meditation labyrinth and a beautiful peace garden on the property that was open and easily accessible to the public. I followed the paths to a cement bench in a hidden corner of the garden that overlooked their reflecting pool. There I sat huddled in a ball, arms wrapped tightly around my shins with my chin resting on my knees, alone and miserable.

The sun was unable to warm the deep, cold sensation that sank into my bones. After a few minutes, I became aware of Ivy's presence sitting next to me and felt a cooling pressure on my bruised cheek.

I closed my eyes and didn't fight her kindness.

"I'm so sorry," I whispered, the words entirely inadequate.

10

———

Now

I shudder awake to find LaShawna sitting at the end of my bed. Her shoulders are bowed, her head bent low over steepled fingers.

"LaShawna!" I exclaim, beyond relieved. Her presence fills my bones with hope. She is the most beautiful, wonderful person in the world right now.

"Good morning, Sunshine," she says, rubbing her hands together and forcing a smile. "How are you feeling?"

"LaShawna," I repeat stupidly, as though her name is a magic ticket to bridge the space between us. As though her name alone will solve all of my problems.

"Asha," she says. There's a solemn note in her voice. "Tell me how you're feeling, Baby Girl."

"Lost."

It is the truest thing I've ever told anyone.

"Of course you feel lost," she agrees. "But you are not lost, you are found."

"Yes, you found me."

"No," she corrects me with a gentle shake of her head. "You found yourself."

"I'm sorry, LaShawna. I messed up. I screwed up everything. I'm so sorry." The words gush out of me in a breathless, little girly voice.

Reaching forward, she gently shifts my chin to look into her shadowed and weary eyes.

"You did not screw up anything, Asha," she tells me. "You trusted me. You told me everything I needed to know. I let you down."

"What? No!" I struggle for words that will make her understand. Words that will wash away this heavy layer of guilt I now see pressing down on her. "I mean, who would have thought? It still seems impossible."

"Impossible? No." LaShawna snorts in disgust. "No, looking at it now, knowing what we know, it was actually clear as day." She shakes her head, scrubbing both hands over her face. "We should have seen it earlier. I should have seen it earlier." She pounds one fist in the center if her chest to emphasize the words. "But I was too blinded by my own crap. And once the FBI told us what they knew, the truth was right there practically slapping me in the face. Still I acted like a fool! Looking around for any explanation other than the one that was staring back at me."

The depth of LaShawna's fury with herself shocks me.

"No one could have guessed," I reassure her.

LaShawna tilts her head and gives me a half-hearted smile. "I think Mai Tsien guessed."

"The landlady? Really?" That statement is like a little jolt of electricity. On pure reflex, I try to sit up in bed, but the pain slaps me back down. LaShawna moves quickly, pressing both hands into my shoulders.

"Hush, now. Don't do that," she croons in a low, soothing voice. "I'm sorry. Forget I said anything. You just relax and stay still. You're safe now. Everything's going to be just fine." Her hands lightly rub my shoulders as she continues to mutter calming nonsense until the pain subsides.

"LaShawna?"

"Yes, Baby?"

"Who is Vera Birch?"

Wry amusement transforms LaShawna's face, returning a spark of light to her eyes. "Funny you should ask. Vera Birch is the reason I'm here, actually."

"Really?"

"Yes, really." LaShawna settles herself on the side of my bed, folding her hands in her lap. "She doesn't think you like her or trust her very much."

"Why should I?" I ask. "Why should I like her? Or trust her?"

LaShawna nods, as though I've said something very wise. "Yes, why should you trust any of us? Every damn adult in your life has let you down. Every damn one of us! We were supposed to protect you and keep you safe, but we let you down."

"I trust you, LaShawna."

Tears well up in her eyes. "Thank you, Baby," she says in a whisper. Then she takes a deep breath and releases it with a sigh. "Vera is good people, Asha. I know she seems like an odd bird sometimes. But I promise you, that woman is decent to the core and she is here for you. She's here to protect you."

"Protect me? From who ... or what?"

"Vera Birch is an amazing and talented lawyer."

Lawyer? The word startles me, making me squirm, but

LaShawna places one hand on my shoulder and makes soothing noises.

"She told me she was my advocate," I say, making it an accusation.

"Advocate. Lawyer." LaShawna shrugs. "Two ways of naming the same truth. But Vera Birch is also more than those two words. Much more. She has some special qualifications in a case like this. I promise you can trust her with the whole truth." She leans in closer, her eyes searching mine. "The whole truth. Do you understand?

I nod because my mouth is suddenly too dry to allow even one word to slip out.

"You know I really do love you, right?" LaShawna's voice quivers slightly and the tears pooling in her eyes spill down her cheeks. "And I am so proud of you. So proud!"

My own eyes tear up in response.

"Wh-why do I need a lawyer?"

"Because somebody needs to stand up for you," she tells me through clenched teeth. "Someone needs to make you the top priority here. Vera Birch will do that."

There's one more question I need to ask LaShawna, but I can't make myself say the words. Terror is like a boulder lodged in my throat. I search her face, silently pleading for her to answer the question I cannot ask.

Am I going to jail?

Pitiful tears leak out of the corners of my own eyes.

"Okay, now let's not start crying like a couple of fools." She gently cups both my cheeks in the palms of her hands and dashes away my tears with her thumbs.

"Listen to me, Asha. I'm your family, and I love you. But, technically, I'm also still the police. And I'm not your legal guardian. You need to take plenty of time and consult with your lawyer in private before you make any statements to any police officer, even me. Or anyone else. Anyone. At all. Do you hear me?"

"Yes, ma'am," I answer.

She plants a dry, firm kiss on my forehead and gives me one more searching look. "I promise you can trust Vera Birch."

"Yes, ma'am," I repeat.

11

———

Before

I arrived back at the condo a little after two o'clock. Mother's Lexus wasn't in its parking spot, so I dared to breathe a sigh of relief believing no one would ever know about my idiotic and ultimately pointless trip to the library. But as soon as I slipped the key into the front door lock, Mrs. Tsien popped out of her own front door and clapped her hands.

"There's Asha!" she announced to no one in particular and hurried back into her home.

Weird, I thought, pushing my way through my own door. Once inside, I looked back and waited, but her front door remained open and empty. Did she want me to come over? Mrs. Tsien was a tiny woman with arthritis that made it difficult to reach above her head. Sometimes she would ask me to come over to retrieve items off upper shelves or to run a duster over her ceiling fans.

Usually I didn't mind helping her and there was always

some special little treat—almond cookies, a sachet of her own blend of herbal tea or, my favorite, a sweet and salty mix of nuts coated in sesame seeds—but today I just wanted to lock myself away from the world and hide.

So, when she didn't reappear after a minute or two, I shut the door and quickly stripped off my mother's clothing and accessories right there in the entryway, exchanging the overpriced ensemble for an outfit I'd left on the stairs—a threadbare, oversized t-shirt and a pair of leggings with a hole in one knee. I'd just managed to return the dress, satchel, sunglasses, silk scarf and those horrible shoes to my mother's closet when I heard a very familiar tip tapping at the front door.

Mrs. Tsien.

"Crap!" My shoulders sagged and my stomach knotted. I did not want to deal with our kind, generous, and insatiably curious landlady. But she'd seen me come in. I could not possibly ignore her.

As soon as I opened the door, Mrs. Tsien lifted a bamboo tray heavily loaded with pottery dishes and glass jars up toward me. Even though the tray was securely balanced on her forearms, the weight caused her arms to tremble and the items rattled alarmingly.

I stepped forward to relieve her of the burden and delicious aromas blasted my nostrils—roast chicken, garlic, and lemongrass mingled with vanilla and citrus. The knots in my stomach disappeared, replaced by an empty void behind my belly button that growled pitifully.

Either Mrs. Tsien didn't have her hearing aids turned up or she was polite enough to ignore my roaring gut. She smiled at me and tilted her head to one side.

"Mommy said you not feeling too good today," she said

with a little crease of concern between her eyebrows. "Maybe you try to eat something?"

Had she not seen me walk home all dressed up in my mother's silks just a few minutes before? I blinked a few times, unsure of what to say. My stomach chose that moment to let out another roar of protest. Her eyebrows knitted together more firmly and I looked down, embarrassed.

Mrs. Tsien clucked her tongue and reached out one gnarled finger to brush the discolored lump on my cheek.

"I fell down," I said quickly, cringing at the weak stupidity of the lie.

"Hmmm," Mrs. Tsien grunted. "I see."

The expression on her face clearly said she really did see. She saw I was lying.

"When I was your age, I fall down a lot too."

There was something off about the way she said it. Was I imagining the heavy, unnatural emphasis she put on the words fall down?

The fragrant steam from a bowl on the tray was making my mouth water, and I grasped for something to say that would end this conversation.

"I can definitely eat," I said, turning away from her piercing eyes. "This smells awesome."

I hurried to the kitchen and carefully slid the heavy tray onto the breakfast bar that separated the kitchen from the living room. I wanted to pick up the ample soup bowl from the center of the tray and slurp up the fragrant broth, but I forced myself to carefully pick up and examine everything she'd brought—in addition to the soup there was a slice of warm almond cake, a jar of honey, a small bowl of sesame candy, and a box of tea labeled with the words *Comfort Twist Blend* in her scratchy writing.

"This is really great," I said, keeping my eyes averted.

Mrs. Tsien didn't answer. Instead, she quietly entered the kitchen and started filling our teakettle with filtered water from the refrigerator door.

"You eat," she ordered, waving her hand toward the wide ceramic spoon she'd placed next to the soup

She didn't have to tell me twice. The broth, thick with carrots, mushrooms, and tofu, tasted even better than it smelled. After spooning in most of the liquid, I carefully used a fork to loudly slurp up the solids. My mother would send me to my room for that kind of behavior, but Mrs. Tsien had taught me this was proper etiquette in her culture and showed true appreciation for the dish. She stepped forward and rubbed one of her palms over my nappy hair.

"You know what?" she said softly.

I looked up to find a sad half-smile on her face.

"I thought maybe when I got married and moved away from my father's house, I thought maybe I wouldn't fall down so much," she said. "Turns out I fall down more than ever before. For five years, I fall down almost every day. The day my little baby boy fall down we walked away from that house and never fall down again."

My throat felt raw and achy. "I've only fallen down a few times in my whole life," I tell her, focused on keeping my eyes locked with hers. "Really. It's not like that."

She continued to hold my gaze for several seconds before nodding her head twice and patting my hair one last time. Then she turned away and started fussing with the package of tea and bubbling teakettle.

We both knew we were not talking about falling down at all.

After a minute or two of blissful silence, during which I

focused on savoring the flavors in my noodle bowl, I heard her say something that sounded like, "Nobody's perfect."

I looked up, certain she was talking to me, even though her back was still toward me and her hands were still busy with tea preparations. "Did you say something?"

"Nobody's perfect," she repeated more forcefully and shook her head, but she didn't turn around and look at me. "Like that time Bao scared me to death. Don't like to think about that. He must have been five or six years old then. Young enough I needed to watch him at the park. Old enough he didn't want Mommy pushing him on the swings."

Was she really talking to me? Or was she talking to herself? No, I decided she must be talking to me because she was speaking in English. I'd heard her chattering to herself in Mandarin plenty of times. So I sat up and listened, sneaking sips from my soup bowl. I wasn't just being polite. I was quite curious to hear where this was going.

Bao was Mrs. Tsien's son, her only child. He was the father of the grandson who died in a hiking accident. According to Xia, there was some serious family drama between Bao Tsien and his mother that went back many years before the accident. It had something to do with the fact that Mrs. Tsien donated quite a bit of time and money to help girls from Southeast Asia who were not in the United States legally. I thought that made Mrs. Tsien a hero. Bao thought his mother was wasting his inheritance on "dirty girls" who weren't even Chinese. He sounded like a selfish, racist jerk. But Mrs. Tsien's voice as she spoke about taking him to the park was gentle and filled with a mother's love.

My heart ached for this sweet, kindly woman. Especially considering the rest of the history.

When Bao's son dropped out of college and moved into his grandmother's spare bedroom, Tsien family relations went from cool to an arctic freeze. Then the boy went missing, and Bao blamed his mother. Everything went nuclear when Mrs. Tsien brought Xia Celeste into the case. Bao went ballistic, calling my mother a "black devil." Mrs. Tsien slapped his face in front of a room full of people. The only reason I knew about Bao was because my mother warned me never to speak his name. And here we were, chatting about little Bao when he was a boy.

"What happened in the park?" I prodded her to continue with the story.

"I brought a book to the park that day," she said. "One of those silly books with pretty girls trapped in scary houses. I used to read them to help me with my English." At that point she looked back at me, flashed an embarrassed smile, then turned back away. "One minute, I look up and Bao is waving to me from the top of the slide. Next minute, I look up and I can't see him. Maybe it was the book, but all of a sudden I was so afraid something bad had happened. I searched. I called for him. He didn't answer. He didn't come. I ran around and I searched and I screamed his name. Nothing. Still no answer. I was so scared."

She shook her head again and started pouring honey into the tea. I took another sip from the bowl and waited.

"Then, I see his little jacket on the ground next to a bush. It was a bright red jacket, very easy to see. I fell down on my knees and screamed 'Bao!' like I was a crazy person. All the other mothers stood up. Any mother would know that sound, that horrible sound, of a mother who lost her child. Then—"

Mrs. Tsien spun around with her arms out wide. "Out jumps Bao! 'Surprise!' he says, 'I tricked you, Mommy!'"

She dropped her hands and settled them on her hips.

"All the other mothers smiled and laughed, some shaking their heads. Then they all went back to their day. I tried to make my face like theirs. I tried to smile but terror was still pounding." She made a fist and beat it against her chest several times. "I grabbed his hand, and I marched him out of the park. I was so furious; I couldn't see straight."

"I marched him all the way home, three blocks, no stopping. All the time he's crying, 'What's wrong, Mommy?' And I can't say anything. We get home. As soon as I shut the door, I spanked that boy like I never spanked him before."

She crossed her arms over her chest, and turned away again, staring down at the tea. The reasoning behind this story was now crystal clear to me.

A wave of relief passed through my body.

Her voice was soft, barely above a whisper when she spoke again. "I was crying and screaming at my baby boy. 'Don't you ever do that again. Don't you ever hide from Mommy again' and swatting at his backside over and over and over. I smacked his bottom. I smacked his back. When I heard the sound of my hand slapping his little legs, I stopped." She shrugged. "Shame filled me. I hated myself at that moment. I don't think I ever hated myself so much. I let him go and dropped to the floor, and I just cried and cried. I cried so hard Bao hugged my back and tried to make me feel better. You know what? Only made me feel worse."

When she stopped speaking, a heavy silence surrounded the two of us.

"Nobody's perfect," I echoed her own words back to her.

She turned to smile at me with a glimmer of moisture on her lashes. "Nobody's perfect," she repeated firmly. Then she rubbed her hands together and said, "Ready for tea?"

"Always."

And that was that. I breathed a sigh of relief, feeling certain the subject of the lump on my cheek was now closed.

Once my belly was filled with soup, cake, and three cups of Comfort Twist tea, which turned out to be a blend of chamomile, rose hips, and dried citrus peels, my sleepless night caught up with me. No matter how hard I fought the heavy wave of exhaustion, my eyelids would not stay open. It was impossible to hold up my head without the assistance of my right elbow.

Mrs. Tsien nudged me awake and guided me to the couch where every throw pillow in the house was heaped up to create a soft nest. She covered me with one of her own crochet shawls, and I thanked her.

At least I think some gratitude slurred out of my mouth before I plummeted into oblivion.

12

———

Before

The sound of voices arguing in harsh, guttural whispers woke me up. Groggy and disoriented, I wiggled around knocking several of the pillows to the floor. The white rococo clock above the fake fireplace showed the time as a quarter after four, which caused me to blink in confusion.

What was going on?

Something wet touched my right arm, and I turned my head to look into a pair of liquid brown eyes. As soon as he saw I was conscious, Kota smiled at me, his pink tongue lolling out of his mouth while his whole body pulsed with the wagging of his tail. He blew a gust of doggy breath in my face.

I knew instantly he wasn't on duty. It wasn't just his relaxed body language; it was the yellow and blue Cal State collar around his neck in place of the harness and badge he wore during work hours.

"Hi, boy," I whispered, not ready for any human attention yet.

His tail wagging increased, slapping against the coffee table. I snaked my left arm across my body to bury my fingers in the thick fur on his chest. In turn, he gently touched his nose to the lump on my cheek and gave it a very gentle lick.

Everything that happened over the past twenty-four hours came back to me, causing tears to well up in my eyes. Kota placed his muzzle across my chest and sat down, as though he were guarding me and comforting me at the same time. He was the sweetest, most wonderful, most intelligent dog in the history of forever. Wrapping both arms around his muscular shoulders, I sucked in a few breaths; partly to control my emotions and partly to enjoy the warm musky doggy scent of him.

"I love you," I whispered, and his tail thumped on the floor in response.

"Don't tell me to calm down!" LaShawna's voice cut through our moment of bonding.

Another voice, Mrs. Tsien's voice I was pretty sure, murmured a few words I couldn't quite make out.

"She'll be lucky if I don't kick her happy butt into the next county. Where is the bitch?"

"Oh, crap," I breathed into Kota's fur.

Kota readjusted his head and muzzle on my chest and let out a sigh as though he agreed with my sentiment. I raised my head and looked around. The main floor of the condo was empty of any other humans and mostly in shadow because the window shades were drawn with the curtains pulled closed to block out most external light. There was one slice of golden daylight spilling across the entryway where the front door was open a crack. As I watched the door, a shadow flashed across the opening then flashed back.

Mrs. Tsien's voice continued in a steady, soothing stream of murmured words. I strained to listen and thought I heard her say "nobody's perfect" and "having a tough time."

LaShawna's shadow flashed past the door three more times, and I knew she wasn't buying whatever Mrs. Tsien was selling.

Despite that, I heard her say, "Okay, Mai. I hear you," in a much calmer voice. "Thank you for everything. You know how much I appreciate you, right?" There was a long pause, then, "You go on home and rub some of that cream your doctor prescribed on your joints. I can tell you're sore today. You go rest. I'll take it from here."

I eyed the stairs up to my bedroom. My heart raced. I seriously considered throwing my body over the back of the couch and racing up to my bedroom before LaShawna pushed open the door.

Kota must have sensed my flight plans because he settled one paw over my stomach and turned his head to look at me with one eye. His command was clear. Stay. I would have laughed if I weren't feeling so sick.

The slice of sunlight bloomed into a full blast when LaShawna walked in. I raised a hand to shield my eyes and she said, "Good, you're up." Then she made a circuit of our condo opening the curtains and raising the blinds until we were bathed in afternoon sunlight.

Kota stepped away from me and made his own circuit of the room before settling down beside the couch again. I sat up, careful to keep the left side of my face pointed away from Officer Simmons.

"That's not going to work, little girl," LaShawna said, settling into a purple velvet chair directly across from me.

"What?" I asked, watching her out of the corner of my eye.

"What?" She looked at Kota. "'What?' she asks."

Kota slapped his tail against the floor three times in reply.

LaShawna rubbed one hand over her tight cropped curls and looked toward the kitchen. The afternoon sun streaming in really emphasized the lines of exhaustion etched in her face and picked up the hints of gray in her dark hair. She'd always seemed invincible to me, like a powerful Ashanti warrior queen etched in basalt. Even though her sharp, sculpted features had not changed, she suddenly seemed weathered, worn around the edges.

"I'm sorry, LaShawna," I said automatically. "I saw the news. Was it tough? Finding her?"

She turned back and looked me over carefully. "I didn't have to do that part. I'm not exactly an official part of the case."

"You're not? Then why—"

"I'm personally involved," she said. Then she scrubbed both hands over her head and groaned.

The image of her at the prayer vigil with one arm around Jazz Brennan flashed through my mind. "Are they your friends? The Brennans?" I ventured.

"Not exactly," she said, then made an impatient slashing motion with her hand. "Never mind that for a minute; we'll get there. Quit trying to avoid the elephant in the room. Let's talk about your face." She touched her left knuckle to her own cheek.

"I fell," I said, pouring all the false frustration I could muster into the words. I'd had a little time to think about my story since my conversation with Mrs. Tsien. "I tripped on the stairs and banged my face on the banister. It's no big deal."

LaShawna didn't blink. Her face was impassive. "If it's no big deal, why didn't you go to school?"

"I didn't feel like it," I said. Hearing the lame excuse come out of my own mouth almost made me cringe. I heaved a sigh and tried again. "I was sore this morning and I felt self-conscious, you know? Stupid."

"Okay. If that's all it is, then why did your stepbrother contact me last night and insist that I check in on you today?"

"Zack did that?"

"Yes, he did. Mr. Zachary Warner, who has never spoken to me in my life, left two separate voice messages for me—one on my personal phone and one on my work phone. You have any idea what he said?"

All I could do was shrug and wait.

"Mr. Warner says I should pay careful attention to how your mother is treating you. On the personal message, he went into a little more detail. He told me about an incident last year, back in Ohio. Said if he hadn't stepped between the two of you he isn't sure what would have happened."

"I'm sorry, LaShawna. He shouldn't have bothered you."

Her eyes popped wide open, the whites glowing around fiery topaz. She pushed her face forward, staring at me in disbelief. Her lips were a tight line. We sat like that for several uncomfortable seconds. Then she shook her head and looked back toward the empty kitchen.

"I should have known. It was right there in my face, but my damn head was buried so far down into this mess ..." Her words drifted off and another stiff silence settled between us.

It was nearly impossible not to fidget, not to twist at the

curls around my ear or chew my nails. Instead, I scratched under Kota's jowl and waited.

"He knew," LaShawna said, and I looked back at her. She focused on her partner. "You knew exactly what was going on, didn't you, Kota?"

Again, he slapped his tail three times in response.

LaShawna looked back at me. "I ran out of here yesterday like my butt was on fire, ready to tear apart every construction site in the Silicon Valley. But Kota didn't want to go. Once we were outside, he balked at getting in the car. Kept looking back at the front door, then looking at me. But I ignored the signals and ordered him into the car."

I opened my mouth to say something, but she made another impatient slashing motion with her hand.

"We were here for forty minutes before you came home from school. Your mother clutched that shoe and huffed and puffed like a pregnant woman giving birth, but she couldn't get anything. Nothing. Kept insisting Ivy was probably alive. I kept insisting she try again. Then you came in."

LaShawna leaned forward and clasped her hands between her knees, never taking her eyes off my face. "Your mother told the truth about one thing. It's probably the only true thing she said yesterday, but I didn't listen. I. Didn't. Listen. Shirley Simmons, or Xia Celeste, or whatever she wants to call herself, doesn't fall into involuntary trances. She never loses control. You made that up, little girl."

My mouth went dry as the sweet Comfort Twist tea I'd enjoyed earlier fought its way up my throat.

"But you found her. You found her in the concrete exactly like Mom—"

"Exactly like *you* said. You." LaShawna lifted her clasped hands and extended both pointing fingers at me. "You knew where to find her, didn't you?"

I shook my head, but LaShawna kept on going. "There was Kota, all tense and on guard, staring at a corner. Not at me, not at your mother, not at you. He was staring at that corner of the room." She waved one arm toward the corner between the kitchen and the living room, the corner where I'd first seen the mass of flickering, frantic images that was Ivy Brennan desperate to break through. "Then there was you, little girl, with your eyes as wide as pies, looking like you wanted to crawl right out of your own skin and run away, telling me what you mother said a week ago. A week ago? Why the hell would you look so torn to pieces over something cryptic your mother babbled out a week ago?"

LaShawna stood up and looked down at me. "She was here. Ivy communicated with you yesterday afternoon right here in this room, didn't she?"

I folded over until my forehead touched my knees and started sobbing uncontrollably. Kota whined and whimpered and tried to burrow his nose in where my face was pressed to my legs. I felt the couch shift as LaShawna sat next to me. Her hand rubbed a figure-eight pattern around my shoulder blades.

She said, "Relax, Kota. Let Asha have a good cry. Hush, now. Let her get the poison out."

So that's what we did. I continued to sob, part of me amazed I had so many tears left in me. LaShawna rubbed my back, humming a tune that sounded vaguely familiar, and Kota rested his muzzle on the back of my neck.

Eventually, the tears tapered off into hiccups and I lifted my head. Kota bathed my sticky cheeks with his tongue. LaShawna walked to the kitchen and returned with a packet of tissues and a glass of water. After I'd had time to mop all the goo off my face and drink a few swallows of the water, LaShawna looked around.

"Is anyone here now?" she asked "Ivy? Or any other visitors?"

I shook my head and hiccupped into the glass.

"All right, well, I still think we need to get out of here. I'm feeling claustrophobic and you could use a little cleansing. Let's take a ride."

13

Before

LaShawna's private vehicle was a battered Jeep Rodeo plastered with bumper stickers. A large dog crate was always in the back, but Kota usually rode shotgun with a special doggy seatbelt harness. I started to climb into the seat behind his, but LaShawna took my elbow and pulled me back.

"Give me a break," she said, but her tone was warm.

After repositioning Kota's harness and draping a hairy Mexican blanket over the seat behind the driver, she waved me into the front passenger seat. Then she got in and said, "Let's hope this hunk of junk can take us where we need to go."

She always said that every time she started the car when I was with her.

I made my face smile back like I was supposed to, but my heart wasn't in it.

The traffic heading north on 280 was horrific, but that

was normal for Silicon Valley. The whole highway system was a massive mess of cars. I'd never get used to it. Never.

LaShawna gripped the wheel and wove her way through the cars like she was navigating an obstacle course to get to the commuter lane where the traffic was slightly less terrible and we could actually get the car moving over thirty miles an hour in short spurts.

I sat tense and alert, waiting for more questions. When none came, I started watching my mother's cousin out of the corner of my eye.

There was a vague similarity to the shape of their eyes, their sculpted cheekbones, and their long necks, but LaShawna's close-cropped hair was natural. She would never sit still for a thousand-dollar weave. I couldn't detect a trace of makeup.

Lines of exhaustion were still etched in her face and her mouth was a frown of concentration, but she struck me as truly strong and beautiful in a way my mother could never be.

LaShawna wiggled her fingers at the car radio. "Turn on some tunes if you want."

"Where are we going?"

"To the sea," she said.

"San Francisco?" I asked, a fission of panic running up my spine. I'd visited the city three times since we'd moved here. The first two times had been heavenly, but the third had been a nightmare. A screaming ghostly nightmare.

LaShawna raised her eyebrows. "Is that a note of fear I hear in your voice? Afraid of earthquakes? Or the dearly departed that seem cluster in the city by the bay?" She laughed. "Don't worry. We're going to Santa Cruz."

I relaxed a bit, then something occurred to me. "What

do you know about the dearly departed and where they cluster?" I asked.

"Up there? Or anywhere?"

"Anywhere," I said. "You put a lot of faith in my mother. And now you're just accepting some of the same coming from me. What do you know about—?" I made jazz hands around my head. "All this?"

She flipped on her signal and took the exit for Seventeen South toward Santa Cruz, braking as the traffic slowed to a crawl. I thought she'd ignore the question, but then she said, "Has your mother ever told you how we met?"

The question confused me.

"Well, you're her cousin." I said. "What's there to say about that?"

"Your mother and I come from a large family that doesn't exactly keep in touch. Between us we probably have at least twenty cousins we've never met."

"Twenty cousins? Are you kidding?" I asked, flabbergasted.

"Probably more," LaShawna said ruefully. "Could be quite a few more. I don't mess with all that genealogy stuff."

"You're the only cousin I've ever met." Her lips tweaked into a bitter smile. "I'm pretty sure you're the only cousin she's ever mentioned. You and Aunt Lettie. That's your mother, right?"

"Oh dear," LaShawna said.

"What? Tell me."

"Aunt Lettie wasn't a blood relation to either of us, but we both loved her dearly. She was a wonderful woman." LaShawna took one hand off the wheel and pressed it to her chest. "A wonderful, wonderful woman. She saved us."

My head was spinning. "But she wasn't your mother? Or Mom's aunt?"

"She was our great aunt by marriage. She married Harrison Simmons. Let me see now ..." She tapped two fingers over her lips, squinting to remember. "Harrison was the oldest of five children. Or maybe it was seven children and five of them were boys. That sounds right. Shirley's grandfather Clem was the youngest of the lot, or at least he was the youngest son. My grandfather Joe was born somewhere in the middle of the brood. Doesn't matter where. Point is, Harrison was your great grandfather's eldest brother. And Lettie was Uncle Harrison's second wife. They married when they were both over fifty. Both of them lost their first spouses kind of early." She shot a quick look at my puzzled face. "You've really never heard any of this before?"

"No, I thought Aunt Lettie was your mother," I mumbled.

"I wish," LaShawna said. "My mother was a mess. It wasn't so bad when my dad was alive, but when he died she went to pieces. By the time I was your age, my mother had been in and out of jail for drugs, theft, and prostitution. That woman was a real winner. My grandmother took me in whenever Mommy Dearest was on the skids, but then Granny got sick." The last word seemed to catch in LaShawna's throat, and she had to clear it.

"The state tried to put me in a foster home, but Aunt Lettie showed up in her big silver Lincoln and took me to her home in Atlanta instead."

"I thought she lived in Decatur, Georgia," I jumped in, reaching out for something that was familiar from my mother's version of history. "That's where Mom escaped to when she left her parents behind in Alabama."

"That's right," LaShawna agreed. "Decatur is a city in its own right, but it's been swallowed up whole by Atlanta sprawl. So I just say Atlanta to make it easier for people to understand where I'm talking about." She looked over at me and winked. "Your mother, on the other hand, likes to say we're from Decatur because it's a little more posh than plain old Atlanta."

"And Miss Lettie was a well-known spirit medium, right? That's why Mom ran to her."

LaShawna shot me another sideways look. "That's what it says in your mother's autobiography," she said in a flat deadpan voice.

"What does that mean?" I asked, frustrated with this shell game.

"Aunt Lettie had the Gift. No question about it. And plenty of folks knew she had the Sight, so they came to her for guidance and advice. That's all true. But the way your mother wrote about Lettie in that autobiography makes it sound like she was some smarmy mystic medium swathed in scarves and staring into a crystal ball. Like a cheap, carnival fortune teller. If Lettie ever read that book of your mother's, she'd have pitched a fit."

"Why?" I asked, genuinely perplexed. I loved the chapter in Mom's book about her time with Aunt Lettie. It reminded me of the part in every great adventure story where the student learns from the master. It was Luke Skywalker moving rocks with Yoda. It was Karate Kid learning blocks by doing chores for Mr. Miyagi. It was Harry Potter falling into a bowl of Dumbledore's memories.

"Letitia Simmons was a respectable business woman. She operated a quaint tea shop where she served watercress sandwiches and dainty sweets to proper Southern belles. There was a private salon behind the tea room where she held very private, highly confidential consultations. Mind you, there was no sign anywhere in or on that building to let anyone know she was a medium. Heaven forbid!"

Unconsciously, LaShawna's voice had slipped into a Southern drawl.

"Aunt Lettie never advertised her services. In fact, she didn't even charge a set fee, though many of her regular clients paid her generously. Aunt Lettie was extremely selective about her clients and extremely protective of everyone's privacy. She wouldn't have dreamed of appearing on television, let alone on a reality show. Your mother's show would have given her a coronary."

LaShawna threw back her head and laughed. I squirmed. That television show was truly awful. Beyond embarrassing. Like the *Unhaunted* article said, Xia Celeste spent most of her time throwing tantrums on camera and rarely did any psychic sleuthing. It was mortifying.

"One thing Aunt Lettie impressed on me and your mother," LaShawna continued, "was that any decent person with the ability to help people in trouble—whether that ability came from the Sight or from more mundane resources—has a duty to help. Payment or no payment. Lettie was always willing to help the police if they came calling. She was very insistent on that point. It was part of a sacred trust. Your mother has always done her best to honor that trust. That's probably why I became a police officer myself."

"Did the police visit Lettie often?"

"Well, we are talking about the South. Even if Atlanta tends to be more enlightened than the rest of the region, not too many police officers came knocking on Lettie's front door."

"Did they come to the back door?" I asked.

Lashawna gave me a wicked smile. "Smart and sassy. That's what I like about you. Yes, there were a few knocks at the back door. And that's all I'm going to say about that."

"Were you going to tell me about the first time you met my mom?"

"I remember that morning very well," LaShawna said, keeping her eyes forward. "It was very early in the morning, so early it was still dark. Rain had been coming down day and night for over a week, and I was worried about having to wade through water to get to school." She looked over and shrugged. "That was my senior year of high school. I was very concerned with my 'do." She patted her close-cropped hair.

"And?" I prompted.

"Somebody started ringing the bell down on the ground floor. You know we lived above Lettie's tea shop, right?"

I nodded. In my mother's book, Aunt Lettie's home sounded like a vanilla and lemon-scented paradise.

"No one used that bell except deliverymen, and it was far too early for a delivery. Police officers and clients who came without an appointment always knocked politely. But that old doorbell started ringing over and over like something was on fire. I was sure Aunt Lettie was going to skin somebody alive when she flew down those steps in her red bathrobe. I didn't want to miss the show, so I tiptoed out to listen at the top of the stairs. There, looking up at me from the bottom of the stairs, stood a scrawny girl with the biggest, saddest eyes I had ever seen."

"My mother?"

"Yes, your mother. She was the same age you are now, but she looked much younger, no older than twelve. I took one look at that pathetic creature and thought, *Now there is someone who's been put through worse than anything my mother did to me. She's all alone in the world.*

"But she had parents."

"Who's telling this story? You or me?"

"You," I said, slumping back in my seat. "But she does have parents. They were strict and super religious, but she has parents."

"Yes, she had parents." LaShawna rubbed one arm thoughtfully, shooting a sideways glance in my direction. "And they weren't just strict, Asha. They were torturing her."

"I know. I read the book." A sudden thought occurred to me. "All that stuff, about the preacher's punishments and her mother turning a blind eye, that's all true, isn't it?"

"Yes, as far as I know," LaShawna agreed. "Actually, I have a suspicion it was worse. I think she skimmed over some of the ugliest bits."

I stared at her with my mouth open, aghast. "Worse?"

LaShawna held up one hand toward the sky. "All in the name of Jesus." She pronounced it *Jay-sus*. "I can still hear the desperate old woman who brought your mother to Lettie's door. She kept saying, 'They were trying to exorcise her, Lettie! Look at the marks on her. She's just an innocent child with the Gift. You've got to do something.' So of course Lettie did something. Shirley moved in with us immediately."

"Wait? Who was this old lady? I thought Mom made it to Decatur all on her own."

"That little white lie served two purposes." LaShawna held up two fingers. "First, it made her story sound better, more empowering. Second, it protected the woman who helped her. Preacher Simmons was a dangerous man to cross, and she was headed back to his county."

"But you're sure the exorcism story is true? You saw the marks?"

LaShawna grew silent, frowning intensely at the road ahead. As we climbed up into the Santa Cruz Mountains, the traffic thinned enough that we could drive at a normal pace.

"Yes," she said quietly. "I saw the marks. Doesn't matter what you call it—exorcism, torture, or plain, old-fashioned child abuse—what those people inflicted on a fifteen-year-old girl was pure evil. I wasn't a trained investigator at the time, but I am now. And I can tell you beyond a shadow of a doubt that Shirley endured horrific abuse over a long period of time. Maybe that's why I keep forgiving all her lies and crazy schemes and juvenile tantrums."

LaShawna looked over and lightly touched the lump on my cheek. "Doesn't excuse her taking a swing at you, though. That's going to stop."

"I tripped and fell on the stairs," I repeated without much conviction.

"Right." LaShawna's tone clearly implied she wasn't ever going to buy that explanation. "The point is, you asked me what I know about living with the dead. My answer is living with Aunt Lettie for four years and your mother for one taught me quite a bit about the voices of the dead." She shook herself and straightened her shoulders. "Let's get ourselves to Santa Cruz first, then we can talk about all this some more."

She flipped on the radio and refocused intense attention on the road. I stared out the side window, my head swimming with everything she'd just told me. Did I want to talk about this old history anymore?

Everything LaShawna said since she appeared in the doorway of our townhouse was like a string of explosions ricocheting through my body. The longer I tried to sit still and absorb the shocks, the more raw and damaged everything seemed. But it was all a distraction from the real problem. It didn't matter if my mother's family included one cousin or one hundred cousins. It didn't matter if Miss Lettie served up tea and sandwiches or secret séances. It really didn't matter if my mother crawled to Decatur on her hands and knees or was rescued by a Good Samaritan. None of this mattered. None of it.

An annoying little voice kept whispering in my brain.

You're going to have to tell LaShawna everything. Everything you saw. Everything you know. Everything.

DREAD WASHED OVER ME WHEN LASHAWNA MERGED ONTO Highway One. Suddenly, the thought of the Santa Cruz boardwalk, of walking through a crowd of normal, happy people laughing and gobbling fried Twinkies, made me want to throw up. But LaShawna passed the exit for the boardwalk.

"Where are we going exactly?" I asked, anxiety making my voice wobble.

"What you need is a salt cleansing, not salt water taffy and beach volleyball." She smiled at the confused frown on my face. "Seabright Beach is low key and ..." She jerked her thumb over her shoulder toward Kota. "Dogs are allowed. So Officer Fuzzface can have a little fun."

Kota started wiggling and whimpering, slapping one paw on the armrest of the door closest to him.

"What's wrong, Kota?" I asked.

"He's not upset; he's excited," LaShawna told me. She fiddled with the switches on her own door until the back windows rolled down. Kota immediately stuck his head out and sucked in a huge intake of air before huffing out his mouth and sucking in more air through his nose. His hindquarters lifted off the seat as his tail beat a wild staccato rhythm. He looked so silly, I surprised myself by giggling.

"He just figured out where we're going," LaShawna told me with a smile. "Usually, when it's just the two of us, he figures it out much earlier and fusses like this for twenty minutes. But he was distracted today; he's worried about you."

"That makes two of us," I said, staring down at my lap, feeling pitiful.

"That makes three of us," she corrected. "No, hold on." She lifted one hand and used her fingers to count off. "Me, Kota, stepbrother Zachary, and Mai Tsien." She wiggled all five fingers at me. "There's quite a few people worried about you."

"But not my mother," I said. The words tasted bitter in my mouth.

LaShawna sighed deeply and dipped her chin a few inches.

"Your mother never really learned how to worry about other people," she said.

"Because of what her parents did to her?" I asked.

"Maybe. Or maybe it has something to do with focusing all her energy on messages from the dead."

We lapsed back into silence while LaShawna exited the highway and navigated toward the public parking area designated for Seabright Beach. Despite everything, the sight of golden sunlight on sand and surf lifted my spirits.

When Mom told me we were moving to California, she'd made a big deal about living less than an hour from the beach. She'd made it seem like we'd be visiting the beach all the time. In reality, I'd only seen the Pacific Ocean three times since moving here, and two of those times the beach had been wrapped in chilly, gloomy fog. But today,

Seabright Beach was so Instagram perfect, it was mesmerizing. When I stepped out of the car, I had to lean back against the door to drink it all in. Following Kota's example, I inhaled deeply through my nose and exhaled through my mouth.

While I stood still and absorbed everything, LaShawna was busy. After clipping a leash on Kota's collar and releasing him from his travel harness, she opened the back door to gather beach towels, bottled water, and dog toys into a backpack. The sound of the door slamming and automatic locks jolted me back to reality. LaShawna slung the pack over one shoulder and pressed Kota's leash into my hand.

"Come on, little girl. Let's get our cleanse on."

"What is a cleanse?" I asked her. "Am I supposed to know?"

LaShawna shook her head. "Your mother," she said, cryptically. "Just follow me."

As we followed the happily dancing flag of Kota's tail toward the water, LaShawna explained that Aunt Lettie had taught her about salt cleansing during her years in Decatur. Apparently, Lettie had been a big believer in the power of sea salt and water to wash away the negative energy that came from working with restless spirits and many of the bereaved clients who travelled from all over the south for her guidance.

"Of course, we didn't have easy access to this kind of beach in North Georgia. What we had was a claw-foot Victorian tub and a closet full of big blue boxes of sea salt. The first time I dragged myself home from school feeling like a bag of dirty gelatin because some of the girls had found out about my mother and were giving me a tough time, do you know what she did?"

I shook my head.

"She marched me upstairs to her master bathroom, turned both taps on full blast, dumped a heaping pile of that salt into the water, and ordered me to remove my shoes and socks. I remember thinking *This is it. This is where I figure out the old lady is crazy.* Then she made me stand in that tub, fully clothed in my school clothes, while she scooped up wet globs of salt and rubbed my hands with it. When she rubbed it into the crown of my head, I was horrified." LaShawna smiled and scrubbed one hand over top of her short-cropped hair. "Back in those days, I had hair. And I would spend stupid amounts of time trying to hot comb that hair smooth. I had not yet figured out I was never going to look like Naomi Campbell."

I touched my own messy corkscrews. "Obviously I'm not real worried about my hairdo today."

We stopped a few feet from the surf. Kota jumped and frisked at the fringe of the water, but he stayed close enough not to pull on the leash. LaShawna dropped her bag and turned to me. She gently clasped my upper arms and looked at me steadily.

"I like the hair. I'm not a big fan of the dark circles under your eyes and I'd like to kick Shirley's ass for that purple goose egg on your face, but I like the natural look on you. With those sassy freckles and that gorgeous butterscotch complexion of yours, you have such a unique beauty, Asha. I wasted too many years and too many tears trying to look like pictures in magazines. Don't waste your time trying to look like someone or something you're not. That bun you normally wear on top of your head makes you look so ... uptight."

I swallowed hard to push down my annoyance. That bun was perfect for dance class and made me feel like the ballerina I'd always dreamed of being.

"So, what's next?" I asked. "Are you going to rub salt water on my hands and head now?"

She shook her head and stepped back, releasing my arms. "What Lettie did worked, but it felt weird. I won't subject you to that." She reached out and pulled Kota's leash from my loose grip. "Just take off your shoes and walk through the surf a bit." She waved her hand toward the waterline that stretched south behind me. "Kota and I will stay here and play fetch. Go walk as far as you need to walk. Take lots of those deep breaths I watched you taking up by the car. Dip your hands in the water as often as you like. Rub some on your arms, your neck, and the top of your head until you start feeling better.

Try to clear your mind. It's easier said than done. Aunt Lettie told me repeating one word over and over can help. I like to repeat the word *release*. You know, like I'm releasing all the negative garbage? But you can use any word you want. Lettie liked the word *peace*. Yogis think *ohm* is a magical word. Come back to us when you feel ready, okay?"

I nodded, looking around, feeling conspicuous and uncertain.

"Don't worry about anyone watching you or thinking you're weird," LaShawna said, startling me by how accurately she'd read my thoughts. "This is Santa Cruz, California, Baby. Everyone is weird. And everyone is way too concerned with their own selves to be paying any attention to you. Just focus on breathing and walking and releasing."

She pulled a sleeve of brightly colored balls and an oversized slingshot contraption out of her backpack then clucked her tongue at Kota. "Come on, Kota. Let's play!"

I stripped off my shoes and socks and started walking away from them through the foamy surf. The water was icy cold. Despite what LaShawna said, I still felt awkward and weird, but at the same time I was also thrilled to be there. I'd dreamed of this experience while we drove cross-country last summer. Breathing in salty air and golden sunshine was pure pleasure. The tight knots in my chest and gut started to loosen up a bit. I kept walking, the rhythm of my footsteps soothing as a warm bubble of hope rose in my chest. Yes, this could work. This was working.

An alien thought popped into my head.

We loved the beach.

Although my eyes were wide open, my surroundings dimmed, then disappeared. Suddenly the sun felt hotter. I felt the grit of sand along the backs of my legs. My nostrils burned with the chemical sent of suntan lotion and bug spray. All around were people. Too many people. Just beyond my toes there was a blonde little girl in a bright pink swimsuit and striped sun hat. She was intensely focused on sculpting a sandcastle, her lips pursed together tightly. Love, pure and sweet, swelled in my chest.

Jazz.

A shadow fell across her and two hands scooped her up. The squeal that came from her mouth made my stomach cramp painfully.

No!

"Come on and play with your Uncle David in the waves, Jazzy."

Jazz went still, like a limp doll, as he settled her on his shoulders. She stuck her sandy fingers into her mouth and looked down at her unfinished castle. Her face was the definition of misery.

No, no, no!

My whole body sprang into motion, launching myself toward the two of them. "Take me! I'll play, Uncle David. I'll play."

His mouth twisted.

"Now, don't be jealous," he said in a big voice. Thick, moist fingers hooked under my armpit as he leaned in close; I felt his breath in my ear. "Don't worry, you're still my princess," he said as one finger swept under my bathing suit and stroked the tender skin near my pounding heart.

ALONE AGAIN ON SEABRIGHT BEACH, I STUMBLED THROUGH the shallow surf. After spinning in a circle to make sure no one was near me, I walked deeper into the ocean until it was up to my knees and plunged my hands into the frigid water, desperately splashing and rubbing the water up past my elbows. I cupped by hands together and scooped up water to splash on my face, my neck, and the top of my head.

"Release, release, release, release." Teeth chattering, I repeated the word over and over in rapid-fire desperation with no noticeable effect. Finally I stood up and screamed, "Go away!" into the wind. Then, in a much softer voice, "Please."

Ivy's response came to me like a distant echo.

Tell her.

Again, I spun in a circle. A woman jogging with a chocolate Labrador shot an annoyed look in my direction, but she didn't say anything or break her stride. I looked back to where LaShawna was launching another ball into the ocean as Kota splashed after the target in hot pursuit. They were like tiny toy figures in the distance, and neither appeared to have heard my screaming.

Tell her.

That's when I realized this whole cleansing thing was never going to work until I came clean with LaShawna.

LaShawna sat on a beach blanket with the soles of her feet pressed together, her hands gripping her ankles as I stuttered and stammered my way through explaining the images Ivy had shown me. Starting with the moment I arrived home to find her police car in the guest parking spot and a strange shadow around the front door, I poured out the whole horrible story – every image, every feeling, every word, every smell.

As she listened, LaShawna remained stone still, utterly silent, unblinking and unmoving. She did not interrupt. She never asked a single question. Even when I struggled to find the right words or fell into long miserable silences, she did not move or speak. When I finally finished describing the beach scene I'd just witnessed, her eyes were burning with an intense fury.

I looked down at my legs and waited. And waited. And waited.

"Please say something, LaShawna."

The silence stretched on until I was ready to scream.

When she finally spoke, her lips barely moved and her voice was so low I couldn't hear the words. So I leaned closer to her.

"What did you say?"

LaShawna cleared her throat. "She tried to tell me."

I sat back, startled by the ferocious anger in her voice. "Ivy never told you, though. You would have listened, if she told you. I know you would have."

LaShawna closed her eyes. "She was in my volunteer youth group for two years. Two years. And I never suspected. She always seemed like such a strong, healthy, poised girl. I had no idea." Her topaz eyes opened, blazing.

"Then, about a month ago, she started asking me these unsettling questions. She told me she was tutoring a younger girl, and there were signs ... oh my God! It's such a cliché. Any police officer worth anything knows it always starts as something that happened to a friend. I told her she could call me, any time, day or night to talk about her friend." LaShawna made exaggerated air quotes around the last two words. "I gave her my card. I should have stopped everything. I should have found a way in."

"You did," I said, the words sounded more confident than I felt. "That's why she wanted me to tell you. She trusted you. She still trusts you."

LaShawna leaned forward, scrubbing both hands over her eyes. "I should have done more."

Kota whimpered, unhappy with his partner's misery.

"Was it a mistake to tell you?" I asked in a soft voice.

Officer Simmons popped back up to a straight spine. "No, it is not a mistake." Then, in a softer voice, "You were absolutely right to tell me. Thank you. I just needed a moment." She stood up and brushed the sand from her legs.

"I am going to take that bastard down."

14

Now

THE RATTLE AND SQUEAK OF A CART BEING WHEELED INTO THE room draws my attention to the door. The girl behind the cart is young, with glowing sun-kissed skin, glossy black hair, and impossibly white teeth.

"Hi, Asha!" she sings out. "I'm Fiona. How are you feeling?"

I look down at the IV, tubes, and wires taped to my right arm, then survey the neon pink cast encasing my left.

"Super," I answer.

"It's lunchtime!" she announces as though this is the most exciting development in the world. "I'm going to be your mealtime assistant today. Let's see what we have."

She proceeds to go through the contents of the tray as though she is a game show host revealing valuable prizes. Asha has won apple juice, blueberry yogurt, chicken broth, and chocolate pudding in today's lunchtime lottery. Lucky me.

"I'm not really hungry," I tell her.

"I'm not going to leave until we eat something," her sing-song voice is pitched down a bit, but her sickening-sweet tone still makes my teeth ache. "Nutrition is absolutely critical in the recovery process. How about this yogurt? It has protein to build strength and calcium for your bones."

"Fine," I agree, just to shut her up. Then I have to endure ten more minutes of her perkier then perky personality as she pushes spoonful after spoonful of thin, watery yogurt alternating with sips of warm apple juice. Her next project is the chicken broth. It's cold, bland, and nauseating. I press my lips together and shake my head like a toddler refusing to eat peas as Fiona tries to offer a second taste.

When Vera Birth appears in the doorway, I'm actually relieved to see her.

"I can come back when you're finished eating," Vera says.

"No!" I cry out, like a drowning victim going down for the third time. "Stay. I'm done now."

Fiona's eyebrows pucker as though she is deeply disappointed in me. "What about your pudding?"

"I'm really not hungry." The words are addressed to Vera. So is the pleading look in my eyes. Without hesitation, Vera responds to her cue by bustling over to my bedside and directly addressing the cheerleader pushing disgusting food at my face.

"Thank you, Fiona," she says firmly, tapping the girl's volunteer nametag. "You can go now."

"Oh, okay!" Fiona agrees with a shrug. "Bye, Asha. See you soon."

As soon as Happy Girl clears the doorway, I look back at Vera. "Is there any way to be sure she never comes back into my room?"

"I'll take care of it," Vera promises.

"Really?" I ask, surprised.

"Really." Vera nods with absolute assurance. She sets her messenger bag in the upholstered chair, pushes the rolling bedside tray with the remains of my lunch to the far wall, and firmly closes the door to the hallway before returning to my bedside. In that short time, fear and dread wash over me in waves. I'm grateful to Vera for banishing Fiona, but, despite all of LaShawna's assurances, anxiety is pounding in my ears.

Vera stretches one hand toward me. For a split second, I think she is trying to shake my hand. Then I realize she's handing me a card. It's a simple white business card with the outline of a bird in flight etched in pale gray. No, not just any bird. It's a crow. The card declares her to be *Vera Birch, Chief Counsel, QFWC Foundation.* Every hair on my body stands on end. There were deposits in my mother's bank account from QFWC Fund. And the mysterious email exchanges with E. Quinn, Trustee. Now Vera, who is supposed to be my advocate and lawyer, is handing me a card that says she is the Chief Counsel. I press the card between my thumb and forefinger as hard as I can to stop my hand from shaking.

"Have you ever heard of the QFWC Foundation?" she asks.

"No." The denial is automatic.

"But you have heard of the Quinn Family Trust, have you not?"

"Of course I have," I say, relieved to find myself on familiar ground. "Everyone in Moonville knows the QFT."

"Do they really?" she asks with an enigmatic smile.

I'm irritated. It feels like Vera is smugly amused by some obvious ignorance on my part while she enjoys superior knowledge from behind her immense purple glasses.

"Well, why don't you tell me what I should know," I challenge her.

"Okay, here's what I think you need to know right now," she agrees brightly, showing no sign of offence at my belligerent tone. "High-level version. The Quinn Family Trust was created by Violet Quinn to manage a substantial portfolio of assets. In addition to the historic sanatorium and estate in Moonville, Ohio, there are many other assets not as well-known—other properties, business enterprises, and global investments, not to mention plenty of good old-fashioned liquid assets like cash and bonds. In a nutshell, it's a very wealthy trust. Much larger than the average citizens in Moonville realize. For instance, not many people know that the Quinn Trust quietly operates a philanthropic foundation currently known as QFWC, but the Foundation has been through many iterations and gone by many names over its long history."

"Long history?" I ask.

"Don't get me started. I can rattle on about the history for hours. I'm a history geek! But I'll try to focus on what's important here. The Foundation's origins are much older than the Quinn Trust. In fact, it predates the Trust by nearly one hundred years. Its history and guiding principles are deeply rooted in the most important social and political movements of the nineteenth century—Reformist, Abolitionist, Suffragist, Spiritualist."

"Whoa. That's a lot of big -ists," I say. "Why have I never heard of it? Why doesn't anything important come up under Google searches?"

As soon as the words are out of my mouth, I want to snatch them back. The only reason I Googled her foundation was because I saw the deposits in my mother's bank account. I watch Vera for any sign of a gotcha moment, but she simply nods.

"The Foundation's mission has always relied heavily on confidentiality and discretion. We like to fly under the radar. Spiritualists, Suffragists, and Abolitionists – they were all well-known for being loud and proud and in the public's face. Yes?"

"I guess so."

"You guess so?" Vera narrows your eyes at me. "Has your mother never sat down with you and taught you the full history of the Spiritualist Movement and how it entwined with important political and social reforms like education, women's rights, and anti-slavery?"

"My mother isn't exactly excited about history like you are," I answer cautiously.

"That's ... disappointing." Vera sighs heavily, and I suspect I've failed an important test.

"But your foundation sounds very impressive," I say tentatively, trying to steer the conversation back into clear waters. "I mean, obviously, I know about those groups. They did lots of great things." Oh yuck! I sound like such a suck up.

"Yes, but some great things are better done unobtrusively. The Foundation, in all its various iterations, has quietly contributed for over a hundred and fifty years."

"And now you're the Chief Counsel."

"Yes." She nods and flashes another smile. This time her smile seems a bit bashful. "Lofty title. La-ti-da." She rolls her eyes. "Actually, my little legal branch of the foundation is a rather new thing. Based on some pro bono legal work I was doing, I wrote up a proposal and submitted it to the foundation for funding. Next thing you know, the funding is approved and I'm the Chief Counsel. Bippity-boppity-boo."

She giggles merrily, her disappointment in my lack of education seems to be forgotten for now.

"What was your proposal? To be a fairy godmother?"

"To do things like this. To help people like you." She opens her arms wide, palms facing upward.

I shake my head. "That's not an answer."

"It's the answer I'm giving you right now. Perhaps I'll tell you more as it becomes appropriate." She makes a cutting gesture to indicate the topic is closed.

"Did your proposal have anything to do with the *Unhaunted* website?" I blurt out the question before I can think too hard about the implications. "Are you The Professor?"

Time seems to stand still. I keep my eyes locked on Vera's face as she tilts her head and studies me.

"Yes and no," she says finally, breaking the stare down. "I started that website and I continue to contribute to it and support the mission statement, but it's an outside interest. Totally separate from the Foundation. Now I think it's time to focus on this situation; it's time to talk about you. I'm here to represent your best interests. The QWFC Foundation will pay any and all expenses related to my representation. Neither your mother nor your father nor any other member of your family will ever owe money for my services. Your mother has agreed to this arrangement, but you can still decline my representation. You can tell me to go away at any time. Do you understand?"

"I guess so."

"Another guess so, Asha? Either you understand or you don't," Vera says briskly. "You're an intelligent young lady. Tell me what you don't understand."

"Why do I need a lawyer?"

I pluck at the bedsheets, struggling the spit out what comes next.

"Am I ... in trouble?"

It's a stupid question. Of course I'm in trouble. What I really want to ask is, am I going to jail? Will there be a trial? Will people find out about our crazy nightmare family? Will I have to tell a room full of strangers about the terrible visions Ivy showed me?

When Vera doesn't answer me immediately, I peek up at her. Her expression is perplexed.

"I'm trying to think how to answer that," she admits with a quirk at the corner of her mouth. "The quick and easy answer is no. You are the victim of a crime. Everything you did, you were defending yourself and others. You are not in trouble with the law. No one wants to do anything that will harm you any more than you've already been violated." She nods briskly to emphasize her words, then retreats to the upholstered chair and sits, sighing deeply.

Violated. The word echoes in my chest.

"On the other hand, it's going to *feel* like you're in trouble," Vera admits. "This is an unholy mess. There's no way to avoid a few more painful bumps in the road before it's over."

An involuntary gasp squeaks out of me. Vera holds up both hands as though she's surrendering. "Very bad choice of words, sorry. I'm here to minimize the pain, not make it worse. I'm not exactly defending you at this point. That's why I introduced myself as your advocate."

"What kind of pain?" I ask her.

Vera smiles with her whole mouth and tips her head toward me. "That's why we need to talk. But before we start digging into this, we need to very clear on one point. Have you ever heard of attorney-client privilege?"

"I've seen a few episodes of *Law and Order* where it was put aside."

Vera chuckles. "Do I really need to tell you that's fiction?"

"No." I flash a weak smile. "I get it. You're my lawyer. You can't tell anyone anything I tell you in confidence. Even if I tell you I murdered twenty people and buried them in my basement, you can't tell anyone else."

"Exactly," Vera agrees.

"As long as it's just the two of us, though. A third party eliminates expectation of privacy."

"Wow. Listen to you, Jack McCoy," Vera teases. "You're correct. So if Fiona Happypants comes back in with more pudding, don't tell me anything you wouldn't want the world to know. Got it?"

"Okay, got it." I swallow painfully and stare up at the ceiling to steady my nerves. "Where do we start?"

"We start at the beginning." Vera removes a bright blue clipboard fitted with a brand new legal pad from her messenger bag and clicks a ballpoint pen, ready to take notes. "Why don't you tell me about the first time you heard the name Ivy Brennan."

And right there, I have a decision to make.

Will I tell her exactly what happened that first day when I came home to find a dead girl in my living room? Will I expose my mother's lies? Or will I hide behind my mother's version of this ghost story?

15

———

Before

The night after I told LaShawna everything, I slept the deep, exhausted, dreamless sleep that only comes to someone who has been trapped under the weight of the world then found a way to escape.

That was the magic of LaShawna. She may not see ghosts or hear the voices of the dead. She may not have x-ray vision into the darkest secrets of someone's soul. She certainly couldn't outrun a speeding bullet or leap tall buildings in a single bound. But LaShawna knew how to listen, knew when to believe. And when she looked into my eyes and said, "I've got this," I knew absolutely and without a shadow of doubt that she would stand up for us. For all of us. For Ivy and for Jazz and for me.

Yes, that was the magic of LaShawna ... and Kota, too. They had this. Little girls would be saved. Bad men would pay. And I would be able to go back to my regularly scheduled, screwed up life.

The next morning, the sunlight streaming though my bedroom window seemed lighter, brighter. There wasn't the slightest hint of a shadow in my room. No tree branches sprouting across my walls. No whispering in my ear. I was alone. My relief was tinged by a hint of sadness. I didn't want anything to do with Ivy Brennan when she first appeared. With her perfect blonde Barbie doll face, I did not want to invite her in. But in a very short time, I'd grown to love her a little. So there was a twinge of sadness at her absence. And yet I wanted her to move on, to be at peace. Of course I did.

Three sharp knocks on my bedroom door startled me, then my mother burst into the room full of bubbly energy.

"Good morning, Daughter Dearest," she sang out, hurrying into the center of my room then twirling to face me. A white silk robe embroidered with cherry blossoms swirled with her, fluttering around her arms and bare legs. I'd never seen the robe before. It looked expensive.

Her golden coffee skin, bare of any makeup, glowed to perfection from head to toe. Obviously, she'd spent lots of time at a spa yesterday. And her hair! I blinked, unable to believe my eyes. She traded in the usual ultra-smooth Brazilian weave for what was supposed to be a more "natural" look—a glossy mass of loose corkscrew curls that cascaded over her shoulders. She twirled one curl with a pink-tipped finger. Add a new manicure to the tally.

"What do you think?" she asked. In the morning light, I could see dollar signs hovering in the air around her.

"Wow," I said, truly dazzled by her new version of glamour even while my stomach clenched in anger at all the money she must have spent to create this transformation.

She giggled. She actually giggled. I'd never heard my mother giggle outside the presence of a man in my entire life. If I didn't know better, I would have thought she drank a bottle of champagne for breakfast. But that wasn't Xia's kind of thing. It was more my father's sort of behavior.

In that moment, I was much more afraid of her than I'd ever been during one of her howling rages. What she said next confirmed my fears.

"Big things are afoot, little one," she told me, spreading both hands wide on either side of her face. "Big things."

"What sort of things?" I asked, the words tasting like burnt ash.

"First things first," she said, suddenly all business. "We're going to have to work fast, get some basic training in quickly."

"Basic training?" I echoed, the dread in my stomach threatened to swallow me whole.

She fluttered her fingers at me. "You know, what we talked about yesterday. Time to begin your training, my young apprentice." Her eyes darted around the room briefly.

"We're alone," I reassured her.

"Good. Wait here." She rushed out of the room, leaving me feeling weak and dizzy. What on Earth was she up to? I didn't trust her, or this whole friendly, fluttering performance she was putting on. She hurried back in and thrust a shrink-wrapped, book-sized box in my face. I took it from her and stared at the words and images printed on it.

"A henna tattoo kit?"

She nodded, then handed over a few folded papers and fluttered her fingers at me again. "Blue ink would be better. Actual tattoos would be best, but you're only fifteen. This will have to do for now."

I stared at her.

She tapped the folded papers once with a pink nail. "These are protective symbols, ones I've used with success."

Then she tapped the box. "Take your shower first and get your skin very dry. No oil or lotion. Choose one or more symbols that speak to you. Draw them on your skin where no one will be able to see. I like to protect this core area."

She pressed the fingertips of her right hand to the area between her navel and breastbone. A corresponding twinge erupted in the same area of my body, and I suddenly realized that was where I'd felt the most powerful resistance when I'd first encountered Ivy.

"Over the heart is good too." She dipped her fingers under the lapel of her robe and flashed the skin over her own heart where she had a colorful and intricate tattoo of an Egyptian scarab. She'd had the tattoo for years, but I'd never connected it with its true purpose – protection.

"Back of the neck and tailbone are also good protection spots, but you don't have time to get that fancy. Just pick something easy and get it done. You'll need thirty minutes for the paste to dry so get a move on."

I continued to stare at her, locked in place.

She snapped her fingers at me. "Move it, move it, move it," she ordered, a familiar edge of impatience creeping into her voice, pushing aside the sickening sweetness I did not trust.

"I'm going to be late for school."

"Not if you move quickly. I'll drive you."

She'd never driven me to school in my entire life. Not once. Not even for my first day of kindergarten. I'd walked through thunderstorms and snowdrifts back in Ohio. In California, the worst I'd had to contend with was a light drizzle. But I always walked. And now, on a beautiful clear spring morning, she was going to drive me to school? What was going on?

Alone in my bathroom with the henna applicator ready

to go, I scanned the pages of protection symbols. Most of them were way too complicated for my meager artistic ability. As much as I admired the Eye of Horus or the swirling ram's horns in the Adinkra symbol for strength, there was no way I could paint either of them on my own midsection without making a muddy mess. In frustration, I decided to try a Google search on my phone to find simple protection symbols.

As soon as I activated my phone, multiple alerts came up. A preview of a text from Zack appeared.

What is that woman up to?

"I wish I knew," I whispered. But I needed to complete the task at hand before reading and responding to any messages.

I quickly decided on a basic arrow tattoo—one line with a triangle tip and three slashes to indicate the feathers. It was a Native American protection symbol and well within my artistic comfort zone. I drew one large arrow across my middle with very thick lines, a smaller version over my heart, and two tiny arrows on the inside of my forearms, halfway between my wrists and elbows. The instructions told me to allow the henna paste to dry for at least thirty minutes before washing it off. So I spread a clean bath towel on my closet floor and, moving very cautiously to avoid smearing the paste, lay on my back on top of the towel as though I was sunbathing on the beach. The whole situation felt silly. To distract myself, I opened the messaging app on my phone.

Strung out and exhausted after the emotional scene on the beach with LaShawna, I'd slept through most of the car ride home and stumbled blindly to my bed like a sleep-walking zombie without checking my phone the night before. Now I found a long scroll of messages waiting for me. The first message from Zack had come in a little after nine o'clock the previous evening. That meant he started sending messages after midnight his time. A fission of unease fluttered through my body.

9:08 PM: *Hey. RU there?*

9:16 PM: *G-pa Elton is here at the clinic. V upset. Been calling you and Xia 4 hours. No answer? No call back?*

9:17 PM: *Where RU?*

"I was sleeping," I tell the phone.

Switching over to the call log, there are two missed calls with corresponding voice messages from my grandfather's home number. The man refuses to "fool around" with a mobile phone. The first voice message came in around seven-thirty in the evening California time.

"This is Elton Kidwell. Your grandfather." Even though his deep, gravelly voice was familiar and comforting, like the stuffed bear I used to sleep with as a little girl, it was also oddly formal—stiff and tight. "You need to call me as soon as possible, young lady. As soon as possible. You hear me? That woman, your mother, has put something on the internet. We need to talk. Call me. Doesn't matter how late. You need to call me."

He's angry, I realized with a pang. My grandfather is never angry. He's Mr. Calm Cool Collected in all situations. He's always ready with a joke to diffuse any tense situation. And now he sounded really angry over something Xia put on the internet.

Big things are afoot, little one.

In the second message he sounded even more upset.

"Asha, this is your grandfather again. Call me immediately. Please."

There was a third voice message from Zack's mobile time-stamped around nine o'clock. It was basically the spoken version of his text messages. Grandpa Elton's raspy voice was grumbling in the background, but I couldn't make out the words. The tone and pitch in his voice made my teeth hurt. He was obviously very upset. The man had a heart condition. It wasn't healthy for him to be so distraught.

And yet, a telephone conversation with my grandfather was simply impossible at that moment. I loved the man dearly and felt horrible he was disturbed over me, but I could not call him. Even with his hearing aids turned up full blast, telephone conversations with Elton Kidwell required practically yelling into the phone. My mother would hear every word. No, that would *not* work. But I couldn't ignore him and leave the man to stew in his obvious distress all day.

Switching back to the text messages, I scanned Zack's remaining texts. The gist of all his messages was that Xia had relaunched her website with a video about the discovery of Ivy Brennan's body. She was taking credit for providing the police with information that led to the discovery which outraged Zack and didn't bother me one bit. What did bother me, what made the arrow symbol on my midsection burn and itch, was the revelation that Xia had mentioned my involvement on her website and then on Twitter.

That was why my grandfather was in an uproar.

9:49 PM: *Website says "My daughter's talent is starting to bloom. Together, we were able to pierce the veil of darkness around Ivy's spirit. It was a team effort."*

9:51 PM: *Seriously? Team effort?*

9:52 PM: *X also tweeted "My little apple didn't fall far from the family tree" with a link to website.*

9:59 PM: *Lots of commentary and retweets flying. Many asking about you.*

10:05 PM: *What is that woman up to?*

"I don't know, but I'm going to find out," I muttered to myself. Thumbs flying, I fired off a quick string of texts back to Zack.

Hey Zack. I'm fine.

All good here. Promise.

In bed early last night.

Got 2 get 2 school now. Running late.

No access 2 phone 2day.

Can't call G-pa now.

Can U call him? Tell him all OK in Cali.

Tell him will call after school.

K?

Several tense seconds went by before he responded.

U promise? All safe and ok?

Yes! Promise!!! I typed back.

Got 2 go! U call G-pa?

My heartbeat throbbed in my ears as I waited for his reply. What would I do if he refused to call my grandfather?

K. Will do.

But U call G-pa right after school.

Then call me.

Don't text. Call!

THINGS GOT EVEN MORE BIZARRE WHEN I HURRIED downstairs dressed for school. On the breakfast bar, I found half of a grapefruit, a mug of green tea, and a white box with a purple bow on top.

Xia stood on the other side of the bar sipping from a mug of coffee, her eyes watching me with an intense cat-like pleasure, waiting for me to react. Skin prickling, I approached the items.

"Is this for me?" I asked, pointing toward the iconic white box with the Apple logo clearly visible.

"It's the newest iPhone," she bust out. The look on her face was smug, confusing me.

"Oh, then it's yours," I said, feeling stupid.

"No, silly girl, it's yours. I had Todd pick it up yesterday. It's all set to go. He charged it up and left some notes for you. Your number. How to set your security code. Blah, blah, blah. All that stuff techie boys think is so important."

"Todd bought me an iPhone?"

"No, I bought it. Todd just dealt with all the annoying details. He likes doing that sort of thing. Men usually do." She checked her watch. "Hurry and eat. You can take the tea with you."

Dutifully, I stepped over to the grapefruit and started spooning the sour sections into my mouth. As I chewed and swallowed mechanically, my brain scrambled to think of a way to bring up Xia's Twitter and website activity from yesterday. The problem was that the smart phone hidden in my bathroom was a secret. Without mentioning its existence, there was no way I could know about my mother's most recent online activity. Likewise, I couldn't ask her why she was ignoring my grandfather's telephone calls. Without the secret phone, I could not possibly know about them. But now I owned a phone that was not a secret. I eyed the pristine white box.

"I can't believe you bought me an iPhone," I said. And it was true. I really could not understand why she'd been so generous. I was the only kid in school who didn't carry some form of smart phone in her backpack, but Xia could have bought something much cheaper. Considering our financial situation, which I also could not mention to her, she should have bought a much cheaper phone. "I hope you didn't pay for data. I heard it gets expensive if you're not super careful."

"No data," Xia barked with a pointed look. "Just talk and text. For now. If you really need it, you can access the internet using the wireless when you're here at home."

"That's great," I said, pushing some enthusiasm into my voice. "That's all I need." Shoveling in more grapefruit, I pasted a thoughtful look on my face. "Am I allowed to take the phone to school?" I asked, trying to sound innocent. Even though the school forbid the use of phones during school hours, I could hide in the girl's bathroom and call Grandpa Elton during my lunch period.

"Of course, that's why I'm giving it to you now. I'll text you where to meet me after school."

I froze. "You're going to pick me up after dance team rehearsal?" A ride to school and a ride home? Again, this was totally unprecedented.

"No, Asha, you're going to meet me immediately after school. As soon as that final bell rings, you need to hustle your butt outside. We have an appointment. There's no time for girly hobbies this week. I told you, big things are happening. There's a whole new world opening for us, but we have to move quickly. Jump on opportunity while the opportunity is hot. We'll see how things go before I make a final decision about when you're going to quit dance team."

Quit dance team? And there it was. Boom. There was the fist in the face I'd been waiting for since she first flounced into my room full of bubbles and brightness. When the blow came, it knocked me into stunned silence. I never bothered to ask for any details about the new opportunity or the mysterious appointment she had planned.

THE SCHOOL DAY WAS A BLUR OF CURIOUS FACES AND superficial conversations where I made my face smile while my heart sunk down to my shoes. Every time someone asked about the fading bruise on my face, I recited my story of tripping on the stairs.

So embarrassing, right?

Most smiled back without a trace of suspicion, eager to tell me what had happened in their lives while I was gone. Brittany had a new crush, Emily was grounded for failing an Algebra test, and Ella was "totally devastated" because her orthodontist had proclaimed her braces would have to stay on for an additional six months.

Envy, pity, and annoyance battled for dominance in my topsy-turvy brain as I listened to the details of my so-called friends small, boring, and utterly normal lives.

In Spanish class, I stumbled through reciting a poem I could have pronounced perfectly two days earlier. I doodled chains and barbed wire entwined with ivy instead of taking notes in biology class. I failed my own Algebra quiz.

Suddenly, I was jerked out of my stupor when someone grabbed my arm outside my fourth period study hall.

"Hey, you're Asha Kidwell, right?"

I looked up to find a girl wearing a black t-shirt decorated with colorful sugar skulls, too much black eyeliner, and messy pigtails streaked with purple. I couldn't remember her name, but I knew she was a senior whose art had won awards. Catalina? Katarina?

How did she know me?

"Um, yes?" My voice sounded like I didn't know my own name.

"Your mother is Xia Celeste, right?"

It wasn't exactly a secret, but I didn't spread that personal detail around and my mother certainly didn't participate in any parental activities to support the school. However, the look on my face must have told this girl she was right.

"Awesome," she said, smiling at me. "I loved your mother's TV show. Sucked when it got cancelled. I'm glad she's back in the spotlight." She waved her phone at me. A new publicity photo of my mother with her new curly hair stared back at me.

"Yeah," I said, feeling utterly stupid. "It's great."

Her face grew serious. "Well, not great about the dead girl. But Xia deserves some recognition, right? Maybe it will get her a new show."

A new show. That was my mother's deepest, most passionate desire.

"Anyway, I am definitely going to be there this weekend. Good luck."

Where this weekend? Good luck with what?

Before I could formulate a sensible question, another image caught my eye, stealing my breath away. Ivy Brennan was at the end of the hallway, glaring bullets at me. A couple of bulky football players passed between us, then she was gone. The sullen self-pity that had kept me in its grasp all day disappeared in a surge of foreboding.

Something was wrong.

"Gotta get to class," the purple-haired girl said and hurried away, leaving me speechless and staring at an empty corridor.

I didn't have a class to scoot off to. This was my lunch period. Instead of moving toward my locker to retrieve the brown bag Xia had thrust at me when she dropped me off at school, I walked in a daze to the place where I'd seen Ivy seconds before. There was a lingering chill in the air, but no other sign of her. The bell rang, causing the hallway to clear quickly and I was left alone. A flickering light in the girl's bathroom caught my attention. A girl I didn't know quickly exited the bathroom with a nervous look over her shoulder and scurried away. As the door swung shut behind her, a shadowy silhouette appeared in the thick, smoky glass at the top third of the door.

Ivy.

I hurried into the bathrooms, only to find the room empty. Every single stall door hung open, the light remained bright.

"Ivy?" I whispered anxiously.

As soon as I spoke her name, the lights dimmed and the temperature in the room cooled.

I stood transfixed as the shadows of bare tree branches snaked up the bathroom walls, surrounding me. Ivy appeared in the mirror, her face furious.

Wake up. Her voice boomed in my skull. *Stop hiding.*

Ivy's image in the mirror was replaced by a rapid-fire series of memories. My mother clutching Ivy's shoe. LaShawna's shattered glass. Zack saying, "Xia stole money." Mother's bank account. Internet images of missing girls. Mrs. Tsien saying, "Nobody's perfect." My mother's publicity photo.

Everything was moving too quickly. The room swirled and tilted. The last thing I remember is my head hitting the speckled linoleum floor.

THE SCHOOL NURSE DECIDED I NEEDED TO GO HOME FOR THE rest of the day. Apparently my mother didn't agree with that decision. Curled up on a cot near the nurse's office with an ice pack pressed to the back of my head, I listened to one side of their telephone conversation. It wasn't going well.

"Ms. Simmons, your daughter has fallen and hit her head. The blow was hard enough to knock her unconscious for a full minute. I cannot simply tell her to get over it and go back to class."

Silence, broken by fingers tapping against wood.

"I'm sorry if this is inconvenient for your business. You didn't provide a secondary emergency contact for Asha. You are the only parent or guardian I can call."

Another silence, the fingers tapping furiously.

"Yes, I am certain this is necessary." The nurse's voice was getting positively icy.

"Yes, you can call me back."

After she recited the phone number, the nurse slammed the phone down with a decisive bang and emerged to check on me with a false smile plastered on her face.

"How are you feeling, Asha?"

"I feel fine," I lied. My head was pounding. "I really could go back to class."

"No, you really can't." Her voice was gentle but exasperated. I'd never met the school nurse before that day. She was a surprisingly tall, boney woman with iron gray hair cropped very close to her scalp. "Even if you feel perfectly fine, which I doubt, it's a liability issue."

"I'm sorry about this."

Before she could answer, the phone rang and she returned to her office.

"Hello, this is—Yes, Ms. Simmons. Yes, you'll have to send a signed release note authorizing him to pick her up from school. What was the name again? Todd Vanderhouse. How do you spell that?"

I groaned inwardly. She was sending Todd the Toad to pick me up.

Luckily, the Toad wasn't any happier about this errand than I was.

"Xia is seeing a client right now," he told me when I plopped down in his expensive sports car with the ice pack still pressed to my head. His bulging watery eyes scanned me nervously, as though my head might start spinning around and spewing pea soup any minute. "She suggested we go to the mall?" He sounded uncertain about this plan, and I had absolutely zero interest in the mall.

It was child's play to convince the Toad to take me home. All I had to do was hint at how horrible I would feel if I threw up all over his lovely leather interior.

"Mrs. Tsien will let me stay with her until Mom's client leaves," I assured him. "Mom won't even know I'm there."

The Toad was so visibly relieved, I almost laughed out loud.

A massive navy blue Cadillac SUV was parked in our designated visitor's spot when the Toad pulled into the parking lot.

"Looks like her client is still here," he said unnecessarily. Was I imagining it, or was there a nervous edge in his voice? I shot him a surprised look. "I'll just wait here to be sure your landlady is home."

Mrs. Tsien was home. She arrived at the door looking flustered and confused.

"Asha? What are you doing home this early?" Her voice was unusually sharp.

"I fell at school. Hit my head," I explained, lifting the melting ice pack from my head to wave it in the air. "The nurse said I had to go home, but Mom's busy with a client. Can I sit with you until the coast is clear?"

Mrs. Tsien's brows furrowed. "Oh, dear." She shot a look over her shoulder, then shrugged and opened the door, waving me in. "You poor girl. Come in and sit down. Do you want some tea?"

I followed her, feeling relieved to be in her familiar space, until I realized Mrs. Tsien had another visitor. I froze in shock. Sitting at the island between her living area and kitchen sat a girl hunched over a pad of paper. The girl didn't look up or acknowledge my arrival in any way. She was busy sketching, her whole body focused on the effort. Only the top of her blonde head was visible, but I instantly recognized her wild tangle of hair. My breath caught in my throat.

Jazz.

"This is Jasmine," Mrs. Tsien said, waving her hand in the girl's direction. "Jazzy, honey, this is Asha. She's not feeling well so we're going to let her rest here for a while, okay?"

Jazz continued to sketch without looking up.

"Don't be insulted, Asha," Mrs. Tsien said softly, patting my arm. "Jasmine lives in her own world. Up here." Mrs. Tsien gently touched one arthritic finger to my temple. "Her auntie is a family friend. While her auntie is seeing your mother, she's sitting with me. Now let me get you some tea."

I nodded automatically, not really interested in the tea. Mrs. Tsien bustled into the kitchen, and I stepped closer to Jasmine. She was drawing an intricate pattern of ivy leaves inside the outline of a running girl. It was a complex and beautiful sketch.

My baby sister is amazing, Ivy said in my head. *I don't care about their stupid spectrum.*

On the spectrum. That was how people politely referred to children and adults with autism. Puzzle pieces started to click together in my head. I hadn't made the connection before because she was so avid and engaged in those early memories where it was just her and Ivy interacting. But then I remembered the image of Jazz spinning and yelling. Her intense focus in building the sand castle on the beach. *She doesn't like touching.* Not just David's touching, but any touching. During the news conference and in those pictures of the prayer vigil online, she was always looking away from people with an expression of fierce concentration that didn't quite match the heartbreak of the moment. Jasmine Brennan was autistic.

Silently, I agreed with Ivy. Her sister was amazing. Not only was the art she was creating extraordinary, but this girl was navigating in a terrifying world filled with noise. And yet she was able to stay so calm, focused, and determined.

Say hello to Asha, Jazzy. She's our friend.

Jasmine's head popped up. "Hello, Asha," she said in a robotic voice.

I blinked in surprise. Could she hear Ivy? "Hello ... Jasmine?"

"Call me Jazz," she instructed, then twisted her head toward the kitchen. "Auntie Mai? Do you have a red marker and also a black marker?"

"Sure, honey. There's some colored pens in the drawer over there," Mrs. Tsien answered. She shot a nervous smile in my direction without meeting my eyes. Why was she so nervous?

I watched with my heart in my throat, as Jazz fetched two Sharpie pens in the requested colors, flipped the page in her sketchbook, and started a new drawing. The red Sharpie sat next to her elbow, unused, as she focused fierce concentration on her new project. The black marker flew over the page. Her movements were swift, assured, and decisive.

When Mrs. Tsien brought a steaming cup of tea to me, I realized I was rooted to the same spot watching Jazz sketch with no concept of how weird I might look. I tried to think of something to say, but nothing came to mind. Mrs. Tsien didn't seem to notice my silent confusion. Her eyes were glued to her front window where she could clearly see our front door across the parking lot.

The whole situation was surreal. If my mother was currently in a session with Jazz's auntie, then that meant she was in a session with Ying Brennan. Was she passing along false messages from Ivy? My stomach soured. To distract my thoughts, I tried to sort out the missing links of this situation.

According to Mrs. Tsien, Ying Brennan was a family friend. Jazz had just called Mrs. Tsien Auntie Mai. That implied a close relationship. But the term auntie could be used as a respectful and affectionate form of address that didn't necessarily mean they were relations by blood or marriage. But there had to be some history, some link I was missing here. I remembered Ivy's ghostly image sitting in Mrs. Tsien's red rocking chair, staring at her with wistful eyes. When I used the Mandarin words to wish Mrs. Tsien good night, Ivy had responded with the Mandarin words for sweet dreams. I had never laid eyes on Ivy Brennan before her spirit appeared in my living room. And yet, she obviously knew my landlady.

My mind went back to the previous summer. As my mother drove us across country to our new home, she told me about our new landlady. She told me about the grandson who had died, whose mortal remains my mother helped locate. She told me about the ugly scene between Mrs. Tsien and her only son, Bao, where he called my mother a black devil. And she told me about the rift between mother and son due to Mrs. Tsien's charity work with female refuges from Southeast Asia. Dirty girls, Bao called them, who weren't even Chinese.

Dirty girls.

My mouth started speaking before my brain could sort through the implications. "Mrs. Tsien?" I asked. "There's a project I need to do. For school. For my Civics class."

"Sure, honey," she patted my leg, still distracted. "You can work on your homework up at the counter with Jazz."

"No, actually, I was hoping you could help me. I have to do a project that explores one aspect of modern immigration issues," I lied.

Her brown eyes focused on me, suddenly very sharp and attentive. "I came to the United States over fifty years ago," she said. "That's not modern."

"But my mother said ..." I stopped and swallowed over a dry throat. "My mother said you help women who come here from Southeast Asia. I thought maybe I could do a project on your work?"

"No." She shook her head with a frown. "That is not appropriate for your school project."

"Not appropriate? Why not?" My nerves were jumping. I was getting close to something important here, I could feel it. A cool sensation tickled the back of my neck, and Ivy appeared in the kitchen. She was standing behind her sister, watching the sketch emerge. She looked up at me and winked, then leaned in close to whisper something in the younger girl's ear.

Jazz slapped down the black marker and looked up. "Because it's sex slaves," she declared.

"Jazzy!" Mrs. Tsien snapped, clearly startled and upset. "What do you ...? How could you know ...?"

"Auntie Mai," Jazz interrupted the old lady's sputtering

protests with an air of exasperated patience. "I know all about the sex slaves. Auntie Ying always tells us how lucky we are to live here in America, with all the food and all the protection and all the money Uncle David spends on us." She focused her fierce stare on me. "Ying was born in Vietnam. Her mom sold her to a Chinese man as a sex slave."

"Jasmine!" Mrs. Tsien protested, appalled.

Jazz shrugged, unmoved my Mrs. Tsien's protest, and continued her narrative in a flat, unwavering voice. "The Chinese man changed her name to Ying and brought her here on a private airplane and locked her in a room. But she escaped. She hid in empty houses and ate food out of trash cans until one day she heard two women speaking in Vietnamese at a gas station. She asked them for help. They took her to one of Auntie Mai's friends. Auntie Mai and her friends help lots of these sex slave girls, but they don't like anyone to talk about it. I guess it's illegal or something."

Two spots of color flared on Mrs. Tsien's wrinkled cheeks. "That's not why we don't talk about it," she scolded Jazz. "It's not nice conversation."

Jazz shrugged again, picked up the red marker, and started scribbling. Ivy looked up at me with a wicked gleam in her eye. What did it mean?

We all sat in silence for several minutes. The only sound was the scratching of the red marker on paper. I was shocked, unable to say anything sensible. Mrs. Tsien looked as though a terrible weight was pressing down on her shoulders.

"I think it's wonderful that you help them," I finally said. "I think you're a hero."

Mrs. Tsien regarded me with glistening eyes. "Some of the girls are so damaged," she whispered. "So damaged. No matter what we do, we can't save them."

I didn't know what to say to that, so I kept my mouth shut.

"Looks like the session is over," Mrs. Tsien announced too brightly. She stood up and brushed her hands over her arms as though brushing off the whole ugly conversation.

I turned. Ying Brennan was emerging from our townhouse; the enormous sunglasses from the press conference still hid most of her face.

"Time to go, Jazzy," Mrs. Tsien said, clapping her hands together twice.

Jazz slapped down her red marker and sighed.

Outside, my mother extended her hand. Ying Brennan stared at it before taking it in a loose grip and shaking it up and down twice. The tiny woman looked like she was eating dirt.

"Asha?" Jazz was standing next to me with an unhappy but determined look on her face.

"Yes, Jazz?"

With one violent yank, she tore the drawing out of her pad and pushed it toward me. "VeeVee wants you to have this."

Behind her, Mrs. Tsien gasped and pressed her hands over her mouth. "Oh! VeeVee. That's what she called her sister."

I looked down as Jazz marched out the door. The sketch showed a girl, clearly Ivy, surrounded by a tangle of tree branches. Her hair was a blowing in the wind, her face set in fierce determination. Everything was rendered in bold black lines except for the girl's dress, which was a sweep of pure red.

I stood, clutching the drawing to my chest, and hurried to Mrs. Tsien's front porch. Jazz climbed into that gigantic SUV without a backward glance in my direction.

"What did she give you?" Mrs. Tsien asked. Without a word, I handed her the drawing.

"Oh," my landlady said, then, "Oh my." Something in her voice made me turn around and look at her closely. Her skin was ashen, her eyes shocked.

"What is it?" I asked.

"The red dress," she whispered. She handed the sketch back to me and shuffled back into her own townhome, shaking her head and muttering in Mandarin. Two words caught my attention. Nü Gui. I folded Jazz's drawing and pointed my feet toward my own front door.

My mother didn't look the least bit surprised to see me. In fact, she looked almost delighted.

"There you are," she announced, as though she'd been looking all over for me.

"Hello, Mother," I answered like a good little girl and walked past her.

I made a beeline for the bookshelf where we kept several beautiful coffee table books related to ghosts, folklore, and the supernatural. I found the book I was looking for – *Around the World in 80 Ghost Stories* – and flipped through the glossy pages until I came to the section on China.

"What are you doing?" my mother asked.

"Looking up something for school," I lied.

"You actually managed to get some classes squeezed in before you passed out?"

I ignored her barb and concentrated on finding the ghost story that Jazz's drawing had brought to mind. The fact that Mrs. Tsien has reacted so strongly to the black and red sketch told me I was on the right track.

A dual image of a beautiful Chinese woman with long black hair glared back at me. On one side, the woman was wearing a long red dress. In the other, she was wearing a long white gown and her skin glowed with a pale green tinge that suggested a ghostly apparition. Yes, this was the ghost story.

Nü Gui: a vengeful female ghost. This ghost is believed to be the spirit of a woman who committed suicide while wearing a red dress. She experienced some form of injustice when she was alive, such as being abused, and she returns to take her revenge. Frequently depicted as a succubus-like creature.

No, that didn't quite fit.

The picture looked right, but the description didn't match Ivy at all. She definitely didn't commit suicide let alone put on a red dress to die. On the other hand, Ivy was abused. And why did Mrs. Tsien look so rattled by that picture?

"Asha, are you listening to me." My mother's voice snapped me out of my thoughts.

"Sorry, Mom. What did you say?"

"I said, since you can't stay on your feet for a full day and that dragon at school just had to send you home, we can go to your appointment early."

"Is it a doctor's appointment?" I asked.

Xia laughed merrily, as though I'd made a huge joke.

"No, this is much more important than a doctor's visit. You need serious help."

16

———

BEFORE

THE SERIOUS HELP I NEEDED TURNED OUT TO BE A THREE-hour appointment at Bright Chakra Spa and Salon located on a heavily traveled strip of The Alameda, just north of downtown San Jose. It wasn't the sort of posh place my mother would trust for her own polishing and preening, but Xia declared it was "good enough to clean up a fifteen-year-old kid." Three Korean women, all chattering in their native language, worked on my hair, skin, and nails while I felt a little like Dorothy preparing to visit the wizard.

But who was the wizard in this story?

Xia disappeared for most of the time, saying she would be nearby if I needed anything. I assumed she was visiting the new age bookstore a few doors down from the salon. They hosted a very successful book signing and psychic event featuring Xia Celeste during the first month we lived here. Mrs. Tsien's words about "another psychic event" came back to me. And then the girl who had stopped me in the hallway.

I am definitely going to be there this weekend. Good luck.

The inkling of a dark suspicion started to form at the edges of my mind.

My mother reappeared in time to oversee my first lesson in applying mineral makeup. "She needs to look natural," she reminded the aesthetician at least five times, tapping her on the shoulder. The woman nodded and smiled toward my mother, then rolled her eyes at me.

"You beautiful girl. Don't need much anyway," the woman whispered while my mother was distracted by a display of exotic nail art.

When she was finally satisfied with the results, Xia handed me a *Forever 21* bag and sent me back to the salon's changing room. Inside the bag I found a simple white eyelet A-line dress and a pair of silver ballet flats. Once I had exchanged the salon's black smock for the new outfit, I stared at myself in the mirror.

My hair, thinner and less shiny than my mother's weave, had been relaxed into similar corkscrew curls that crated a dark nimbus around my face. My fingers and toes were polished in the same subtle pink Xia was currently wearing. My skin, though paler than my mother's and still sprinkled with freckles, had a hint of cinnamon glow. The bruise on my cheek had been artfully blended away. These chattering women had done a great job, and I tried to feel good about the way I looked, I really did try, but all I could feel was a numb sense of defeat.

The dim, calming light in the room started to flicker erratically. A harsh chill snaked over my bare arms. In the mirror, the empty air behind my right shoulder seemed to darken, swirl, and shift until a faint impression of Ivy appeared in shades of gray behind me.

Stop this, her voice whispered. *Stop her.*

Three sharp knocks on the dressing room door caused me to jump and nearly knock over a vase of white willow branches. The lighting and temperature in the room snapped back to normal, leaving me feeling hollow and dizzy.

"Come on, Asha," my mother's voice barked from the other side of the door. "We don't have all night. Move it!"

"Coming!" I yelled back too loudly, then swallowed several times to push down a wave of sickening anger and frustration.

Ivy had reappeared at my school. She seemed to be following me, warning me of something. She definitely wasn't resting in peace. Something was wrong.

And I was busy playing dress up with my mommy.

DESCENDING DRAGON MYSTIC BOOKSTORE WAS A TINY NEW age shop wedged between an aging movie theater that specialized in Bollywood films and a tattoo parlor named Illustrated Woman in the same strip of shops as Bright Chakra. The proprietress of "The Dragon," as most patrons called it, was a relation of our landlady, a cousin or a niece, who was also called Mrs. Tsien. She was a short, plump woman with shiny cheeks and short, spikey black hair liberally streaked with platinum blonde highlights. I called her Little Tsien, a nickname she found absolutely hilarious. Probably because she was over forty years old and weighed more than twice our landlady's weight.

When my mother hustled me over to The Dragon after

my makeover, I wasn't surprised. What stopped me in my tracks was a banner covering the store's main display window that read *Special Event—Xia Celeste Here Saturday! Psychic Detecting: Shadows, Secrets, and Lies.*

Decorative skeleton keys and an overabundance of exclamation points were used to list additional details:

Anatomy of a murdered ghost!

What is truth without Truth?

When mediums become prey!

Insider secrets the police don't want you to know!

Book signing starts at 1:00!

Presentation starts at 2:00!

This event will sell out! Reserve your seat today!!!

Limited private sessions also available with prepayment!

Wine and cheese reception starts at 4:00!

Finally, at the very bottom of the banner was the announcement that had frozen my body and soul in place.

Guest Appearance: Come meet Xia's gifted daughter, Achsa Celeste.

Achsa Celeste? Anger and disgust simmered in my gut. Achsa Sprague was a famous American Spiritualist from the nineteenth century who wrote arcane poetry and traveled all over the country going into trances to deliver messages from the afterlife. At least one of her lectures had brought her to Moonville. There was a drawing of her in our public library standing next to Granville Quinn. While he grinned broadly, Achsa looked like she smelled something rotten. According to my father, my mother wanted to name me Achsa but he had fought her until they compromised with Asha. I was grateful my father refused to saddle me with such a weird, ugly name. And now Xia had christened me Achsa Celeste, her gifted daughter. Yuck.

Xia swept open the front door of The Dragon and

announced with a dramatic flourish of one arm, "Here we are!"

Unable to move or speak, I stared at her in shock, my mouth opening and closing without a sound like a fish trapped on a dry, sandy beach.

"Come on, my lovely, don't be shy!" The playful brightness of her voice was in direct contrast to the cold glare in her eyes. She grabbed my arm and yanked me inside.

"Ta da!"

Thankfully there was not a crowd waiting inside the store, just a few people grouped around the cash register to politely ooh and ahh over my transformation. If this was supposed to be my coming out party, it was decidedly underwhelming by most standards. But with my brain still reeling from my latest encounter with Ivy Brennan and my chest pounding like it might explode, I felt like a trapped animal standing in a circus ring surrounded by a sea of eyes.

"What's going on?" I asked through clenched teeth in a breathy, low voice only Xia could hear.

Instead of answering, she wrapped an arm around my shoulders and firmly maneuvered me toward the tiny group. "Asha, you know Mai's cousin Zenaida, of course."

"You look pretty, Asha!" Little Tsien smiled with sincere enthusiasm.

"Thanks," I mumbled.

Little Tsien indicated a younger version of herself standing behind the cash register. "This is my daughter, Jade. She's my new media and events coordinator."

Jade flashed a wry smile in my direction. "Which is a fancy way of saying I know how to post things on social media, and I'm required to perform unpaid slave labor for special events," she told me in a flat American accent.

"Unpaid? Who pays all that college tuition then?" Little Tsien shot back.

My mouth said, "Hi, Jade." My brain screamed *You have no idea about slavery, college girl. I'll trade places with you any day!*

A plump middle-aged woman with curly neon orange hair stepped forward and patted my shoulder. "Don't you look like your mother's daughter, Achsa?"

"Asha," I corrected her automatically, at the same time wondering why she'd put a strange emphasis on the words *look like.*

"This is Rhiannon," my mother said, her tone dismissive. "She pretends to read Tarot cards here for money." The frank rudeness made my face burn, but Rhiannon just chuckled.

The great Xia Celeste was always fond of telling anyone and everyone that Tarot cards, pendulums, Ouija boards and other "superficial toys" are crutches used by frauds to fool the masses. She also claimed using props could weaken and even kill a genuine medium's connection with the other side. Considering her recent failure with Ivy, she probably had that wrong. Or maybe she had it right. Either way, the rudeness wasn't necessary.

"We can't all be as talented as you are, Xia," Rhiannon said with a twinkle in her eye. There was that odd emphasis again—this time, in the way she said the word *talented*—that made me suspect she was actually saying something else.

Mother twirled away. Rhiannon looked at me, then furrowed her brows and leaned in closer.

"Oh, dear," she said under her breath. "You might want to take a salt bath."

What was it with these concerned women and their salt baths?

NEXT MY MOTHER PULLED FORWARD A WILLOWY, PALE-SKINNED girl with short platinum blonde hair. The girl's eyebrows and eyelashes were nearly translucent, making her avid gray eyes disconcerting. Wearing a sage green tunic, white leggings, and a silver web of chains draped across her forehead, she looked like she might have escaped from the elven village of Rivendell from Lord of the Rings.

"And this lovely creature is the amazing and talented Shea McLaren!"

The sickening overabundance of sugar dripping from my mother's tone told me Xia's true opinion was that this creature was neither lovely nor amazing, but she needed something from her.

The girl didn't smile or say a word. She looked me over from head to toe, then lifted an expensive digital camera that looked like it weighed half as much as she did before stepping back to focus the lens on my face.

"Shea is an award-winning photographer," Xia continued, "and she creates these wonderful live-action films based on Irish folk tales. Her YouTube channel has over a million followers. Isn't that amazing?"

My mother's tone managed to convey true disbelief that the girl was so successful, mixed with a healthy dose of raw envy.

"Amazing," I echoed back.

Shea looked up from the digital display on her camera and announced, "You're very photogenic," in a flat tone of voice that would have been more appropriate if she had said, "You have spinach in your teeth."

"Oh, um ... thanks?"

"Being photogenic is a very good thing," Shea told me in

a neutral voice. Then she stepped closer and looked into my eyes with an intense, wide-eyed stare. "My next project is going to be about college girls living in a haunted Victorian mansion in Pacific Heights. Your mother gave me some ideas. She said you would have some, too."

"Well, I'll try," I said "Is that what we're doing here tonight?"

Shea snorted loudly. "No, this is real life ghost stories," she said. "Your mom is helping me. I thought it might be fun to help her, too. We're going to take a few publicity pictures to help promote your new channel then block out some shots for Saturday."

"Oh ..." Even to my own ears, my voice sounded strange.

"Todd thinks we should start our own YouTube channel," Xia explained, swooping into the space between Shea and me. "I'm not convinced, but Shea thinks it's a good idea and she's agreed to help us feel our way, so to speak. There are idiot ghost hunters and so-called ghost whisperers all over the Internet and television. It's mostly garbage, but genuine talent isn't enough to attract followers in the current media environment. That's why I've agreed—"

She broke off, giving me a mock-stern look, and placed a hand on her own chest.

"That's why I've agreed to let my baby girl stretch her wings."

She was making it sound like I'd been begging her to step into the spotlight to talk about dead people in front of cameras for years when I'd been ducking away from this sort of thing my whole life. The few times I've had a meaningful communication with a ghost, there was no audience watching every move. My throat closed up, making it nearly impossible to breathe.

"We'll see how this event goes on Saturday," Xia said. "If

it's a success, we could create something totally unique to modern Spiritualism."

Right. Then, together maybe we could rule the galaxy as mother and daughter.

Xia placed her hand on my shoulder, discretely digging her nails into my shoulder blade.

"What a great idea," I chirped like a puppet on a string, even though the words burned like acid in my throat.

The next hour whizzed by in a blur of activity I barely understood. While Xia and I posed for publicity shots, Jade Tsien moved the central bookshelves, which had cleverly hidden wheels that locked and unlocked, to open up the center of the room. Xia and Shea engaged in a serious, intense series of discussions that encompassed lighting, sound, camera angles, and blocking every movement.

This thing was getting nearly as complicated as my last dance recital.

To my intense relief, my part in the production was small. After learning my cue to enter the room, where I would stand during the presentation, and a few helpful do's and don'ts from Shea, I was left alone to poke around the edges of the store while Jade was pulled in to discuss more detailed logistics that I simply could not follow. I picked up a few books and looked them over without really seeing the words printed on the cover ... until my hands found a large illustrated novel that nearly knocked me on my butt.

White Crow Chronicles Book One: The Murder Garden. Story and illustrations by Lucy Sloan.

I'd followed Lucy online for years, but this was the first time I held one of her physical books in my hands. A ripple of excitement passed through my entire body. Looking around furtively to make sure my mother wasn't paying any attention, I slipped into the narrow space behind the bookshelves and flipped to the back of the book to find her author photo and bio. My eyes widened in shock, and I may have even gasped out loud. The picture on Lucy's blog showed her wearing a white feather mask. The only other pictures I'd ever seen of Helena Sloan's daughter were taken when she was very young. This was Lucy Sloan now, in her twenties, and she looked so much like my Aunt Nicole it stole my breath away. Her skin was lighter, her nose slightly narrower with fewer freckles, but the overall resemblance was insane. Lucy's hazel-green eyes could have been my aunt's eyes. Had my grandfather or my father seen Lucy Sloan recently?

If ever I doubted it, this picture was solid proof.

Lucy Sloan is closely related to my father's family. Closely related to me. In that moment, I was absolutely sure of it.

I looked out from behind the bookshelves, feeling desperate.

Xia was absorbed by her performance with Shea and didn't show any sign she even knew I was still somewhere in the room.

A burst of rapid-fire knocking drew everyone's eyes to the store's main entrance. I seriously considered dropping the book into my *Forever 21* bag. Even though I had some money saved and could buy it, my mother would go into a howling rage if she saw the author's name.

Little Tsien hurried toward the front door, making slashing X-movements with her forearms. "Sorry, no, we're closed," she said toward whoever was knocking.

I couldn't do it. I couldn't steal from Little Tsien, even if I did plan to pay her later. Regretfully, I replaced the book on the shelf. Maybe there would be a chance on Saturday to buy the book without Xia seeing it.

When Little Tsien got to the front door, I heard the deadbolt chunking open, then murmured explanations and apologies. I only caught a few words. "Closed early ... private event ... come back tomorrow."

A tearful, wavering, high-pitched voice cut through the room. "Xia Celeste? Is Xia Celeste here? I am Ivy's auntie. I must speak with Xia Celeste. I will pay very well to speak with her."

The voice sliced my skin like a thousand shards of broken glass.

Watch out! Ivy's warning was loud in my brain.

"Don't let her in," I whispered. No one heard me.

"It's all right, Zenaida," my mother said, stepping to the center of the open store as though she were a gladiator about to do battle. She clasped her hands in front of her chest and unleashed a deep sigh of resignation. "Let her come in. I'll speak with her."

Then she shot a pained look around the room. "Asha? Where are you?"

When she looked the other way, I quickly slipped out from my hiding place and took a few steps toward the middle of the room. "I'm right here, Mom."

"Come here, Asha." She snapped her fingers. "Stand by me. You'd better learn how to deal with this."

Learn how to deal with what? Xia had just finished a session with this woman a few hours ago. What was going on?

17

BEFORE

WHEN LITTLE TSIEN STEPPED BACK TO LET OUR DESPERATE
visitor into the bookstore, my first thought was how
different she looked a few hours earlier. Ying Brennan was
much more frail and tiny than she appeared in the news
conference and the online photographs I'd clicked through
the day before. Her clothes – loose silky pants that looked
like they were going to fall right off her body any second and
a green floral print blouse – were wrinkled and disheveled.
Strands of hair had escaped from her sleek ponytail and
clung to the dampness on her cheeks and neck. The worse
part was her eyes, no longer hidden behind sunglasses. Not
only were they red and swollen, they looked impossibly
large in her narrow face. And afraid. She looked utterly and
completely terrified. Every fine hair on my body quivered.

What was going on here? How could this woman be so
terrified?

"Do you know who I am?" she asked Xia in crisp formal English though her voice wavered a bit.

"Yes, we do," Xia answered calmly, wrapping one motherly arm around my shoulders. "You are Ying Brennan, wife of David Brennan, and aunt to Ivy Brennan."

I twitched slightly at her words. What was this? Xia's arm tensed on my shoulders. It was a clear message to stay quiet and still.

Ying blinked once and seemed to grow even more unsettled, visibly shaking. "Did Ivy tell you about me?"

"Why are you here, Ying?" Mother asked instead of answering.

"I saw some comments posted online. They say you speak to the dead. They say you sent the police to our door. I want to know if this is true."

No, Ivy whispered in my ear. *Liar.* Icy air snaked up the back of my neck, sending an involuntary shiver down my spine. I nodded in agreement. This was all one big fat lie.

"And if it is true?" Xia asked. "What will you want then?"

Behind Ying Brennan, I could see the interior of the store reflected in the plate glass windows that faced the darkening street. In the ghostly reflected scene, shadows gathered and swirled behind my right shoulder until Ivy's image formed, glaring back at me in the reflection.

Do something, she snapped at me. *Stop her.*

"Mother," I gasped.

Xia looked at me, her eyes popping with impatience. She took one good look at me and relaxed slightly, her lips curling into a sympathetic smile. "It's okay, Asha," she said calmly. "Just breathe. Everything's under control."

Liar! Ivy's electric retort crackled in the air between us though my mother's expression was unfazed. Either she was an incredible actress, or she remained blissfully unaware of Ivy's presence.

Ying stood still, eyes darting between us. Her whole body was tense, quivering. The girl with the serene smile who had stood next to David Brennan was gone. She looked every bit as miserable as I felt. When she finally spoke, her voice was so tight it sounded like her throat might tear open.

"When I was a young girl, there was an old blind man who lived in our village. He lived alone and did no work, but he never wanted for anything. The people in the village took care of him. They built his house, gave him food, clothing, and plenty of tobacco for his pipe. And yet, no one liked him. When people saw him, they would turn and hurry away before he could get close or they would stop and stare at the ground until he passed by.

"It was very puzzling to me, so one day I asked my mother about it. She told me the man could talk to the ancestors. Not just his own ancestors. Any family's ancestors. That was why people honored him. And that was also why people feared him."

Ying grew silent, eying us with an expression that brought an image into my head – a butterfly trapped in a spider's web. Why was she so fascinated and afraid of us? Or was it all part of an act?

What had happened in her session with my mother?

"Did this old man ever talk to any of your ancestors?" Xia prompted her.

"He came to my grandfather's funeral and spoke to my grandmother. He said Grandfather had buried some valuable items under our chicken coop. The next day, we dug up a metal box filled with gold and jade jewelry. My grandmother never knew about the box or the jewelry until that day. No one did. From that day forward, my family gave him fresh eggs every week. Every time they sent me with the basket, I would set the eggs next to his door and run away as fast as I could, always feeling the cold breath of death on the back of my neck."

"But he helped you," I said. "Why were you afraid of him?"

My mother gave me a sad smile, patting my shoulder. "Hush, now. Don't let it hurt your feelings."

Her voice was so gentle and loving that my eyes quickly scanned the room looking around for Shea McLaren. Sure enough, while everyone had been focused on Ying's dramatic entrance, Shea had started filming. I quickly dropped my eyes to the floor and mumbled, "Sorry."

"It's all right, but you'd better let me do the talking with Mrs. Brennan," Xia said, her voice perfectly pitched to convey firm patience. She redirected her attention to the tiny, miserable girl.

"I take it you're not here to give us some eggs and run away, Ying. So I'll ask again. What do you want?"

"I want to know what Ivy told you. I want to know everything she told you."

"But—" I started.

No, Ivy's voice snapped again. *Don't say a word.*

"There's not much I can tell you, Ying. I'm sorry." Xia removed her arm from my shoulder and stepped forward two paces. Ying's eyes grew even larger. Her weight shifted onto her heels. It looked like she was fighting her instinct to step back. "Ivy conveyed her message to me in a very ... unusual way."

Stop her, Ivy ordered. I looked up at the dead girl's image in the store window and shook my head slightly. She didn't want me to talk. What did she want me to do?

"What do you mean by unusual?" Ying asked, swal-lowing hard and giving every appearance she was struggling to hold her ground.

"A concerned person brought a personal item that belonged to Ivy to me and asked if I could connect with her, figure out where she was. At that point she was only known to be missing, you understand?"

Ying nodded and bit her lip.

Ivy continued chanting her refrain of *liar, liar, liar, liar* until I thought my ears would explode.

"At first, I couldn't get anything," my mother continued. "In fact, I was starting to think Ivy had to be alive and was probably hiding somewhere. Just as I was ready to give up, my daughter touched my hand." She looked at me and lovingly took my hand in both of hers. "Immediately an image came to me, or, more accurately, this image slammed into my brain. It nearly knocked me right out of my chair."

"What image?" Ying asked, leaning forward.

"I saw ivy vines cast in concrete. It was a pretty image, actually. But it made my head hurt. I felt real physical pain right here." She tapped two fingers to the middle of her forehead. "And I think I said something. I don't really remember ..." She shook her head, then turned toward me. "Maybe my daughter remembers. She was right there when it happened."

Every eye in the room focused on me. I swallowed over a rough, dry throat and struggled to ignore Ivy's reflection flickering frantically, her repeated orders to keep quiet.

"You said, 'Why is there Ivy in the cement?'" I answered in slow, unsteady tones over the noise of Ivy's protests echoing in my skull. Why was Xia asking me to contribute that particular lie to the whole fiction?

"And then it was over." Xia snapped her fingers at Ying. "No further connection. No more images. No words. Nothing. However, what I said electrified the person who had brought the personal item to me. That person said something about an uncle who owned a construction company and rushed away with barely a thank you. The next day, we learned about the discovery of Ivy's body the same way most people did, on the live news feed."

My mother squeezed my hand in an iron grip. Silence stretched to an uncomfortable length while my mother and Mrs. Brennan continued to make eye contact. Finally, Ying nodded and swallowed hard yet again. "Please tell me, who was this concerned person?"

"Oh, I'm sorry, Ying. I can't tell you that. We always maintain strict client confidentiality." Mother's voice didn't sound the least bit sorry.

We? I thought.

"Can you tell me what the personal item was?"

"I don't think that would be a good idea, either. That detail might point to the person who brought the item to me. Total client confidentiality is absolutely essential in our business."

Our business, I thought.

Ying continued to stare at the two of us with a fascination that seemed horrible to me. "What if I wanted to bring you a personal item that belonged to Ivy? Will you try to connect to her again? For me? I will pay double your normal fee."

"Before I answer that, I think you should tell us exactly what you hope to accomplish. What are you hoping Ivy will tell you?"

Nothing, Ivy screamed.

A throbbing headache pulsed in my temples.

"I'll pay triple the fee," Ying said, reaching into her voluminous purse.

My mother dropped my hand and pressed both palms toward Ying Brennan. "No! Stop that." Her words echoed Ivy's repeated protests. "This isn't a matter of money. In fact, I'm not even sure we could ethically take any money from you. You've endured a terrible shock. Look at you, you're barely keeping yourself upright. I don't want to do anything or promise anything or give you any false hope that will make this horrible situation any harder for you. Tell me what you're trying to—"

"My husband didn't kill his niece!" Ying broke in. The desperation in her voice was practically obscene.

In the reflected scene, I could see everyone in the store shift and fidget in various degrees of embarrassed discomfort. Everyone that is except my mother, who simply nodded.

"I thought so," Xia said calmly.

Ying became more agitated. "No, you don't know," she said, pointing a shaking finger. "My husband loves those girls. He loves them way too much! He spends so much money on them; I got mad about it. I told him we will have our own daughters. But my husband always keeps those girls safe. When their mother died, he took them in. He would never hurt those girls."

Apparently startled by the other woman's verbal onslaught, my mother stepped back, bumping into me and stumbling over my feet. I grabbed her arm to steady her. "Oh dear," she said under her breath, throwing a quick, conspiratorial look back at me.

I ducked my head behind her right shoulder and whispered, "Ivy is screaming for this to stop." *Can't you hear her?* I wanted to add.

My mother nodded her head once, indicating she'd heard me, then took my left hand in hers as she turned back to face the panic and desperation in the other woman's face.

"I didn't say your husband hurt anyone, Mrs. Brennan." Xia spoke the words slowly and clearly, as though she was explaining something to a small child. "I never said anything like that."

"Not you. The police say it. They say terrible things to us." Ying stopped, bending forward from the waist to choke out loud sobs.

Little Tsien cautiously approached and patted the young woman's back clumsily while looking at my mother with a question in her expression. My mother shrugged and shook her head. Whatever the question was, Xia didn't have the answer. After several uncomfortable seconds, Ying Brennan forced herself to stand upright again.

"They interrogated my husband. They searched our house. They're treating us like dirt. This is ruining our family. It is ruining our lives!"

"Ying, listen to me," my mother said gently.

"I want you to talk to Ivy, Miss Celeste. I want you to find out who did this to her."

No. Liar. Stop this. Stop her. Ivy's protests continued to pound a non-stop litany as the throbbing in my head grew worse.

"Even if it worked, even if I was able to communicate with Ivy and she was able to tell me exactly who killed her and how it happened, then what?" Xia asked. "Your husband can't use a ghost's testimony as a defense."

"I can hire my own detectives." Ying jutted her chin forward, defiant. "If I know who is guilty, it will be easier to tell them how to prove David is innocent."

"Sweet girl," my mother's voice dripped saccharine-sweet insincerity. "What if your husband is not innocent?"

"He is innocent. He must be innocent. Nothing else is possible." Despite the absolute confidence she was trying to put into her words and body language, the wobble in Ying's voice said she wasn't entirely certain. "Please, help me."

My mother turned to look at me again, rubbing her forehead thoughtfully. I tried to shake my head slightly without making it too obvious. She frowned.

"Here's what we're going to do," Xia said, turning back toward the desperate woman. "Find one small personal item that belonged to Ivy. Something she would have worn or kept close to her most of the time. Put it in a plastic zipper bag and leave it with Zenaida Tsien here at the store." Xia pointed at Little Tsien and the older woman smiled at Ying.

Ying's brows furrowed. "Leave it here?"

"No offense, but your energy is ... wow." Xia's hand fluttered over her chest. "If there's any chance of getting a reading, you cannot be with me. I'm going to need some time alone with the object in a safe, quiet, private environment. If I get anything – any new images or information that might help you understand what happened to your niece – I will set up a private session here at the store to discuss the situation. Then and only then will you decide if I have helped you and whether or not you want to pay my normal fee. Not double or triple, just my normal reading fee. That's my best and only offer. Do you want to try this?"

Ying nodded her head vigorously. "Yes. She had a favorite watch, a very nice sports watch for timing her running. I'll bring that."

"Perfect."

With that decided, Ying Brennan let Little Tsien gently guide her back out the front door, giving the other woman a half-hearted wave before locking the deadbolt.

"I'm curious, Xia" Rhiannon spoke into the heavy silence

that descended as soon as Ying was gone. "What are you going to do if Ivy Brennan tells you her Uncle David killed her and buried her in a cement foundation?"

Xia spun toward the other woman and smiled with her best effervescent charm.

"First, I will call Ying Brennan and tell her the reading failed and I have no new information for her at all. Second, I will call the same concerned person I mentioned earlier and let that person know exactly what happened to that poor child."

18

———

Now

"WHOA! WAIT A SECOND. I DON'T UNDERSTAND." VERA holds up a hand to stop the flow of my story. "That scene between your mother and Ying Brennan in the bookstore … it was all a lie?"

I nod, chewing on my bottom lip.

"Why did your mother agree to stage such an elaborate performance? Why did Ying participate? What was the purpose of that whole charade?"

"It was Xia's idea."

Vera's eyebrows popped up and she clicked her ballpoint pen over and over furiously, waiting for me to say more.

"The camera," I explain. My stomach cramps as I stare down at the sheet covering my battered body. "It's always about the camera. Getting the shot, you know?"

"No, I don't know." Vera leans forward and peers at me closely. "But it seems to make some sort of twisted sense to you. Can you explain it to me?"

I sigh deeply and force myself to look up into her magnified eyes, even larger now with disbelief.

"Did you ever watch my mother's TV show?" I ask. "Or any reality TV investigations about real hauntings?"

"I'm more of a historical drama and documentary fan." Vera smiles. "Not quite the same thing."

"Actually, a documentary is kind of like what I'm talking about," I say, warming to my subject. "In a documentary, someone sits in front of the camera and looks through the lens to tell the audience 'this happened, then that happened.' Then the story cuts over to actors re-enacting what the person just talked about. But in reality TV, the commentary happens after the event. In theory, the camera catches something real happening as it is actually happening. Then someone looks through the lens and tells the audience more about what was captured on camera."

"Okaaaaaay," Vera responds, looking puzzled.

"Problem is, lots of times, the real thing that really happened doesn't get captured by a camera. So you need to re-enact what happened. Only this is reality TV. So you don't use actors, you use the real people. This was sort of like that."

"Sort of?" Vera asks.

"Right. My mother told me Ying had come to her earlier that day with pretty much the same story about her village and the same questions about Ivy. Only her request was very different. She didn't want Xia to help her prove her husband's innocence. She wanted my mother to prove David Brennan was guilty."

"Wait." Vera clicked her pen one more time and started writing on her legal pad furiously. "When did Xia tell you this?"

"In the car. On the way home from the bookstore that

night." I waited until Vera's pen stopped moving before pressing on. "Mom said she could tell Ying was terrified of her husband, not just terrified for him or what might happen if he was arrested, but terrified of him. So Mom convinced Ying to come to the bookstore that night and stage a sort of re-enactment of their session. Only, they changed the script, so it looked like Ying was making a plea for her husband's innocence."

Vera shakes her head then tilts it to one side. "Again, I ask why? Why change the script?"

I shrug. "Mom said a suspicious wife begging for proof that her husband was guilty would make people hate Ying. But a fearful wife, begging for proof of her husband's innocence, would make people want to protect Ying and punish David."

"I see," Vera says in a neutral tone.

"My mother is a big fan of Truth with a capital T."

19

BEFORE

"THERE IS A HUGE DIFFERENCE BETWEEN SAYING SOMETHING that is factually accurate and telling someone the Truth, with a capitol T," Xia declared, forming a capitol T with her hands as though she was asking for a time out on the basketball court. "We are in the business of spreading Truth, Asha."

We were sitting cross-legged on the living room couch, both of us turned sideways, to face each other. Between us, there was a copy of my mother's first published book, multiple Post-it note flags stuck out from the pages, and a blue file folder.

After her performance with Ying Brennan, my mother had ended the planning session at the bookstore, pleading mental exhaustion from our encounter with "such a sad and desperate creature." We'd hurried home to eat a late dinner – California rolls from a supermarket deli – before starting on the lesson that Xia assured me would be the most important lesson of my entire life.

Despite the importance, or maybe because of it, I was having trouble focusing on my mother's words. My head was swimming, and the ache in my temples simply would not go away.

On the short drive back to our condo and during dinner, I'd listened to my mother's explanation of the staged scene in the bookstore and tried to make my mouth form the words that would tell my mother what I knew about David Brennan. I wanted to give voice to all the ugly things I'd seen and felt through Ivy's perspective. But the words that had flowed out of me when I'd come clean with LaShawna stayed lodged in my throat and chest, refusing to re-emerge. For her part, my mother seemed uninterested in anything I had to say, waving away both weak attempts I'd made to open the topic, saying, "We'll discuss that later."

Instead, we were discussing Truth and I was fighting to listen and stay awake. Apparently, my distraction was obvious. My mother snapped her fingers three inches in front of my face.

"Repeat what I just said," she ordered in a drill sergeant's voice.

I was able to parrot the words back to her, but, when she asked what those words meant to me, my tongue got tangled in my teeth.

"Asha, pull it together." She delivered a hard push to one of my shoulders, causing my aching head to jerk painfully. "We've got work to do, young lady. You cannot fall apart every time a weeping widow begs for help."

"She isn't a widow," I snapped back. "She's a scared little girl who married a child molester!"

My mother sat back, eyes wide, nostrils flaring.

"Are you sure?" she asked.

I nodded, then my whole body slumped until my cheek rested against the back of the couch. Unshed tears turned my vision watery. "I saw ... I mean, Ivy showed me—"

Xia cut off my words by pressing one hand over my mouth. "Not another word. I don't want to hear it. Does LaShawna know?"

Again, I nodded.

Xia removed her hand from my lips and stood up. "Go upstairs and splash some cold water on your neck and face," she ordered, pointing toward the stairs. "You need to shake this off and get your head on straight." She marched into the kitchen and rooted around in the cabinets until she found a bag of Hershey's miniatures. She tossed a handful of the candy bars into my lap. "Eat these. Sugar helps. Come back down here in ten minutes ready to apply some focus. This is bad, but it's not the end of the world. In fact, it's all the more reason why you need some basic training." She snapped her fingers at me. "Move, move, move!"

When I emerged from my bathroom a few minutes later, the sound of my mother's angry voice stopped me in my tracks.

"We had a deal, LaShawna. No sex crimes. Ever! How dare you drag this garbage into my house!" There was a short pause, then, "You didn't know? Really? Is that supposed to make me feel better? You damn well should have known! It's supposed to be your job."

Sour bile rose in my throat. I looked back into my brightly lit bathroom and yearned to crawl back into my closet, plug my ears and block out everything.

Instead, I tiptoed toward the stairs, every movement slow and careful. At the bottom, Ivy suddenly appeared and stared back up at me, her expression sad and hollow. Vertigo gripped me, and I had to grab the wooden banister to stop myself from falling headlong down the steps.

"No! Don't you dare!" My mother's voice snapped my attention back to her tirade. "We're busy right now. If you have anything to tell Asha, you can tell me. I'll decide if she needs to hear it."

Ivy nodded at me. Whatever it was, I needed to hear it.

"Don't you threaten me, LaShawna Simmons. Haven't you done enough damage to my daughter's life?"

Mother's angry words trailed behind me as I tiptoed back to my bathroom and fished the secret phone out of its hiding place. As soon as I switched it on, the screen lit up with a series of text messages from Zack. Ignoring them, I pulled up LaShawna's mobile number and fired off several short texts to her.

Shaw its Asha
Dont tell mom
This is a secret phone
from my dad
whats going on?!?!

Downstairs, my mother screamed, "Oh, no! You did *not* just hang up on me!"

I closed and locked the door to my bathroom as quietly as possible and turned on the cold water tap full force. The phone buzzed in my hand with LaShawna's reply.

On my way
Me: *Not a good idea*
X will go crazy
LaShawna: *I'll handle her*
Sit tight
Be there in 10

My finger hovered over the screen. Part of me wanted to argue with LaShawna, to tell her not to upset Xia any further. Why couldn't she text whatever she needed to say? But the other part of me wanted to see her, wanted her to stand between me and Xia's wrath, and, most of all, wanted to find out what she had to say about David Brennan and tell her about the weird encounter with Ying.

I opened the trail of text messages from Zack and scanned the bubbles. The messages were all variations of "Where are you" or "Call me."

"Asha!" Xia bellowed from downstairs, causing me to fumble the phone a few times before capturing it in both hands and pressing it to my pounding chest. "Get down here."

"Coming," I yelled back, then quickly switched off the phone and dropped it back into the box of tampons.

Downstairs, I found my mother pacing between the kitchen and the living room areas like a caged animal. I stood at the bottom of the stairs, in the exact spot where Ivy's image appeared a few minutes earlier, careful to stay alert and out of my mother's way. Ivy didn't seem to be with us, but I could feel a lingering fission of sadness in the air. Minutes ticked by slowly.

Eventually, Xia stopped pacing. She took a deep breath and faced me, both hands planted on her hips.

"We have three hard and fast rules," she announced. "The rules are there for a reason. I've learned most of them the hard way.

"Rule number one." She held up one finger. "We don't deal with sex crimes. If we're getting images or messages of any kind that seem like they belong on an episode of *Special Victims Unit*, we shut down. We block it out. We walk away. Do you hear me?"

"But how? How do we shut down and block—"

"Shut up and listen to me," she snapped, making a

slashing motion with her hand. "This was not your fault. It's LaShawna's fault for bringing it here. It's your father's fault for refusing to deal with your gift before you were confronted by this kind of ... horror. We'll talk about how to shut down and block in a minute. For now, just listen.

"Rule number two." She held up two fingers. "We don't visit violent crime scenes where one or more victims have died. If you happen to stumble on a scene accidentally, you shut down. You block it out. You walk away. Got it?"

"Yes," I answered quickly, not because I understood exactly how I was supposed to follow these rules, but because that was the answer she wanted to hear.

"Rule number three." She wiggled three fingers at me. "We are not police property. We are not avengers. We are not in the business of solving crimes. Sometimes the messages we relay can help the police, if they're willing to listen. Most aren't. Sometimes the messages right a wrong and some-times crimes do get solved. But that is not our business. Earlier, when we were sitting on the couch, right before you dropped that ugly little bomb on me, I told you what we are in the business of doing. What did I say?"

My brain struggled to remember.

Spreading Truth, a voice whispered in my ear. It wasn't Ivy's voice, but the familiar comforting sound of Aunt Nicole.

I repeated the words to my mother and she lifted both hands above her head. "Hallelujah! There it is. Say it again."

"We're in the business of spreading Truth," I said again, a little louder. *But what does that mean?* I thought, swal-lowing down my frustration.

"And is telling someone the Truth always the same as saying something that is factually accurate?"

"No?"

"That sounds like a question, Asha, not an answer."

"I mean ... can you give me an example?"

"Why, yes, I can. In fact, I've given you quite a few examples." Xia scooped up the copy of her first book that had been sitting on the couch between us earlier and flicked one of the Post-it note flags that stuck out of its pages. "I've marked several passages that illustrate what I'm saying. I want you to read these passages before you go to sleep tonight. In the morning, I'll expect you to be able to explain the difference between regurgitating facts and speaking the Truth. That is part one of your homework for this evening."

"I'm really not going to school tomorrow, am I?"

Xia squinted at me and shook her head. "Tomorrow is Friday. Our first public event together is Saturday. Here's another Truth for you, little girl. Nothing in the world is half as important to our future as this event on Saturday. Nothing. Do you hear me?"

"Yes, ma'am."

"Then repeat it back to me."

I straightened my shoulders and forced myself to look directly into her eyes. "Nothing in the world is half as important as this event on Saturday."

"Is any poor little dead girl, be that Ivy Brennan or any other weeping willow, more important than this event on Saturday?"

"No, ma'am," I answered, the words tasted acrid on my tongue.

"Are your grades more important than this event on Saturday?"

"No, ma'am."

She smiled with an evil light in her eyes. "Is your next dance competition more important than this event on Saturday?"

"No ma'am," I repeated yet again, my nostrils burning with suppressed fury and disgust.

"Are you ready to hear the second part of your homework assignment for tonight?"

Outside, a car pulled into the parking lot, its heavy tires rolling to a stop in the parking space directly in front of our condo. It was a safe bet LaShawna had arrived, but my mother's intensity didn't waver.

"Remember the three steps? Shut it down. Block it out. Walk away." She ticked off the three commands on her fingers. "You asked me how to do that. Well listen up. Here's the secret. It's a matter of preparation, practice, and self-control.

A car door slammed and the jingle of Kota's dog tags approached our front door.

Xia picked up the blue file folder that had been sitting next to her book and waved it on the air. "This folder contains a worksheet that will help you figure out exactly what you need to visualize for shutting down and blocking unwanted spirit communications. What works for one medium won't work for another. You need to figure out what works for you. Fast."

The doorbell rang, followed by a blast of urgent knocking. Somehow, instinctively, I knew it would be a huge mistake to react to the visitor in any way, so I kept my focus on Xia. It wasn't hard, because my mother was finally telling me something I desperately wanted to know.

"Some mediums visualize a switch they can flip off. Some come up with elaborate guardians that defend and protect. Some use colors, white light, curtains, protective symbols, or force fields out of their favorite sci-fi movie. Whatever works, works. It's just that simple and also that difficult."

A second round of knocking was followed by LaShawna's voice. "Open the door, Xia."

"The second item in the folder describes mental exercises that will help you practice your new visualizations. The exercises will strengthen and defend your mind," Xia continued, unruffled. "The second half of your homework assignment for this evening is to complete the visualization worksheet, then practice at least one of the recommended exercises. Got it?"

"Yes, I've got it," I promised, eying the blue folder with suspicion.

She extended the book and the blue folder toward me. I took both items and hugged them to my chest.

A third round of knocking and doorbell ringing erupted. "Xia, maybe you've forgotten that you gave me a spare set of your keys. I'm counting to five. If this door isn't open before I finish counting, I'm coming in. One!"

The right side of my mother's lips quirked up in a half-smile. "Is anything LaShawna has to say more important than our event?"

"Two."

"No, ma'am," I answered, returning her half-smile even as my stomach churned.

"Three."

"Good girl," Mother said, then turned and walked briskly to the front door.

"Four."

Xia unlocked and opened the door as LaShawna said, "Five."

"I told you we're busy," Xia addressed her cousin in a flat tone.

"And I told you it's important." LaShawna dropped Kota's leash and he trotted around the perimeter of our condo's main floor, thrusting his nose into every nook and cranny.

"Does he have to go to the bathroom?" Xia asked, wrinkling her nose with displeasure.

"No, Shirley, he's checking the perimeter to be sure we're secure."

"Why?" Mother and I asked at the same time.

LaShawna stepped inside and bolted the front door.

"Here's a better question, cousin dearest," LaShawna turned on my mother, speaking through gritted teeth. "How in the world did your name get all over the internet as being the anonymous source that led police to Ivy Brennan's body?"

My mother shrugged one shoulder. "I have absolutely no idea."

"Really?" That one word carried a heavy load of sarcasm and disbelief. My gut twisted in response.

"Really," Xia answered back, "but it's brought us the most wonderful surge of publicity right before this event on Saturday."

I remembered Jade Tsien saying *I know how to post things on social media.* Had she helped spread Xia's victory messages?

"You need to cancel the event on Saturday."

Xia burst out laughing. "Don't be absurd."

"What's going on LaShawna?" I asked, unable to stay quiet.

Her topaz eyes focused on me, softening a bit. "After what you told me the other day, Asha, I convinced the lead detective on this case to look at David Brennan from a new angle. As soon as we started looking, some things started to come to light. I can't tell you any details; I shouldn't say anything."

"But you will say something," Xia said, crossing her arms, "Or else you wouldn't come barging in here yelling threats like a one woman S.W.A.T. team."

LaShawna shot my mother a nasty look before focusing her attention back on me.

"Rich Uncle David isn't just a pervert. He's a pervert who knows how to connect with other perverts and make lots of money."

"Okay, that's enough," my mother said. "How many times do I have to tell you we're done with this mess? No sex crimes."

"What if this mess isn't done with you?" LaShawna shot back.

"You have this disgusting man in custody," Xia answered. "You'll figure out a way to send him away; you always do. Why do you have to come into our home spewing this filth?"

"David Brennan has an airtight alibi for the window of time when his niece was killed."

I waited for Ivy's voice to respond, to scream her favorite accusation, liar, in response to LaShawna's declaration, but nothing happened.

"No, that's not possible," I said, my voice sounded small.

"Find a way to break his alibi," my mother said, waving one hand dismissively.

"The pervert doesn't even know he has an alibi. He refused to account for nearly eighteen hours on the day and evening his niece died, saying he was driving around looking at properties all over the Bay Area with no witnesses or receipts to support his story."

"Liar," I whispered.

"Yes, he's lying," Xia agreed.

"Exactly," LaShawna said. "However, his actual activities were recorded on extensive surveillance videos which are currently in the custody of a special FBI task force. His activities that day, while entirely disgusting, immoral, and illegal, do not include kidnapping or killing his niece."

Mother and I stared at her in stunned silence.

"That's not possible," I repeated.

My mother shook herself. "David Brennan is a very rich man. He could have paid someone to get rid of her."

"Sure, but there's no evidence of that," LaShawna replied. "And that's why the FBI insisted David Brennan be released from our custody ..." She checked her watch. "Forty five minutes ago."

"You let him go!" My mother was outraged.

"We had no choice," LaShawna replied, suddenly looking tired and defeated. "And now he's out there, free to think about all those provocative comments posted all over the internet that claim Xia Celeste led police to his door. You need to cancel this event."

Although she looked disturbed and ashen, my mother shook her head. "No, LaShawna. That isn't going to happen."

"Shirley, stop being a moron. It gets worse." LaShawna reached inside her jacket and removed a rolled up sheet of paper. I saw that it was the picture of two men talking. I drew closer and reached for the picture.

"What is that?" Xia asked.

"This is a picture taken by the FBI two weeks ago. It's a picture of David Brennan at a construction site talking to a very dangerous man. This man is involved in horrible things. Drugs, extortion, human trafficking – you name it, he's got a finger in it."

I reached out and stopped LaShawna from waving the picture. Something about the image had caught my attention, and it wasn't David Brennan's ugly face. The other man looked faintly familiar. Then I saw the thick white scar running through one eyebrow.

"Oh, it's him," I said, finally placing the face.

"What do you mean 'it's him'?" asked LaShawna. "Who him?"

"Did Ivy show you this man?" my mother asked.

"No, I saw him at the library. He was ... he seemed nice."

Both women were looking at me in horror. Finally, LaShawna broke the spell.

"What library? When?"

"The public library here in the Rose Garden. He was in the computer room with me. Yesterday. Before we went to the beach."

20

Before

Sleep felt impossible that night. Not because Ivy haunted me, but because she was silent. I whispered questions, begged her to come. Nothing. Worse, I could hear my mother pacing endlessly in her own room. The sound of her restlessness reminded me of her book and the lessons she'd told me to practice. *Perhaps,* I thought, *there's something in there that will help break down this miserable wall of silence.*

When she first swarmed into my life, I wanted nothing more than for Ivy Brennan's spirit to move on into the light. Now I feared she'd found her peace and would leave me behind in a shattered, violent mess. So, while my mother's medium exercises emphasized protection, putting up limits and force fields and closed doors, I sat and focused my mind on opening doors and sending out signals.

In the heavy silence, I heard a song – the bittersweet ballad from the eighties about roses and thorns, cowboys, and sad songs. When I was lonely, Aunt Nicole used to curl up at the end of my bed and sing it to me. Years later, the song still worked its magic. My body eased, almost against my will, and my limbs felt loose and languid. My eyes became heavy. Around me, the ghostly shadows of tree branches grew, stretching across the barren white walls of my bedroom. I could hear the wind in the branches, smell the damp earthy smells of the woods back in Moonville.

Sleep now. The words drifted over me like a sigh. So I curled myself into a nest of covers and let myself drift away.

Hours later, I was torn from sleep by the sound of a slamming door. Startled and disoriented, I sat up with my heartbeat pounding in my throat and temples. Last night's revelations from LaShawna came back to me, including the disorienting sight of Kota checking the perimeter of our condo.

"Mom?" I called out. I kept my voice low but loud enough that she would be able to hear me from her bedroom. No answer came back, just eerie silence. Moving cautiously, I crept to my bedroom door and listened with my ear to the hollow wood. Nothing, No sounds came back to me. Scanning my room, nothing even remotely resembled a weapon, until my eyes fell on my house keys. Zack took me to a self-defense class at the YMCA right before we moved here and the instructor had harped on the right way to carry your keys in a darkened parking lot. I picked them up and laced the keys through my fingers, the ends protruding as I made a fist. The sensation gave me a tiny boost of confidence. Not much but enough to carefully open the door to scan the hallway.

No one was in sight. My mother's bedroom door was wide open. Even though I knew it would be empty, I checked there first. The grainy picture of the bad man LaShawna had shown us last night stared back at me from my mother's dresser, a bizarre sight among the usual chaos of lotions, potions, and makeup. His cold eyes sent a shudder down my spine. Was it possible I was wrong? I had thought the man who spoke to me in the library was so kind. But no, the distinctive scar through the man's left eyebrow was exactly the same as I remembered it. His words had sounded kind, but I hadn't really looked into his eyes. I'd focused on the scar, the scruffy sweater, the low voice. I turned down the surveillance photo and crept out of mother's bedroom to the top of the stairs.

Everything looked normal and undisturbed down below. I scanned the living room, the open kitchen, and dining area while I descended the stairs, step by cautious step, with the keys gripped in my fist.

"Mom?"

Nothing. No sound or movement. I hurried to the front door and found both the knob and the deadbolt locked, but the security chain was dangling open. Even though LaShawna regularly told us the chain was next to useless against a serious attacker, I shot the chain back into place. A quick look through the fish-eye peek hole showed that the parking space directly in front of the door was empty.

On the counter, I found a scribbled note.

Asha,

Appointment up in San Francisco. Back by 2:00. Jade Tsien might stop by with items for the event. Make sure you eat plenty and practice your homework. Do not call LaShawna.

X

She can't even sign a note as Mom?

Feeling reassured and yet abandoned, I hung my keys on

a proper hook and started scavenging through the kitchen for breakfast. It was just like my mother to order me to eat "plenty" but then leave me to fend for myself with a mostly empty fridge and pantry. There was cereal but no milk. Butter and jelly but no bread. Cheese but no crackers. God forbid we keep any fresh fruit or eggs in this house. I couldn't even find a snack pack of trail mix or granola bars. I was seriously considering a can of tomato soup when I heard a familiar ripple of polite taps at the door. Through the peep hole, I saw Mai's bamboo tray filled with food. With my mouth watering, I hurriedly opened all the locks and flung open the door.

"Hello, oh!" I stumbled back, shocked as Ying Brennan peered back at me from behind the bamboo food tray.

"Hello." She gave me a watery, uncertain smile, "Asha?" She spoke by name carefully, as though it were an exotic word.

"My mother isn't available right now."

"No, she's at the studio recording voiceovers. Sounds very exciting. This is for you." She lifted the tray toward me and the smell of scrambled eggs made my stomach rumble. I stepped backward into the house and Ying followed, passing me to set the tray of food on the counter before turning back around. Her face, her voice, everything about her was so different from the day before. She made me feel off-balance and weird.

"Thank you?" I pushed the door fully open and waited for her to leave. Instead, she clasped her hands together and smiled at me.

"Auntie Mai isn't feeling well this morning. Her arthritis is very bad. She wanted to bring you some breakfast, to get your strength up for the big show tomorrow, but she has so much pain. I said I would do it so she could rest. Mai does so much for everybody else, you know. Never thinks about herself. Aren't you going to eat?"

Despite my earlier hunger and growling stomach, I did not want to sit down to eat that food with Ying Brennan watching me. But I couldn't ask her to leave me alone. Feeling trapped, I walked over to the tray and made a bit of a show of sniffing the air above the tray. The scent of jasmine mingled with the eggs.

"Is this Mrs. Tsien's jasmine green tea?" When she nodded, I forced a big, goofy smile on my face and scooped up the warm clay mug, cradling it in my hands. "Thank heaven for caffeine," I said, my voice sounding idiotic and false in my head, and took a huge gulp. The bitter taste that filled my mouth almost made it impossible to swallow. Almost. But I forced the stuff down. Mai makes her jasmine green tea with wildflower honey and a touch of almond milk. This stuff tasted like chewing on green tea bags and perfume.

Ying's sad, watery smile faltered. "Something wrong?"

"Oh, no. It's just hot." I fanned my face. "Hotter than I expected."

"We could put some ice in it, if you want?" She pointed toward the refrigerator at the far end of the kitchen.

I want you to leave, I thought. My skin was crawling. Instead, I said, "No, that's okay. I like hot tea. I'll just take smaller sips." To prove my point, I took a loud sip of the evil brew. The bitterness crawled up my nostrils. I blinked and smiled to cover my misery.

She smiled politely and nodded. Her eyes never left my face. It felt like she was searching for something. To cover my embarrassment, I drank more of the tea. Maybe, once I swilled that stuff down, I could get her to leave. My tongue and nose were starting to get numb to the flavor. So I took another serious swallow and smiled at her.

"Thank you for bringing this," I said, waving the mug toward the tray. The glob of eggs on a plate no longer looked appetizing. It looked snotty. My stomach roiled and churned. "It was very kind of you, with everything ... that's going on."

"Fetch water, chop wood, make tea."

"I'm sorry?"

"It's a Chinese proverb," she explained, tilting her head to one side. "Like those English signs you see everywhere. You know the ones. Keep calm and carry on?"

"Oh! My grandpa used to say, 'Hit the ball and drag George.'" As soon as the words were out of my mouth, I wanted to grab them back. Why would I say that to a woman whose whole world was falling apart?

But she smiled and clapped her hands together once, as though I'd said something brilliant. "Yes, exactly. I love that joke."

"You love that joke?" I repeated her words, feeling wooden and stupid. "You've heard it? Really?"

It looked like she was going to say something else, but she suddenly yelped and started patting around at the pockets of her loose silk jacket and pants. Eventually, she pulled out a phone that was faintly buzzing on vibrate. One look at the glowing screen and her face puckered into an expression somewhere between worry and annoyance.

"I need to do this," she said vaguely and turned away from me, one finger pecking carefully at the screen.

While she was diverted, I looked around the living room and kitchen, wishing a nice houseplant would suddenly materialize so I could easily ditch the rest of the tea. Of course, Xia doesn't believe in plants or pets. ("They just die on you, Asha!") For a few seconds, I seriously considered dumping what was left in my cup into one of my Converse All Stars. *There's not that much tea left*, I told myself. I could wash the shoes later. It's not like I'd be able to wear them with that "pretty, pretty princess" outfit Xia bought for our psychic family circus. But, in the end, good manners won. I could not make myself pour out the tea and risk insulting that tiny, frail, tragic person. Instead, I gulped down the rest of it, right down to the last gritty dregs, and then clumsily placed the clay mug back on the tray, causing a clatter. Ying looked over and gave me a distracted smile. She swirled one hand toward the tray, indicating I should go ahead and eat.

The eggs still looked snotty but there was a slice of almond cake that looked like it was cut from the same cake Mai gave me on Wednesday. And I was relieved to see there was also a small glass of orange juice on the tray. I sipped the juice slowly, allowing the sweet tart liquid to rinse around in my mouth and wash away the nastiness of the tea. It worked, and I started to feel a little less nauseated. In fact, the juice made me feel so much better that I was able to nibble on the almond cake. It was dry, missing the warm honey syrup Mai drizzled over it before serving, but the cinnamon almond flavor was still pleasant. While I nibbled cake, I used the fork to move the eggs around the plate hoping to make it look like I'd taken some bites.

"Yes, I love that joke." Mai suddenly materialized beside me at the counter, setting her phone down next to the bamboo tray.

I dropped the fork guiltily, but she didn't seem to notice. Her face looked worried; her voice sounded brittle. She was looking toward Mai's condo, visible through the open front door, with a distant, worried expression on her face.

"Was that Mai texting you? Is she all right?"

"Oh no, Mai is just tired. She didn't sleep well last night, and she needs to take a nap. She does too much. And she eats so much sugar. It's bad for her arthritis. Sugar makes inflammation. I tell her all the time she needs to lose weight and watch out for diabetes."

So that explains the missing honey and syrup, I thought. *Give me diabetes over your nasty tea.* A tiny giggle escaped, and I pressed my fingers to my lips, horrified.

Ying smiled at me ruefully. "You are still young. So lucky. No real worries."

No worries? Could she be serious?

The phone buzzed again, rattling loudly on the counter. Ying snatched it up quickly and said something under her breath. "The police are back at my house again!" she told me. "This is insane. I have to make a call."

When I nodded, my head felt as though it was full of cotton. Ying turned away, and I continued to move my head in slow circles. The magic of the orange juice was wearing off; the fumes from that terrible tea were climbing up my throat and I felt fuzzy at the edges. A heavy blanket of exhaustion was pressing down on me. Another restless night, the morning terror, the freakish discomfort of entertaining Ying Brennan in my living room – it all seemed too much. I rested my heavy head on one elbow, willing the sour feeling in my stomach to settle down.

Ying started speaking rapidly into her phone, her voice tense. I was shocked to realize she was speaking in Spanish. How many languages did this woman know?

"Asha?" She stood next to me, shaking my arm. "Are you done eating? I have to go. The police are there. My poor niece is freaking out. It's bad."

"Jazz?" I said, sitting up as an electric jolt of fear rushed through my body.

"Jasmine is autistic. Her useless mother was a drug addict." Her phone buzzed again, she looked at it, then looked back at me in frustration. "She's starting to hurt herself."

"You go," I said, "I'll take back Mai's tray."

"Yes, thank you!" Ying hurried toward the front door.

I stood, scooped up the tray, and started to follow her. But my feet seemed to have a mind of their own, causing me to stumble and nearly drop everything. Luckily, Ying was right there and neatly caught the tray.

"Better let me take this. It's Mai's favorite mug."

Feeling embarrassed and hopelessly clumsy, I watched from the doorway as Ying quickly deposited the tray inside the door to Mai's condo, then shut and locked the front door behind her. She gave me a distracted wave and fumbled with her keys to the massive SUV as she checked her phone again. She let out a cry and leaned against the door. She looked so tiny and overwhelmed.

"Is there anything I can do?" I asked her. It was an automatic reaction to her distress.

Ying looked at me with tragic, teary eyes. "She's screaming for her VeeVee again. What am I supposed to do?"

A blurry kaleidoscope of images fluttered through the edges of my vision. I could hear a very young child screaming "VeeVeeVee " on an endless loop as she spun in frenzied circles.

"She's pulling her hair and her eyelashes and she's bleeding. The police are storming through our house with their boots and their cameras. They won't leave. They say they have a warrant. Poor Jazz is hysterical. What am I supposed to do? She doesn't like me. She hates me. She only wants her VeeVee."

"I can help." My lips moved before my brain could stop the madness. "She ... we got along when we were at Mai's house. She gave me her drawing, remember? I'm ... I kind of ... maybe I remind her of VeeVee ... I think. I mean I don't look like her, but you know." What was I saying?

Ying had her head tipped to one side, looking at me with a sort of pleased, sort of doubtful expression. "You are like your Mommy, aren't you? You hear ..." She wiggled her fingers in the air, then whispered, "ancestors."

"I can help," I repeated.

Her phone buzzed again. She looked at it, then pressed the screen to her chest and closed her eyes tightly, as though she'd been hit.

"What is it?" I asked, dread and terror pulsing in my ears.

She turned the phone toward me. The picture was mostly a blur of motion and hard to understand at first. But as I looked closer I could see a messy mop of blonde hair and two balled fists pulling at it, one with bloody, bruised knuckles. Peeking out from behind one scrawny wrist was a wide, panicked blue eye. Jazz's terror pierced my gut. Then I was in motion.

"Hold on, I'm coming with you," I yelled over my shoulder as I ran back to the house. I was still wearing the t-shirt and shorts I slept in, but there was no time to change. Instead, I threw on a hoodie, then grabbed my All Stars and the house key. Just before locking the door, I remembered the new iPhone.

The Cadillac engine roared to life behind me. I twisted around, and Ying waved me to come on. I held up one hand and made a mad dash back into the house, tripping and stumbling up the stairs. As I shoved the iPhone in my pocket, I noticed the picture Jazz gave me on my dresser and grabbed it before running out the door. As soon as I climbed into the passenger seat, Ying put the car in motion. There was a heavy "chunk" as the childproof locks activated and the shoulder belt started moving toward my chest automatically.

21

BEFORE

"PLEASE FASTEN YOUR SEATBELT," YING TOLD ME AS SHE pulled into traffic.

My fingers fumbled with the lap belt; my shaking hands made it difficult to close the buckle.

"Are you sure you want to do this?" Ying asked as she stopped at a traffic light. "Jasmine can be quite violent."

I nodded and traced my thumb over the drawing that Jazz gave me. It was a very sophisticated image and it explained why I knew I could help, but for some reason I suddenly felt shy about showing it to her aunt. Ying was quiet then, navigating with extreme caution through the snarl of weekend traffic around the mall. I wanted her to honk her horn, to drive that beast up on the sidewalks to get past the mass of time-wasting shoppers that were between us and Jazz, but Ying appeared to be a very timid driver.

"Maybe we should call your house and let them know we're coming?"

"It's illegal to use the phone and drive," she told me with a disapproving frown at the taillights in front of us.

"You don't think this is kind of special circumstances?"

She sighed deeply, then tore her iron gaze away from traffic to risk one quick, disapproving look at me before refocusing her attention forward. "You want to know what I think? I think American teenagers are ridiculous."

The words were spit out with such hate, I felt like I'd been slapped.

"I mean," she continued in a softer tone, "I can't go driving around like a crazy person every time Jazz has one of her fits. We already have police invading our house. Why would I give another police reason to pull me over? I need to keep calm and carry on!"

The tone of her voice sounded the exact opposite of calm, but I kept my mouth shut. She wasn't really expecting any response. She'd lapsed into her native tongue again. From the tone of her voice, I guessed she was still complaining about police, or me, or the annoyance of American teenagers, but I couldn't understand a word of it. I was acutely aware of the bitter taste of that tea climbing back up my throat, along with a metallic taste pooling under my tongue. Worse, the slow, wobbly motion of the vehicle was making my stomach churn. So I closed my eyes and tried to focus on not throwing up all over this woman's expensive SUV as her voice chattered on.

My mind started to drift. Images from the last few days flickered and shifted behind my closed eyelids.

Dimly, I heard the turn signal and felt the engine accelerating. *We must be getting on the highway now*, I thought. Hopefully, the 101 won't be packed with weekend warriors headed up to San Francisco. I opened my eyes and blinked a few times. My vision felt distorted and blurry. When I tried to rub my eyes, my fingers felt foreign. I stared at them in confusion, then stared at the trees on either side of the road. Trees? I should have been seeing urban sprawl, not trees. This wasn't the 101.

It took a great deal of effort to swivel my head and look at Ying. She was hunched over the wheel, her eyes squinting straight forward, lips still moving. She'd switched back to English, chanting the same thing over and over.

"Fetch water, chop wood, make tea. Fetch water, chop wood, make tea. Fetch water, chop wood, make tea."

A sudden thought struck me. Was she dragging George? The joke is about three guys on a golf course. George drops dead suddenly. The other two keep playing golf, but the game takes forever because they have to keep hitting the ball then drag George with them. I never really thought the joke was funny. At that moment it became horrifying. Was I George? Was she dragging me along in a stupid, pointless game? I tried to ask her, but the words came out as nonsense.

She looked over at the sounds I was making and smiled at me. "How are you feeling, Asha?" Her voice was high and sing-song. She carefully pronounced the two syllables of my name, as though it was two words. Ahsh Ah. Through my blurry, bubble-headed confusion, a terrible cold terror gripped my stomach. "Such a nice, polite girl. You drank that tea right up. Don't want to make the poor, sad, little lady feel hurt."

That tea. That stupid, nasty, bitter tea! I had forced down every last drop. How could I have been so stupid?

"You have manners. I give you that. Someone has taught you to mind your manners!" She raised one finger at the last word and giggled like a little girl.

All I could do was gape at her in horror. She shook her

head and sighed, still looking ahead and not looking at me. "Not like David's girls. They are like wild animals. No manners. No respect. They don't even know how to chew with their mouths shut. And he lets them get away with anything, like they own him. He gives them every most expensive piece of technology any teenager could want. Like they are his first and second wives. I am his wife, but he treats me like I am distant third. Do they appreciate it? No. That stupid girl she just bites and bites and bites the hands that feed her!"

"Ivy! More like Poison Ivy. And Jasmine is no delicate, fragrant flower. She is a monster. It's no wonder. Their mother was a crazy meth addict. Did you know that? Did Poison Ivy tell you that? She was a meth addict, never did one day of honest work. But those girls never know one day of hunger. Not one day. Not one night of going to bed sick from hunger. All because of David. Uncle David's money keeps their bellies full. Keeps a beautiful roof over their heads when meth addict mommy died. And that stupid, greedy girl wanted him to lose everything."

When the edges of my vision started to darken, my helpless fascination with her words turned to pure panic. Arms flailing wildly, I tried to open my door, struggling with my seatbelt, but the door handle refused to operate and my useless fingers wouldn't cooperate.

"Stop that!" Ying barked, slapping at my hand then backslapping at my face.

Clumsily, I pushed my left knee against the gearshift and managed to throw the car in reverse. There was a satisfying grinding, screeching sound, and Ying screamed as we swerved off the road. Metal scraped against the concrete barrier briefly before we came to a stop. She turned off the motor and glared at me, her own breath coming in gasps.

"You are going to pay for that," she hissed at me, spit flying.

I stared back at her, helpless. Fascinated. Somehow, all of the terror and anger had drained away. She scrambled out of the car. The rear door opened and there was some activity. It sounded like she was digging through a pile of tools.

I'm going to die, I thought, testing the idea out the way you would test the edges of an old wound to see if it still hurts. Amazingly, the thought brought no terror. And I found that absolutely mesmerizing. I was going to die. Just like Ivy. Just like my Aunt Nicole. Just like the bossy girl who used to play with me in the woods when I was a little girl back in Moonville. Would I leave a ghost? Would my mother be able to hear me? Would I finally find Daddy?

My door opened and Ying was right there beside me with a mass of colorful bungee cords gripped in one hand. The colors fascinated me, even as she used them to bind my feet and hands together. It was unnecessary. That push of the gear shift was the last of my fight. But I knew my mouth wouldn't form the words, so I just watched her, amazed. This tiny, delicate, doll-like person was going to kill me. Now it was my turn. Once my hands and legs were sufficiently tight, Ying gave me a hard and vicious shove. Then she flashed a tight, polite smile.

"Don't fight. It will be much easier for you if you calm down and do what you're told." She shrugged. "That's the advice my own mommy gave to me the first time she sold me to a man." Then she slammed the door.

In the rearview mirror, Ivy's tearful eyes looked back at me. *Don't cry for me*, I thought. She smiled through her tears and gave a tiny shake of her head. As we looked at each other, a shift started to happen. I didn't understand it, but I allowed myself to relax into it. I'd met too many ugly frightened mixed-up ghosts who struggled against the light. *I won't struggle.*

But Ivy Brennan wasn't taking me to the light.

There was a dizzy moment where time and space stretched. Only Ivy and I existed in the entire universe. There was a soaring sensation, then an abrupt swoop and drop, as though I'd fallen down a shoot right back into my body sitting in the SUV. But it wasn't my body. I was sitting in the same passenger seat, but I was looking through teary eyes at milky white freckled knees. My knees, but they were her knees. When I looked toward the driver's side, Ying was putting the car in park. Light rain spattered the windows behind her even though I knew it was a sunny day.

"Let's talk this out." Ying's voice was an echo from the past.

"No, I'm done talking," Ivy's voice snapped back. "There's nothing to talk about."

A second image, a faint shadow of Ying in the present, climbed back in the car, started the engine, and some distant part of me knew we were in motion again. Even as I saw the past Ying turn toward me with her hands folded, pleading. In a childlike, whining voice, Ying said, "Please, be reasonable, VeeVee."

"Don't call me that! Don't you ever call me that!"

Ivy's hands rummaged in her backpack, eyes still blurry with tears. She yanked out a manila folder and waved it toward Ying's startled face.

"You're not going to adopt these girls."

"Where did you get that?" Ying's tone had lost the wheedling tone, turning harsh.

"There is no way in hell I'm going to let you bring these girls into his house. No way."

Ying tilted her head and smiled too sweetly. "Okay, you found out our surprise. We are adopting these lovely girls. You are going to have two new younger sisters. Don't be jealous. We still love you and Jazz."

"Jealous? Are you crazy?"

"These girls are in an orphanage in Russia. They are very poor; they have very little hope. We have so much to share."

"Stop it, just stop it."

"You would let them starve and suffer when Uncle David could give them so much?"

"You know what he did to me. You know!"

"What did he do? Give you a beautiful home, the best education, every expensive electronic gizmo you wanted?"

"Guilt gifts. He stole my childhood. Now you want to help him steal theirs? You know what he is!"

Ying's voice changed again, dropping to a harsh, guttural tone. "Yes, I know. I know quite a bit. You don't know. You don't know what it's like to be truly hungry. You don't know anything about suffering. Your uncle ... we need to keep him at home. These girls will keep him home."

"You are a freak!" Ivy's hand opened the door. I felt a surge of power in my body as Ivy burst out of the car, ready to kick and spit and fight. I felt light rain kissing her bare arms. Ivy whirled around and gripped the doorframe, glaring back at Ying. "Get away from me."

"Where do you think you are going?"

Ivy took a deep breath, sucking in the cool, rain-sweet air. Outside the car, on her own two feet, Ivy felt restored. She felt powerful. She felt invincible. And I felt everything Ivy was feeling even though some part of my brain knew I was still sitting slumped and helpless in the SUV with Ying driving us to some unknown destination.

"I'm going for a jog. Then I'm going to meet a friend."

"By yourself?" Ying asked, looking appalled. "Isn't this where that that jogger went missing a few months ago?" Despite the alarm in her voice, Ying's words were a little too innocent, a little too nervous. But Ivy didn't seem to notice the false note in her aunt's voice.

At that moment, every part of me wished I could use Ivy's powerful body to reach into the SUV and pound that evil creature's face in. But I couldn't change what happened in the past. Ivy's anger was draining away. In its place I felt a surge of determination.

"Ying, shut up," Ivy's voice was dead even. "Just stop. Stop pretending you give a crap about me. This is over. Stop this, stop him, or run away and find a new American husband to buy you presents. I don't care what you do. I'm going to the police." Ivy slammed the door shut and gave it a good kick to punctuate her point. She stepped back as Ying slumped over the steering wheel.

The outside of the vehicle was splashed with a thick coating of mud along the bottom. And the navy blue color looked black on a gray rainy day. The black SUV with mud obscuring the license plate described in the Amber Alert was her aunt's car all along. Ying must have washed it before Jazz called the police. But why would she do that?

Excess energy was cracking through Ivy's body, firing her legs into motion as she turned away. The coiled tension snapped into motion as Ivy broke into a fast run. Air rushed into her lungs as her arms and legs pumped furiously. I'm a dancer. I've never run over a mile in my life. But I could feel Ivy's exhilaration. I felt her comfort and the soothing release she experienced as her body ran along the trail. Ivy's eyes didn't roam around to give me a good view of the path she was on, but I could tell it was very familiar to her.

Time bent and contracted. Seconds later, I felt the good solid satisfaction of a long run. Ivy was no longer on a dirt path. Black pavement stretched upward toward a misty horizon. She was running with her eyes forward, rushing toward that moment when she would stand up and fight. I heard and felt the slap of her tennis shoes on pavement. Then I heard the rumble of a car engine approaching from behind. Ivy quickly moved to the far left side of the road, with a quick glance over her right shoulder. The movements were automatic for a girl who ran regularly. She had just come around a bend in the road, so the car wasn't visible yet, though it sounded loud. She continued to run, eying the edge of the road to be sure she didn't stumble on the uneven stones at the shoulder where she was jogging.

The engine roared wildly. Tires squealed. Startled, Ivy looked back into gleaming metal and everything disappeared into darkness.

22

———

Now

Doubled over, sobbing, my whole body aches. Breathing is painful. Cool fingers touch my neck.

"Asha? It's all right now. You're safe. You are safe now, Asha. You lived. You're safe."

As the soft litany of Vera's reassurances start to penetrate my grief, a tissue dabs carefully to stem the flow of tears and snot streaming down my face.

"She ... thought ... she ... won!" I gasp out the words, feeling the terrible wrench of loss.

"Good," Vera says firmly. "Good for her."

I look at her, shocked.

"How would you rather die?" Vera asks me, gently brushing the tiny springs of curls back from my damp face. "Feeling victimized? Helpless? Defeated? Or feeling like you just faced down the dragon and victory was in your reach?"

Some small part of my brain whispers that Vera is right,

but I feel too sick and dizzy with horror to speak. Instead, I lift my hands and stare at how violently they are shaking.

"Those salt cleanses never worked for me. Only sweet can chase away the bitter." Vera moves away as I struggle to stop my teeth from chattering. A rattling noise is followed by the familiar crack and fizz of opening a soda. Kneeling beside me, Vera coaxes a cold glass of Coca-Cola into my shaking hands. "A sparkling elixir of sugar and caffeine. It's the only thing that works for me."

After one tentative sip, just to make sure I can swallow the stuff without choking, I gulp down half the drink then press the cold glass to my forehead the way Grandpa Elton always does after mowing the lawn. Taking long, slow, cola-sweetened breaths, I wait until the worst of the shaking passes before attempting to speak.

"Works for you?" I ask, looking at Vera. She has the grace to look embarrassed. "Are you really my lawyer? Is that really why you're here?"

"Oh you poor thing!" Vera settles herself back in her chair to face me. "You've been lied to by just about everyone your whole life haven't you?" I shake my head in protest, but she leans forward and gently places three fingers under my chin, tilting it forward to look into my eyes. "I am indeed a lawyer; I'm *your* lawyer. I have a very real law degree and a private practice, in addition to my work with the QFWC Foundation." Without taking her huge, luminous gray eyes from my face, she leans to one side, fishes a fresh package of tissues out of her messenger bag and hands it to me.

"You also have a very real website aimed at exposing psychic frauds."

"Yes, I do." Vera nods. "To be honest, I think that's part of the reason why Elton called and asked me to step in here."

"My grandpa? Called you?"

"Yes. Elton Kidwell called me because he is aware I have some special qualifications outside of my mundane law practice."

"Special qualifications," I echo her words stupidly.

Vera's smile is warm but tinged with sadness. "Some of my clients can't exactly testify on their own behalf. And some of my clients are normal people victimized by spirit mediums with their own agenda. It's an odd mix, I'll admit. But my particular set of skills is why I want to help you, Asha. You've read the Professor's bio on the website. You know my story."

Taking another swallow of Coke, I eyeball Vera carefully considering my next words. "So you're definitely here to represent me?" I ask.

Vera nods with enthusiasm.

"Or are you representing Ivy Brennan?"

Vera tilts her head to one side and pauses as though she is considering her answer very carefully. "In this case, it has to be both don't you think?"

Eyes burning, I drop my head.

My lawyer nods, rubs her hands over the tops of her knees and takes a deep breath. "This has been a rough day, hasn't it? We can pick this up tomorrow after you've had a night to sleep and recover." She snaps her pen to the clipboard and stands up.

"No, let's get this over with. I'll never sleep with the words unsaid."

23

BEFORE

I WOKE UP IN TOTAL DARKNESS. I WAS FACE DOWN ON something not quite soft that smelled of mold and ammonia. Revolted, I turned my head and blinked my eyes several times. Everything remained pitch black. Panic exploded and I pushed myself up quickly — too quickly. The sudden movement brought on a surge of violent nausea. My stomach contracted, causing me to heave and retch, but only a thin steam of bile came up. I clamped my teeth shut and took short desperate breaths through my nose until the attack subsided.

Feeling a bit more in control, I poked my fingers at the surface under me, pushing outward. It felt plastic yet spongy, like a cheap air mattress. Pushing myself slowly and carefully to my knees, I blinked and used my fingers to explore my own head and neck. Nothing, no covering or blindfold to explain the inky blackness. So I went back to patting the mushy surface below me, tentatively exploring with my fingertips even as my imagination dredged up horrors my fingers might find.

I was definitely on an air mattress; the soft pattern of plastic seams and puffed ridges was familiar. I'd slept on quite a few cheap air mattresses in my time. This one was bare, no sheets or blankets. And it smelled terrible.

The air further away from its surface didn't smell much better. There was a trace of nastiness that reminded me of the dog kennels first thing in the morning. An image of Zack filled my mind so strongly, I almost cried out for my stepbrother. Clamping my teeth harder, I pushed that thought aside and continued exploring.

My fingers finally found a wall running alongside the mattress. It felt both familiar and foreign, with hard ridges running up and down in a regular pattern. The surface was too cold. Making a fist, I knocked lightly. The reverberation identified it as metal. Metal walls?

In the perfect blackness, an image swam in my memory from after I'd told my mom and LaShawna about meeting the man at the library. LaShawna waving a manila folder at my mother and yelling. The folder dropping, pictures spilling out. She'd moved quickly to hide the pictures from me but not fast enough. I'd gotten a good look at the top picture. Now the image was swimming in the darkness, pushing me toward hysteria.

It was a metal shipping container, like the ones they loaded on ships and rail cars, with one end open. Eight girls were huddled together on a stained mattress, their black eyes squinting up into the light.

Eight girls.

"Hello?"

My voice, dry and choked with terror, echoed back at me.

"Hello?" I tried again, trying to make my voice sound calmer. "Is anyone here?" The last word squeaked with terror.

Nothing but echoes answered me.

Inch by inch, I felt my way to the edge of the mattress and found the floor. It felt like smooth metal gritty with dirt. My feet were bare. For a brief second I wondered what had happened to my shoes, but that thought reminded me of my mother holding Ivy's Sketcher in the comfort of our kitchen and calmly babbling about Ivy being somewhere near water when her body was buried in cement in someone's back yard. I shook my head to clear the image, refusing to give in to helpless fury and resolutely placed my feet on the floor.

Gripping one of the ridges on the wall, I pushed myself up, inch by inch, into a standing position, panting through the waves of nausea that threatened to push me back down. The universe seemed to tip and twist around me as pulsing spots swam in the darkness. But I managed to stay upright, refusing to give up this little bit of progress.

The air didn't smell any better from a standing position. If there was no light, was there also no air? Was I currently panting my way through all the oxygen in this hellhole? Fear made my breaths more desperate, and I gulped the rancid, musky air into my lungs. How would I know if the oxygen was running out?

Shuffling forward, I kept one hand in contact with the wall to stay oriented in the total darkness. I searched the perimeter, feeling utterly vulnerable with my bare feet. It seemed like hours before I found the first corner, which felt like a huge victory even though I was still trapped in some sort of metal box. The next wall was much shorter, then the third was the longest of all. When my toes nudged the air mattress just a few steps after rounding the third corner, my earlier assumption was confirmed. I was definitely trapped in some sort of metal box, probably a shipping container like the one in the police photo LaShawna had tried to hide from me. My careful circuit had not found any door or handle or crack that might lead to a way out.

Tears burned my eyes and flooded down my cheeks. Squatting, I felt the air mattress before sitting on the edge. There had to be a way in and out of this black box. There had to be. Ying couldn't have beamed me in here from space. I had to search again, more carefully, feeling high and low for any sign of a latch or handle. But I couldn't make myself move. Instead, I curled up on one side in a pathetic comma and sobbed. As the tears poured out, I screamed nonsense filled with impotent fury.

"Help me someone, please help me" eventually dissolved into "Whyyyyiyiyiyiyi?" until I was limp, my throat raw and aching.

I thought of Ivy then, the terrifying angry spirit that had first assaulted me in my own home. Every sense in my sick body and terrified brain reached out for her, longing for the cool tingle of air that would mean she was there with me.

Nothing happened.

"You did this to me," I whispered into the darkness. "Ivy? You did this. Help me. Get me out of here." Anger boiled up, overpowering the misery. "Get me out of here!" I screamed into the emptiness.

A deep clunking noise startled me, followed by a faint whirring that made me sit bolt upright.

"Hello?"

Warm air brushed my cheek, but it wasn't supernatural. It sounded like a fan of some sort. The air wasn't any cooler, but it seemed a bit fresher. If there was a fan, there had to be some sort of air vent.

Screaming with tears and snot running down my face, I pushed myself upright and worked my way around the circuit of the room again. I was much faster this time since I knew the floor around the edges of my prison wouldn't damage my bare feet. On the far, shorter wall, I could feel a tiny bit of vibration and smelled a slight whiff of fresher air. Reaching up, stretching onto my toes, my fingertips brushed a bolted metal frame.

"Air vent," I said aloud. So I wasn't going to suffocate. Straining upward, I screamed and screamed, occasionally falling silent to listen for a response, then screaming again until my throat and lungs were on fire. When the air shut off, the sound of my gasping breath was thunderous in the silence.

Weak with disappointment, I turned and pressed my back against the wall, sliding down until my butt hit the floor. I tried calling for help again, my voice getting thinner and more desperate until I pressed my forehead to my knees and gave in to a fresh bout of sobbing.

"It's time to stop screaming now."

The tiny voice sounded distant, but it sent a volt of pure adrenaline through me.

"Hello? Who is that?"

Instead of answering my question, the thin wavering voice started singing.

"Itsy bitsy spider went up the water spout." Rhythmic tapping on metal accompanied the words of the familiar song. "Down came the rain and washed the spider out." The wobbling voice, so pure and innocent, was straight out of Ivy's memories. "Up came the sun and dried up all the rain."

An image flashed in my mind – a blonde little girl, spinning and hitting at her own arms. Then I saw the child look up, wild eyes watching me through tangled hair as a pair of hands – familiar pale, freckled hands with bitten nails – created the universal finger to thumb motion from the song.

"So the itsy bitsy spider went up the spout again."

"Jazz?" My voice was a shrill gasp. "Jasmine Brennan? Is that you?"

"You have to sing along."

Again, I saw the younger Jazz Brennan looking up, calmer this time. "Again," she said, trying to imitate the spidery motion of Ivy's hands.

"Ready?" the voice outside asked me. "Now sing." The rhythmic tapping started again. "Itsy bitsy spider went up —" Her delicate voice cut off suddenly. "You're not singing," she complained.

"Jazz, please," I begged, "can you get me out of here? Or can you call the police. Call 911. Tell them—"

"No." Her voice cut me off in a harsh tone. "That's not possible. You have to sing."

Frustrated tears threatened to strangle me.

"I don't want to sing," I choked out. "I want to go home."

"First you have to sing," she repeated stubbornly.

"Please help me, Jazz. VeeVee would want you to help me."

"I know that," she snapped, her voice sharp with irritation. "I am helping. You have to sing. No good having baby fits. You will hurt yourself. Just sing."

Cool air stirred around my neck and cheek.

Sing, Ivy's voice told me clearly.

"Okay," I gasped as hope replaced frustration. "Okay, I'll sing."

"Ready?"

I swallowed hard. "Yes, let's sing."

The rhythmic tapping started again. This time I sang with her from the beginning. My voice was shaking and completely off pitch, but I sang the familiar nursery song as loud as I could.

We finished the first round and Jazz demanded, "Again." So we launched into the silly song again. The whole thing was fully absurd, but by the fourth repetition, I was tapping along with her and feeling a bit calmer.

When the sun came up for the fifth time, a crack of light appeared above me and Jazz's pale face appeared in the opening, illuminated by a faint blue glow.

"So the itsy bitsy spider went up the spout again!" she declared triumphantly.

Behind her, stars lit up the night sky. I stood, reaching my arms upward as fresh air washed down over me. But the opening was too high and well out of my reach.

"Don't panic," Jazz told me just as panic was twisting in my gut. "Stay calm, okay?"

I nodded even though the desperation to claw my way out of the darkness was nearly overwhelming. The weak light from above made the room barely visible. Turning in place, I could clearly see what my searching fingers had already told me. There was nothing in here with me but the air mattress. There was no way up – no ladder or any kind of foothold on the metal walls.

"We're going to sing the song one more time," Jazz told me calmly, drawing my attention back upward.

"I can't get out," I told her, desperate. "Can you get me out?"

"Asha, stay calm," she told me with absolute authority. "You must stay calm. No baby fits. Sing the song one more time by yourself, okay? Just one more time."

I swallowed and nodded. "One more time," I repeated.

"Go," Jazz commanded and disappeared from the opening. I fought back a squeal of protest. "Sing!" I heard her order from outside my line of sight.

So I sang, both fists clenched, voice wobbling, fear churning in my gut. I sang every stupid word of that stupid song. And, at the end of the final verse, a white ladder made of rope and plastic dropped into the room.

"Now it's your turn to climb," Jazz told me. "Like the spider."

I grabbed the floppy ladder and tried to climb out, but the thing swung wildly, making me feel like a ball fighting to escape up a string.

"You have to move slowly, carefully," Jazz's voice told me. "Be like the spider. You are the spider. You can do this."

Breathing deeply, I focused on slow careful movements. One foot up, then the other. One hand, then the other. I was able to make some progress. It still wasn't easy. My muscles were screaming, the plastic covered rope was digging into my bare feet, and all of my limbs were shaking. When the opening was finally within reach, I gripped the frame and felt Jazz place both her hands over mine.

She doesn't like touching people, I thought. *She's doing that to make me feel better.*

"Don't panic," she said calmly. "Keep going one step at a time."

So I did. Once my head emerged, Jazz sat back and hooked her feet under my armpits. It probably didn't make my position any more stable, but I felt more secure. She was using all of her strength to help me pull myself up and out until I flopped down quivering and gasping on the metal roof.

She leaned in close and smiled like a proud mother. "Good job, Asha."

I gave her a weak smile and looked around as she hauled

up the plastic ladder. A dark border of tall trees surrounded us, looming in the darkness. In the starlight, I could make out a small cabin about a hundred feet away. There were no lights on in the cabin, only a flickering television in an upper window. The only other light source came from the stars and a nearly full moon.

When Jazz closed the metal hatch with a reverberating thud, a convulsion of horror ran through my body. Jazz noticed, giving me a grim, tight smile.

"You're out now. Let's make sure they don't put you back in."

"They?" I asked. "Where are they?" I looked back toward the cabin. "Who are they?"

Jazz hunched down in front of me, hugging the rope ladder to her body and staring down at a spot between us. "They aren't here now, but they will be back soon. That's why you have to get out of here."

"Where is here?" I asked, already gathering my strength. I rubbed my legs to get ready to run.

Jazz shrugged. "Don't know for sure. Somewhere between Los Gatos and Santa Cruz. We drive on Highway Seventeen before we turn off onto a terrible twisting road that makes me feel sick. Then we turn on the gravel road that goes back and forth and back and forth through the trees until we get here."

All I could do was stare at her in disbelief.

"They call this place The Station," she continued, still focused on the spot between us. "Like a Cal Trans station? But nobody wants to buy a ticket here." She looked up at me then quickly looked down.

A new slice of fear cut through me.

"Who are they? Who else is here?"

"Auntie Ying brought me here. She calls the man Papa C.

He was waiting on the porch. He was so mad. They started fighting, screaming terrible words. I tried to cover my ears, but I could still hear them." She shot another look up at me, furrowed her eyebrows and spoke on a deep, gruff voice. "Too far, Ying, you've gone too far. This girl is no runaway. Her aunt is a damn cop. What were you thinking?"

Jazz's face smoothed out, her eyes looked above my head, pleading. "I had to bring her here, Papa C," she said in a perfect imitation of Ying's delicate voice. "She's a pretty little thing, a dancer. You can find a place for her on the circuit; I know you can."

"A place for me?" The words tasted rancid in my mouth. "What is the circuit?"

She shrugged. "I don't know, but it can't be good." She glared at my left shoulder. "I'm not retarded," she declared in a flat monotone voice. "They think autistic means retarded."

"I don't think that," I tell her.

"You maybe thought I was a little bit retarded when I made you sing that song." She smiled at my right elbow.

"Right now I think you are a freaking genius, Jasmine Brennan."

She scowled suddenly and threw a quick hunted look behind her left shoulder. "You have to get out of here. They'll be back soon. They never leave me here longer than seventy two minutes."

"How long ago did they leave?"

"They never leave less than thirty six minutes and never more than seventy two."

"Jazz—" I tried to break her train of thought, but she continued on.

"They think I'm retarded. They put baby shows on the television and tell me to stay put in the attic bedroom. They lock all the doors. They put two padlocks on this metal box. The lock on my door was so stupid, easy to break. They don't think I can find the top hatch door and the fire escape ladder and—"

"Jazz!" I yelled, breaking into her strange monologue. "How long have they been gone?"

She looked directly into my eyes then, her own eyes dry and steady but terrible.

"Where is VeeVee?"

I blinked at her, totally confused. She was at the press conference where the police chief announced Ivy's body had been found. I know she isn't stupid, quite the opposite. Then I remembered her drawing of her sister among leaves wearing a red dress. The way she looked at me when she handed it to me and said, "VeeVee wants you to have this."

"Jazz, you know your sister is dead but you're asking me this because ... can you still hear her sometimes?"

Jazz nodded solemnly. "Does that mean she is in hell?"

Her question jolted me. "No! Why would you think that?"

"Some people say ghosts are stuck here. Some people say there is purgatory. Some people say her ghost is forever doomed to suffer." Her words were spoken in the same flat monotone, but I could see her neck pulsing with tension.

"Those people are idiots," I snapped. My own heart was pounding wildly in my throat. We didn't have time for this conversation. We had to run, but she was still hugging the escape ladder to her body and staring down. I took a deep breath and tried to make my voice calm. "Jazz, this is a really big and complicated conversation. We need to get out of here now. We can talk about this when we're safe."

Her face collapsed in a sour grimace.

"Ivy is not in hell, I promise." I tried to touch her arm

but she jerked away, falling back on her butt without loosening her grip on the escape ladder. I held my hands up in surrender. "Listen to me. I don't have all the answers, but I know your sister wants us to get out of here. Maybe she's still here because she wants to save us from these people."

I look around at the dark towering trees.

"We have to get out of here!" My voice was shrill, trembling in panic. "Jazz, please! We have to go!"

With one hand, she reached into the pocket of her jacket and pulled out a small thin object. The blue glow from earlier lit up the space between us.

"Is that a phone?" I asked at the same time she said, "They've been gone thirty two minutes."

I grabbed the phone from her hand and instantly recognized the picture of Misty Copeland on the lock screen. It was my new iPhone. With shaking fingers, I entered my code and opened the dial screen.

"It won't work," Jazz told me. "No service here."

Ignoring her, I pressed 9-1-1 and send. I was shaking so violently, I had to grip the phone in both hands so I wouldn't drop it. The top of the screen clearly said "No Service," but I had a faint memory of my aunt telling me that even if one carrier has no service in an area, any carrier in that area will transmit a 911 call. I waited, breathless, until a "Call failed" message appeared. Tears of disappointment blurred my vision.

"No!" I screamed and dialed again.

"It won't work," Jazz told me, "I already tried." She stood up and tossed the rope ladder over the side. "You have to go now."

When I looked up, I saw she was looking past the small cabin into the distance. When I looked in the same direction, I saw a distant flash of light play across the trees that sloped away from us. "Oh my God, is that—?"

"Headlights," Jazz said calmly. "They're coming."

The rush of pure terror that hit me in response to those words threatened to make my skull explode.

Jazz sat back down and held the ladder. "Go now. Don't run toward the gravel drive." She pointed to the far side of the cabin where there was a break in the shadowy outline of the trees. "Go that way. It's a weedy trail. I think it goes toward Santa Cruz Highway."

I was already climbing down when her words hit me. I looked back at her. "You're coming with me."

"No," she said calmly. "You go. I can delay them and point them the wrong way. They think I'm retarded, remember?"

"No!" I screamed back at her. "They will hurt you. You have to come with me."

"They killed VeeVee. How much more can they hurt me?"

"More! A lot more!"

"Then maybe I'll be with VeeVee," she tells me calmly. "But you need to go now, Asha."

The sound of engines came to us through the distance.

"You have maybe three minutes now," Jazz said.

24

ON PURE INSTINCT, I FINISHED SCRAMBLING DOWN THE ladder, dimly aware it was much easier to navigate when braced against the side of the metal container. As soon as my feet touched the ground, I ran through the weedy clearing in the direction Jazz had pointed. Once I had the cabin between me and the gravel road, I turned around. Jazz's outline on top of the container was clearly visible in the moonlight.

"Jazz! Come with me," I screamed. She waved one arm above her head.

"Good-bye, Asha Kidwell. Good luck."

Headlights slashed through the trees, and the sound of the engine was getting closer. Feeling torn but desperate, I turned and ran away. I left her behind to deal with the monsters and I ran, telling myself I would run until I found a car or a signal on the phone. Then I would get help back to her.

The path through the trees was choked with tall weeds, but the moonlight penetrated the thin foliage above. Ignoring the bite and sting of rough ground and twigs under my bare feet, I ran. Years of ballet had taught me to ignore pain in my feet, and I was frantic to put as much distance as possible between me and the nightmare "station."

The path twisted into a dark tunnel of trees where the moonlight was no longer visible. Stopping to activate the flashlight app on my phone, I heard the sound of distant shouting. They had gotten to the cabin and would be coming after me. I tried to resume running, but quickly got tangled with some sort of vine. Forcing myself to stay calm, I picked my way through the mossy, vine-choked trees, wondering if they would be able to see the weak light on my phone from the cabin.

The trail opened again. Moonlight flooded this section of the path, so I sprinted forward while listening and looking over my shoulder for any signs of pursuit. Without warning, I slammed into a wall of cold acrid air that knocked me backward so hard I fell on my left side. A sickening crunch brought a wave of nausea over me. I bit down my own scream as a terrible howl shattered the night.

Standing over me was a dirty, disheveled girl about my own age. She howled again, making an inhuman sound. Icy knives seemed to slash at my skin as I looked up into her twisted, enraged face. Wild, glowing eyes stared back at me. Her supernatural howling raised every hair on my body.

When I tried to stand up, another icy blast knocked me back again.

"Please, let me go," I gasped.

Her incoherent, guttural howling started to shape into words. "Go back."

"I can't," I whispered, tears streaming down my face.

"They'll kill me."

"Killed me here. Kill you here. Go back."

Again, I tried to push forward and again she forced me back, stunning me with the force of her blow. I'd never encountered a ghost that could assault my senses in such a violent and physical way.

"Please," I begged, sobbing.

She dissolved, then suddenly appeared hunched on the ground next to me. "Look," she growled, pointing into the darkness ahead.

At first I didn't see anything, but then several thin lines started glowing in the darkness. Posts appeared. Then corkscrews of barbed wire twisted through the space between the lines. Everything glowed with a supernatural light, then disappeared again into darkness.

A large egg-shaped pinecone rolled across the path and bumped into my leg. Spellbound, I grabbed the pinecone with my right hand and threw it in the direction where I'd just seen the glowing fence. An explosion of electricity fried the pinecone. It would have fried me if the howling ghost hadn't stopped me.

"Go back," the girl whispered, disappearing into the night. "It's the only way out."

THAT'S THE POINT WHEN EVERYTHING GETS FUZZY. IT'S possible I snapped. It felt like I lost all hope of survival, and I didn't care. Everything drained out of me – all the terror, all the desperation, and all the hope. My brain went to this place, sort of like when I was sitting helpless and drugged in Ying's deathmobile. It was like *game over*. I'd lived my whole life surrounded by ghosts, and now I was going to be one.

Suddenly I was so pissed off. All I wanted to do was claw someone's eyes out before I died.

I remember getting back up onto my feet and cradling my damaged left arm against my body. I remember walking away from the path, away from the electric fence, away from the moonlight, not really sure where I was going. I remember walking like a zombie from tree to tree. I could have walked for hours or ten minutes, I'm not really sure. When two flashlight beams came down the path, I didn't even try very hard to hide. I just stood behind a tree watching them, listening. It was definitely the same Hispanic man from the library. He was wearing the same moth-eaten cardigan.

They weren't in a hurry, just walking casually and chatting in Spanish. My Spanish is practically non-existent despite good grades in class, but I'm pretty sure I heard the other guy say something about pollo frito. As in fried chicken. And I don't think he was talking about his dinner.

I held my breath as they walked right past me. Neither man so much as glanced in my direction. They just assumed they were going to find my dead, fried carcass on the electric fence.

It wasn't funny, yet I had to swallow back a giggle.

Then I heard the screaming.

BY SOME MIRACLE, I MADE IT BACK TO THE RING OF TREES that circled the cabin. My feet were bloody, my left arm was obviously broken, and I was beyond exhaustion. I felt grim and hopeless. Somewhere outside of my line of sight, someone was still screaming. Despite the sound, I couldn't make myself care. I just sort of accepted it, like 'yeah, of course there's screaming' and walked toward the noise. But what I saw in the clearing injected a new spark of energy that surged through me, filling my entire body with renewed hope.

The area was flooded with bright artificial light. Two vehicles were parked in the clearing; an ancient rusted Jeep Wrangler stood beside Ying's SUV. Both vehicles' headlights were on, pointed toward the container. Both vehicles were empty. The driver's side door of the Cadillac was open and a warning chime dinged endlessly as the engine continued to run.

I blinked and rubbed my eyes to make sure it wasn't an illusion. Instinct kicked in as another scream echoed in the night. Crouching down, I circled through the trees to get closer to the vehicles, my eyes locked on that open door. Where was Jazz? As soon as that thought popped into my head, I realized it was Ying who was screaming in her native language. I didn't understand a syllable of what she was saying, but I recognized the crazy in her voice. Underneath Ying's insane screaming, Jazz was chanting "No, no, no, no" over and over. Her voice was low and determined.

I scrambled behind the Jeep because it was closer and peeked around the fender. In the full blast of the headlights, Ying and Jazz were struggling, each holding on to the end of a long, thin, brightly striped object. The end Jazz was gripping with both hands had a wicked metal point. Streams of bright red blood were running down Jazz's face from a gash in her forehead.

In a flash, I realized Ying had been hitting her with an oversized umbrella. White-hot anger burned though my brain, taking over my body. I scrambled across the grass toward a black metal table with two bistro chairs arranged in front of the cabin. Without stopping to think, I grabbed one of the chairs with my good right arm and ran at the two figures locked in battle, swinging the chair for all I was worth at Ying's back.

I'm not sure who was more shocked when it connected, her or me. She went down hard. I just stood there, staring at her, sick to my stomach. I had never used violence against another person in my entire life. But Jazz didn't hesitate. She quickly let go of her end of the umbrella, picked up the key fob that had dropped out of Ying's hand, and pushed it toward me.

"Can you do this?" she asked calmly, as if she was asking me to open a jar of pickles.

I grabbed the key fob as Ying struggled to push herself back up, an inhuman gurgling growl convulsed her body.

"Run!" both Jazz and I screamed at each other.

Once inside the SUV, Jazz triggered the automatic locks and buckled her seatbelt while I stared, momentarily bewildered by the state-of-the-art dashboard. Zack taught me to drive an old Ford panel van with a manual transmission on backcountry roads the previous summer. It was totally illegal, but Zack insisted that every teenaged girl needed to know how to drive in case of emergency. This was definitely an emergency, but this overpriced Cadillac was nothing like the panel van. I was momentarily confused by the fact that I was holding a key fob, but the SUV was already running. In the place where I expected to see a key in the ignition, there was a button.

"We have to go now," Jazz informed me through gritted teeth just before a jolting crack slammed against her door.

Through the passenger window, I saw Ying raise the metal chair I'd just used to attack her with for another swing at the door. On pure instinct, I shoved the automatic gearshift into reverse and stomped on the gas pedal. We rocketed backward, away from Ying, the chair just glancing off the front fender. In startled reaction, I stomped on the brake just as we smacked into something solid.

"Maybe I should drive," Jazz said in her careful monotone.

"No, I've got this," I told her, more to soothe the worry on her face than out of any real conviction. "I can do this. I can do this. I can do this," I chanted as I put the car in drive and swerved away, kicking up dust and gravel.

"Slow down," Jazz ordered. "It's a very twisty road."

"I can do this," I barked back at her, risking a quick look in the rear-view mirror. I saw Ying opening the door to the Jeep.

"I think she's going to chase us," I told Jazz.

"Yes, of course she will," Jazz answered me. "So don't crash. That will make it very easy to catch us. And stop hyperventilating."

As soon as she said the word, I realized my breathing was wild and erratic. I struggled to navigate the first steep switchback of the driveway with one arm and I tried unsuccessfully to control my breathing, constantly checking the rearview mirror for the Jeep's headlights. By some miracle, the headlights didn't appear. I maneuvered through switchback turn after switchback turn, losing count and all sense of direction. We dinged a few trees and scraped the wooden retaining wall that ran along the passenger side several times.

After what seemed like hours, Jazz announced, "We're about halfway to the road now."

"Halfway?" I screamed at her in disbelief and pressed harder on the accelerator. Just then, a figure appeared in the middle of the road, causing me to swerve wildly. A large redwood tree loomed in front of us so I slammed on the brakes and swerved again, causing the SUV to skid sideways into a different tree.

"VeeVee, what are you doing?" Jazz yelled angrily.

Dazed, I looked over to see Ivy still standing in the middle of the road. She was smiling at us in a grim, satisfied way.

The rear window shattered, spraying the rear seats with glass. Both Jazz and I reflexively covered our heads. In the driver's side mirror I saw the man from the library, the man Jazz had called Papa C, holding a revolver and calmly taking aim for a second shot.

Again, I slammed the car into reverse and stomped on the gas. I saw him dive away much faster than I would have thought possible, but I also felt the car connect with something that wasn't a tree or a wall. Shuddering violently, I pushed the gear shift back to D. Then we were hurling forward again, taking the sharp turns way too fast. Jazz screamed at me over and over to slow down and watch out, but I could not do as she asked. It was like someone else was in control. We barreled down the gravel drive, careening side to side, sideswiping more trees than I could count, but I did not stop. I could not stop.

We skidded out of the private gravel drive onto a paved road, but there were no lights or cars in sight. So I kept driving. I drove right down the center of that twisting turning road, alternately hoping and dreading that another car would appear in the opposite direction. When I saw the signs pointing to Highway Seventeen, I should have slowed down. I should have stopped. But I pressed the accelerator to the floor.

The last thing I remember is suddenly emerging on the highway, blinding headlights, squealing brakes and the sound of tearing metal and broken glass.

25

Now

"And here we are," Vera says softly. "You're very lucky to be alive."

"Lucky?" I snap, bitterness flooding my throat. "You call this lucky?"

"Asha?" Vera asks with another puzzled tilt of her head. "You do want to be alive, don't you? You don't ... you haven't glamorized the other side, have you?"

I glare at her. "I'm not going to slice open my veins or swallow a bottle of pills if that's what you're asking."

"Well, that's good," Vera says in a calm, therapeutic voice, "but it's not what I asked. Do you think it would have been better, or maybe just easier, if you had died in that old railway container?"

"No!" I bark at her. "I wanted to get out of there and I wanted to save Jazz, but I didn't want—" My words are strangled off as I stare down, unwilling to finish the sentence.

Vera's fingers touch under my chin. "Asha, look at me."

I glare at her to ward off whatever load of it's-not-your-fault crap this woman is going to shovel at me.

"You did get out of there. Jazz is alive. You did save her."

"I know that." I grind out the words between clenched teeth. "I wanted to help Ivy. I wanted to stop those people from hurting more girls."

"And you did! You did all that, Asha. What you did—"

"And," I scream over Vera's words, "I wanted to do all that without killing anyone else!" I'm practically spitting the words at her.

The reaction on her face—first surprise quickly followed by pity—tells me everything.

"Asha, nothing about this situation is your fault."

"Yes, it is!" I shake my head when she tries to say more. "It is my fault. I drove that huge, nasty SUV into traffic without looking. I didn't think about anyone else. I didn't think!"

Vera's face clouds over in confusion.

"How many?" I ask, my voice shaking. My whole body is throbbing with shame. I am terrified of her answer, but I need to know.

Vera shakes her head, still confused. "How many what?"

"How many people died in the accident I caused?"

"Oh, no! No one died in the accident. Not one person."

"I drove that stupid SUV into traffic. I went the wrong way. There were headlights and horns and screeching metal …"

"Stop. Listen to me Asha." Vera places both her hands on my shoulders and looks into my eyes. "What you are saying is all true. But no one died on Highway Seventeen in the accident. In fact, the only person who was hurt was you. It was late at night. There were only two other cars on that road when you emerged. There were two cars coming toward you. Both drivers managed to get out of your way before you crashed into the concrete barrier that divides the highway. No one was hurt but you because your seatbelt wasn't securely fastened. A third car arrived after you crashed. Luckily, that car was driven by an off-duty paramedic who knew exactly how to manage the scene. And when Jazz told her the two of you were running away from men with guns, she was able to get police and emergency services there very quickly. Why are you shaking your head?"

"Don't lie to me."

"I'm not lying. Not one word I've said is untrue."

"Then tell me who I killed."

She steps back and looks at me carefully choosing her next words.

"Don't handle me," I tell her, suddenly feeling exhausted. "I saw it on your face when I said I didn't want to kill anybody. You looked at me all pitiful and sorry." None of this is Vera's fault, but I want to shake her. "Just tell me who died."

Vera reaches toward me as though she wants to put her hands on my shoulders again, but I shrink back from her and she stops herself.

"Why do I need an attorney? Who did I kill?"

Vera sits in her chair, laces her fingers together, and holds them in front of her chest as though in prayer. "All right. Let's get this over with. You said Ivy Brennan suddenly appeared during your escape down the gravel drive, causing you to swerve, correct?"

"Yes. Why?"

"That swerve caused you to skid and lose control of the vehicle for a few seconds ending with an impact?"

"Yes, on Jazz's side but Jazz is okay, right?"

"Yes," Vera agrees, "Jazz is just fine. She's in much better shape than you. In fact, she remembers that moment too. She clearly saw her sister appear, causing you to swerve and crash. She's very mad at her sister about it and also confused."

I lick my lips, thinking back. "Every time a ghost has redirected me, even violently, it was for my own good. Like in the woods, that poor thing at the electric fence."

"Is that what happened this time?"

"I don't know." I press my back to the pillow and think. "Maybe. Maybe she slowed us down so I didn't kill another driver on the highway. Or maybe that bullet would have killed one of us if she hadn't intervened." I stop when I see the impatience in Vera's expression.

"You remember what she was wearing, don't you?" Vera asks. "Because Jazz remembers very clearly what her sister was wearing when she caused you to swerve."

The tone of her voice is coaxing, pulling me along, asking me to see something that is plainly obvious. I clamp my eyes shut and remember the view through the windshield. Harsh, blue-white halogen headlights illuminating the twisting ribbon of gravel, the weeds and tree branches whipping past. The split second when Ivy appeared out of nowhere causing me to jerk the wheel. My eyes snap open.

"Red dress," I whisper. "She was wearing a long red dress and she was surrounded by tangled branches. Just like—"

"Just like this." Vera removes a folded, tattered sheet of paper from her messenger bag and places it in my hands.

I open it, knowing exactly what I will find and yet still anxious to see the confirmation. Ivy stares back at me from the intricate drawing her grieving sister drew a few days earlier. The red dress. The complex snarl of tangled leaves and branches surrounding her. The hint of a smile on her lips now seems a bit smug. I touch two fingers to the grooves in the paper where Jazz drew her sister's mass of curly blonde hair.

"Just exactly like this," I agree. We sit in silence as I absorb everything, trying to put words to the thing I'm starting to understand.

"Nü Gui," I whisper the words. And yet, no. That's not quite correct. "Wait, Ivy can't be a true Nü Gui," I tell Vera, shaking my head to shake off the dark knowledge bubbling under the surface of our conversation. "She didn't put on a red dress and commit suicide to take revenge on some rapist. She's not a vampire succubus thing. She was a murder victim. Ivy is the victim."

"Yes, Ivy Brennan was an innocent victim. Of course she was," Vera agrees, her tone gentle. "Don't get too caught up in the details. The legend of the Nü Gui is a simple, straightforward Chinese folktale about ultimate justice that's been all but ruined by misogynist garbage and modern cinema. Did you know there's also a modern twist on the folktale? An urban legend that started with a tabloid story?"

"Yes, I know the story. The family of a murdered girl buries the victim in a red dress hoping she'll come back as a Nü Gui and murder her murderer."

"Murder her murderer? That's an interesting turn of phrase. Why isn't that justice? Doesn't a woman have the right to defend herself?"

"My father taught me there's a huge difference between self-defense and revenge."

"Did he?"

"Yes, and he also taught me hauntings are never about revenge."

"Good for him," Vera says without a trace of irony. "And

did he also teach you that women have the power to defend others? Your cousin LaShawna carries a gun. She's trained and absolutely willing to use deadly force if it's necessary, isn't she?"

"Again," I say, feeling annoyed but oddly detached, as though we are debating a hot political topic on television, "deadly force is supposed to be a last resort." A voice in my head is telling me to stop this. Cut to the chase. I fold my hands in my lap and stare deadpan into Vera's eyes.

"We were getting away," I tell her. To my mind, it is a blunt, brutal statement of fact that sums up the entire case against me.

In response, Vera shrugs one shoulder without breaking eye contact.

"Unlike that 'poor thing' at the electric razor-wire fence. Unlike a long list of other girls locked up in The Station before you." Vera takes a deep breath before continuing in a softer tone. "Jazz heard Ying tell Papa C he could find a place for you on the Circuit, isn't that what you told me? Do you know what that means?"

"We were getting away," I repeat, exhausted.

"This is very important, Asha. I can't let you hide from it. What do you think it means to be put on the Circuit?"

"Prostitution." My mouth forms the word but it's barely audible, even to my own ears.

"What did you say? Speak up."

Gritting my teeth, I force myself to speak the words clearly. "Ying was asking Papa C to take me away to ... somewhere and force me to ... to become a prostitute ... a sex slave."

Vera's face softens again. "That's right. That's exactly right. These are nasty, vicious people, Asha. Papa C's real name is Mateo Benitez. Mr. Benitez is a very wealthy man.

Don't let his hangdog face and tattered clothes fool you. That old man is worth millions, and he made those millions destroying lives. I spoke with someone on the human trafficking task force based in San Francisco. They don't know exactly how many people he's enslaved or murdered, but they estimate his victims number over three hundred. Over three hundred living, breathing, innocent people, Asha!"

The tightness in my chest loosens up a tiny bit. "Okay, got it. Papa C was a very bad man. And he was shooting at us when I reversed and hit him, so that was justified. That's what you are trying to say, right?"

"Absolutely justified." Vera nods briskly. "Too bad he only has a broken leg, four bruised ribs, and a concussion. He was spewing some garbage about a lawsuit when they first brought him into the emergency room, but a brief conversation with the FBI agent in charge of this investigation shut him right up."

"He isn't dead? Then that means ... the other guy? The one who said 'pollo frito' when they were looking for my dead body in the woods?"

"Oh, that guy," Vera says airily, waving one hand as though shooing away a fly. "Probably one of Papa C's lieutenants. He must have hightailed it out of there when everything went wrong. They haven't found any sign of the third accomplice. They probably never will."

"So then ... I don't get it."

Vera stares back at me with a look of exasperation on her face. "I think you do. You just told me you know the story of the Nü Gui; you fully understand the symbolism of the red dress. And still, you refuse to see it. Who murdered Ivy?"

"Ying?" I ask in disbelief. "You're saying Ivy caused that SUV to swerve and somehow we managed to kill Ying?"

"Yes."

That one word echoes like a gong in my head over and over. *Yes, yes, yes.* Yes, I have killed Ying Brennan. Yes, I am a killer. Yes, just yes. I wait for the knowledge to crash in, to burn my body down to a single point of cinder. But what I feel is a weird sense of calm.

A stream of words rushes out of Vera's mouth as she tries to dilute the horror behind what she has just told me, but her reassurances are like gnats swarming around my head – annoying and essentially useless.

"We left her behind. At the cabin." I am stating a fact, looking for how all the details fall together. I'm not arguing with Vera. I am simply thunder-struck. "How did she get down there?"

"There was a shortcut, a footpath that ran along one side of the twisting gravel drive. It's the same path Papa C used to get there and take a shot at you. Apparently, he couldn't run as quickly as Ying. She got to that curve in the road first. The investigators think she was leaning against a redwood tree to catch her breath. When you swerved and skidded, Ying Brennan was crushed between the tree and the car."

Crushed. It's a vile, disgusting word.

I squeeze my eyes shut and lie back waiting for some sense of regret or horror to wash over me. But still, I feel nothing more than acceptance; a sensation like the final jigsaw puzzle piece clicking into place. And perhaps a tiny flicker of curiosity over my own acceptance. Will I ever feel any remorse or regret over the death of Ying Brennan? Does this mean I have become a monster like Ying herself?

"Asha, this isn't your fault."

"Isn't it?" I ask her. "Whose fault is it then? I mean, aside from Ying and Papa C and the universe handing them back what they dished out, is there really no one else to blame? Were we all stupid puppets dancing on the end of strings?"

Vera Birch twists one side of her mouth into a sly, lopsided smile. "That, my dear girl, is an excellent question. In fact, you might even say that's the million-dollar question. Is there anyone else who might be at fault for this whole mess?"

"What about Uncle David?"

"All right, yes. David Brennan is a pathetic, disgusting excuse for a man." Vera says these words with a breezy dismissal that makes me grit my teeth. "Don't worry; his days of abusing little girls are over. I promise you that. But that isn't the million-dollar question." Vera leans forward with a ferocious glint in her eyes. "Can you think of anyone else who might be at fault for what happened to you and Jazz Brennan?"

Mai's round smiling face pops into my mind, her eyes clouded with sadness. "I don't believe Mai Tsien knew what Ying was doing," I state with conviction.

"No, she didn't know exactly what Ying was doing, but she suspected something was very wrong in that household. That's why she originally brought Ying to see your mother during the first forty-eight hours of Ivy's disappearance. That's why she kept asking LaShawna, your mother, and even you what was happening with the case. Which brings us closer to the million-dollar question, but we're still not there."

A wave of fierce heat penetrates the sense of acceptance I've been feeling since learning of Ying's death.

My mother's voice from the emergency room comes back to me then. *Don't say a word. Keep your mouth shut.*

"Why is this a million-dollar question?" I ask Vera.

Vera eyes suddenly seem hungry, even a bit dangerous, so I focus on keeping my expression flat and only mildly curious. After a few moments of uneasy silence, Vera sighs and shakes her head, breaking the spell.

"Deep down, I think you know the answer to that question. Or else you can certainly figure it out. You're a very smart girl, and a mind is a terrible thing to waste."

Vera stands up, suddenly very professional and brisk, and replaces the loose items in her messenger bag before hoisting the strap on one shoulder and giving me another appraising look. "Is the great and famous Xia Celeste really another garden-variety psychic fraud? Is she a talented performer with a gift for telling people what they want to hear? Or, if she ever had the ability to hear the dead, how did she lose it? Does she really have some mystic, unprecedented power to filter out inconvenient ghosts? Or is there some other reason why Xia Celeste stopped sharing the secrets whispered to her from beyond the grave? In short, Asha, I think you need to ask yourself what your mother really knew about this whole ugly mess when she posted those comments online and pulled you into the middle of it."

I blink up at her, startled by this short passionate tirade. "You don't like my mother very much, do you? And yet, it seemed like you were on the same side when you arrived in the emergency room."

Vera offers another sly, half-smile. "Your mother knows when to make allegiances that are in her own best interest, and she has a long history of accepting free gifts." She leans forward and gives my right elbow a light squeeze. "I'm your lawyer, Asha. I represent you. Not your mother. None of this mess is your fault. No matter what, please try to remember that. But do think about what I've asked you. Think about that moment when you discovered Ivy's ghost begging for justice while your mother told LaShawna the missing girl was alive and located near a body of water."

"I can't stop thinking about it," I whisper.

"What would have happened if you didn't intervene?"

I shake my head, unable to answer. I don't know what would have happened; can't even fathom the alternate possibilities.

"Think about what you saw in her bank account," Vera continues. "Who has been paying Xia large sums of cash? And why are they paying her? Are they paying to receive messages from beyond the grave, or to silence the dead?"

We are locked in silence for several minutes as I stare at the far wall struggling to come up with something to say, and Vera stands over me waiting. Finally, she retreats in silence. There's a gentle snick when the door closes behind my lawyer.

I'm alone with the echo of Vera's accusations ringing in my head. Every inch of my skin is boiling with shame.

"I don't know what I'm doing." The words blaze out of my throat as I stare up at the ceiling. "What am I supposed to do?"

Cool green light pours over my body.

Pay attention. Speak up. Don't look away.

I squeeze my eyes shut to stem the flow of hot tears.

"Ivy? Is that you?"

Pressure shifts the hospital bed as though another body has settled next to mine. Bands of gentle, cooling pressure entwine with my arms and legs. Fingers of icy air comb through my sweaty coils of heavy hair. A feathery light kiss touches the soft spot between my earlobe and jaw.

I know you. I trust you. I love you.

26

AFTER

ONE WEEK LATER, I AM SITTING IN A LAWN CHAIR WATCHING A
small army of movers in crisp white coveralls swarm over
our townhome. It is fascinating to watch these efficient
strangers pack up our lives in color-coded boxes and carry
them up the metal ramp into the moving truck parked in
front of our door. My chair has been carefully arranged in
the square of green grass beside our unit so I can watch the
movers work without actually looking into the interior
space where most of our worldly possessions are being orga-
nized for the move back to Moonville, Ohio. I cannot make
myself stare into the cavernous maw of the truck's trailer
without shuddering in revulsion, even though its interior is
sparkling clean with no sign of an air mattress or gritty dirt
on the floor.

My mother noticed my discomfort when the back door
of the truck rolled open and quickly set up this outdoor
seating arrangement to make my wait more comfortable.

She even pressed a glass of iced tea into my right hand before she took our moving coordinator on another quick tour of the condo. Xia has been doing quite a bit of noticing me lately and quite a bit of fluttering around, acting like a caring mother should act with a fragile, injured daughter. She even manages to behave well when there is no audience to impress and no cameras around. It's a nice change, but I'm not stupid. This current incarnation of Xia Celeste is an act, a part she'll enjoy playing until she screws up our lives again.

Right now Xia is flying high on the wings of victory, but everybody knows it won't last.

I stare at the sweating glass in my hand as though searching the amber liquid for a glimpse of the new life waiting for us back in Ohio. It certainly won't be the same life we left behind eight months ago. According to Xia, we're returning to Moonville like royalty, like conquering heroes after a successful campaign. Like celebrities casting a glamorous new light on a dying small town. I feel more like a virus under a microscope than any of the glorious pictures she keeps painting, but I've made my decision. There's no turning back now. The contracts have been signed.

Lights, camera, action.

We are going back to Moonville to renovate and restore the historic Quinn Mansion while also investigating the many spirits, legends, and unsolved mysteries that make the Quinn Estate the most haunted property in North America.

That was my mother's big surprise, her next big thing.

She's been working on this deal for months. At the same time I was being kidnapped and held prisoner, my mother was meeting with a massive assortment of lawyers, agents, and accountants negotiating every aspect of the contract for our new reality television series – *Moonville Mediums.* Note the plural. As in more than one. Guess who gets to be my mother's Number Two?

Xia says the production company pitched the series to the network as *This Old House* meets *Psychic Detectives*.

"Isn't it brilliant?" she asks me. "Won't this be fun?"

She doesn't require any answer, but occasionally I do make the effort by molding my face into a smile and forcing a little bit of awe into my voice when I say, "I can't believe this is our lives." It's not exactly a lie.

It turns out Ivy's murder, my abduction, the wild escape driving the wrong way on a California highway, and all the media coverage around the case is pure marketing gold for the new show. Who would have believed it?

Yes, I think I fully understand Vera Birch's hints and questions at the end of our private interview. Vera was right; I'm a smart girl and it didn't take a brain trust to deduce her "million-dollar question." My mother has been accepting large sums of money from her clients, sometimes to expose the truth and sometimes to keep the truth hidden. I know this. And I also know something Vera doesn't realize. Xia has already paid a terrible price for her crimes. The only thing she ever wanted to be was a dazzling psychic detective. Somewhere on this journey, she poisoned her own gift.

But Xia Celeste isn't exactly stupid, either. While I was exposing my soul to Vera in the privacy of my hospital room, my mother hosted a press conference where she tearfully handed over a large donation check to The Polaris Foundation. The check amount was exactly fifty thousand dollars — the reward money Ying and David Brennan originally offered to solve Ivy's disappearance and later, her murder. Ying paid the reward to my mother on the day I encountered Jazz in Mai Tsien's living room. Xia swears she believed the check was an honest reward for leading the police to

Ivy's body and securing her assistance in exposing Daved Brennan as the murderer.

When one reporter asked if she felt any suspicions about Ying's part in the murder at the time, she pressed her hand to her ample chest and looked at the other woman in horror.

"That evil little woman was my client. I thought she was a victim, but the whole time she was using me. Then she attacked my innocent daughter. Can you imagine?"

Xia has the genetic gift of appearing heartbreakingly beautiful while crying. Happy or sad, exuberant or horrified, playing mystic or acting mundane—the cameras love my mother. I'm sure the production company will find a way to use footage from that press conference in the series.

The problem with Vera is that she overestimates the power of truth, justice, and all that crap which means she underestimates my mother. I will never underestimate Xia Celeste again. I'm grateful to Vera for forcing me to face the truth. There's no telling how long I would have let myself ignore those mystery payments in her bank account. But this isn't an issue for the police or for family court. I can't abandon my mother now. Without my ability to back her up, she will create even bigger messes and hurt more people.

I have to stop her; no one else can do it.

Several times over the past week, I've remembered what my father used to say every time Xia started celebrating her next big thing.

"Be careful, Shirl," he used to warn in a soft, sad voice. "Someday the universe is going to hand you everything you think you want, and you're going to figure out the true meaning of misery." He never said it in a spiteful way; my father doesn't have a mean bone in his body.

Thinking of my sweet, shy, troubled father now sends a quick jolt of anxiety through my core.

Another side effect of this incredible media circus that has become my new life is that my grandfather has finally admitted his son is missing. Daddy isn't sitting in a private rehab facility. He isn't on a motorcycle pilgrimage or some weird spiritualist mission overseas. Nathaniel Marcus Kidwell is officially missing. It's one more freakish aspect of this case that keeps the online amateur sleuths and conspiracy theorists posting new and ever crazier theories.

Daddy is missing, but he isn't dead. He promised he would come back to me one way or another. I know what that means now. If he were dead, he'd have come to me. For now I'm stuck in limbo, waiting.

Despite her disappointment in my refusal to tell the police about my mother's bank records, Vera Birch has proven herself to be an incredibly effective advocate. Not just for me, but also for Jasmine Brennan. The police detectives and prosecuting attorney who recorded our official statements were like putty in her hands. One of the officers, a short stocky bald-headed man who reminded me of Mr. Clean, cried during my statement and patted my hand saying, "I have a daughter your age."

A familiar teal Rodeo pulls up to the temporary police barricade at the entrance to our parking lot. I watch as LaShawna flashes her badge and exchanges some words with the officer, gesturing backward with her thumb and holding up three fingers. Officer Ortiz nods and flashes her his megawatt smile before opening the manual wooden gate. We're on a first name basis with all of our special duty protection officers. Officer Ortiz has three daughters, stays up late to watch international soccer, and looks like he belongs in a toothpaste commercial.

LaShawna parks her car next to my lawn chair and leans out her car window. "Quite a change from moving out here, huh?" She's pointing at the small army of movers.

I feel myself relax a bit. She sounds like she's in a more upbeat mood today, which is a relief. Dealing with LaShawna's guilt over what happened has become a burden. She alternates between horrendous despair over misjudging Ying, frustration over not preventing the abduction, and fury with my mother. Even Kota seems to feel ashamed and dejected every time I see him. It is exhausting.

While LaShawna is getting Kota out of his travel crate, a second car pulls up next to the Rodeo. This car is a light green Prius driven by my lawyer. Jazz is sitting in the passenger seat waving at me energetically. The sight of her makes me smile, but I'm also a bit surprised. Her wild tangle of hair has been tamed into two chunky French braids that twist into a pretty bun at the nape of her neck. I touch my own hair that Xia helped me pull into a smooth bun this morning, then point at her.

"I like the new style," I tell her warmly as she marches up to my chair. An unpleasant scene flashes in my mind like a memory–Jazz screaming and twisting away as someone tries to pull a comb through her hair–and I have to clamp my teeth together not to shudder.

This version of Jazz gives me a satisfied smile. "I did it myself. Laura taught me." Laura is a friend of Vera Birch and Jazz's foster mother. I like Laura very much. She's a pale, quiet, unassuming woman with an air of gentle competence. I look behind Jazz, but I don't see her.

"Where is Laura?" I ask.

"She's coming in the other car." Jazz shrugs and pulls up a lawn chair next to mine. I'm momentarily distracted by

Vera. She has her messenger bag on one shoulder and a grim, business-like look on her face as she greets LaShawna.

"Uh oh," I say under my breath. "Looks like Vera has a bug up her butt."

Jazz snorts out a laugh. "She does and you're going to hear about it. Do you think VeeVee would like this dress?"

I look back at Jazz and carefully look over her outfit as she squirms and tugs at her sleeves. She's wearing a cornflower blue dress that matches her eyes with white embroidered flowers down one side. She looks absolutely lovely, pretty enough to make my heart ache, but I know she won't appreciate any gushing.

"Well, it's not red," I say, drawing another snort out of her. "I can't speak for Ivy, but I think you look perfect. Do you feel comfortable?"

She gives me a scornful look. "No."

"Is there anything you could wear today that would make you feel comfortable?"

My question gets a genuine smile, and I feel like I just hit the target and won a prize. "Probably not," she answers ruefully. "I hate cameras."

A shadow falls over my chair, and I look up to see Vera frowning down at me. "Good morning, Asha," she greets me in a brisk voice.

"Good morning, Vera. You look like you've swallowed a toad."

The thing is, I like Vera Birch. Not only do I like her, but I really admire her. Watching Vera handle me, the police, the press, and most especially my mother over the past week has ignited a deep respect for the way she has married her gift and her profession. In fact, I've even started to wonder if I could someday do what Vera does. The idea of being a lawyer who specializes in clients from beyond the grave seems like such a better way of managing the difficult messages. After all, I can't go around running down murderers the rest of my life. And despite the lies I'm currently telling my mother, I have absolutely no interest in the "family business" she wants to build on camera.

But Vera is deeply disappointed in me, and she can't seem to hide it. No matter how many times I tell her I have to deal with my mother my own way, she thinks I'm still hiding from the truth. Maybe some day, if I win this battle and stop my mother's idiocy, I'll be able to make peace with Vera. But not yet. Not now.

"We have a few minutes before the other car arrives and we need to head out. I need to talk with you in private before Ivy's memorial service. Do you need help getting inside?"

She nods toward the condo. I'm still a bit stiff and sore, but I refuse any assistance and follow her into the house. Once inside, we can hear my mother down in her office giving orders to someone. Without pausing, Vera leads me through the kitchen area and into the tiny laundry room tucked behind the refrigerator. I'm a bit surprised, but I follow her into the cramped space.

When she shuts the door, I lean against the back wall and grab my cast with my good arm. "Cozy," I tell her.

"Private," she answers and pulls a yellow folder out of her bag, placing it on the top of the clothes dryer before twisting the dial and pressing start. The machine rumbles to life noisily. "I would have liked to have this conversation in my office, but your mother keeps finding excuses as to why she can't possibly take the time to drive you into the city to see me."

"Sorry about that."

"When are you going to stop apologizing for her?"

"I don't know. Probably when you stop making me feel like I need to apologize for her."

Vera tips her head back and takes a deep breath. "You know," she tells the ceiling, "I could still make a case for removing you from her custody." She looks down at me and shakes her head. "Even without your cooperation, I could do it. LaShawna would back me up and your grandfather—"

"Please don't do that, Vera," I interrupt and place a hand on her wrist. "I know what I'm doing. We're going home, back to Moonville. Xia will have her big break. I know the cameras will be annoying, but I'll have my dance classes and my grandfather and my stepbrother and it's not like here. Moonville is a small town where everyone knows everyone else's business. I love the Quinn Estate; I've always loved it. And now we'll get to live there. Will you please let this drop?"

When she looks at me with the same sad, empathetic expression she used to pull my story out of me in the hospital, I know I've won.

"There are conditions in your contract. Your mother has been provided with a very clearly worded letter that explains the terms of your contract, but she will try to ignore them. I'm going to go over them with you. If I find out these terms are not being honored, I will take action. Do you hear me, Asha?"

"Terms? What contract?"

"We're going over them right now. If you really want to stay in your mother's custody, I recommend you make sure these conditions are met."

As Vera proceeds to efficiently rattle through the special terms she's added to my contract with the production company, I am more and more taken aback. After one week, no, actually after one long, grueling day of confessions, this woman seems to know me better than either of my parents ever bothered to try. To start, it's a huge relief to know I am supposed to be on camera no longer than four hours on any given day and limited to two hours on school days. Regarding school, the contract states I must complete my freshman year with special tutors in a private classroom that will be a camera free zone. I will return to dance classes at my old studio (contingent on doctor approval) three days a week, and I will also have access to a private studio to practice dance one hour every day. Again, all dance sessions are to be camera free unless I am giving a public performance. In addition, I am to be allowed free access to the Warner residence, my old bedroom there, and, if I so desire, I will be welcome to volunteer with light animal care duties under adult supervision.

"Yes! I so desire," I blurt out, tears prickling my eyes.

Vera stops and looks at me sharply. "Your mother may not remove you from dance classes against your will. From what I heard, she likes to threaten you with that, but it's an empty threat. And she may not stop you from visiting and volunteering at the veterinary clinic. However, you are still responsible for taking your limited part in the production. You will be scheduled for some camera time, and you need to be where you are supposed to be on time. Do you understand?"

At first I nod automatically, but then stop and shake my head. "I mean, is all that really legal and binding and everything?" I wave my hand toward her yellow folder and her papers. "The dance and the volunteering with pets at the clinic. Can you really enforce all that?"

Vera gives me one of her wry smiles, pushing her glasses up on her head. "There's more than one interested party involved in the terms of this new television production. You haven't forgotten our conversation regarding the Quinn Family Trust and the QFWC Foundation?"

"Wait, what?" I ask. "What are you saying?"

Vera chuckles. "You didn't think your mother's project could move forward without the approval of the board of trustees, did you? Doctor Warner sits on the board, and your grandfather has spoken to the board on your behalf. To put in bluntly, the current board is supporting your welfare as fiercely as it protects the Quinn Estate."

"My grandfather isn't on the Quinn Board of Trustees," I tell her, amused. The idea of my crusty grandfather sitting in a stuffy boardroom makes me laugh. "He's more like a volunteer groundskeeper."

Vera pops her glasses back on her nose and fiddles with the papers in her folder. "He's got some influence," she says with a dismissive shrug. "Anyway," Vera looks at me while tapping the stack of papers together, "without the Quinn Estate there is no television show. And the Quinn Board of Trustees will support our list of conditions to ensure your well-being. Be prepared. The Quinn Trust has its own list of rules, Asha, many many pages of rules. Both your mother and you will get your own personal copies of their guidelines and conditions, probably laminated and indexed in a three-ring binder. You'll be required to attend an educational session, maybe more than one. And every single change your mother proposes on that property will have to be reviewed and approved by the board." Vera snaps her folder closed and shoves it back into her bag with some force. "I think your mother has some fantasy of floating around the property calling out messages from Violet Quinn, tearing out access ramps and spending thousands of dollars of the Trust's money on crystal chandeliers and hand painted Victorian wallpapers."

I giggle. That is pretty close to Xia's fantasy.

"She's going to have a rude awakening," Vera tells me.

"I'm counting on it," I tell her.

Another worried look crosses Vera's face. She's about to say something else when the dryer buzzes loudly and stops, breaking the moment.

"We'd better get going," I say lightly. "We don't want to be late for Ivy's memorial service."

When we re-emerge from the condo, Xia is standing on the tiny front porch with a tight, false smile plastered on her perfectly made up face. Todd is hovering by her right elbow acting solicitous. There's a new car in the parking lot parked next to Vera's Prius – a dented and rusted old panel van I would recognize anywhere. Just like the tall, lanky guy leaning against the front fender, his surfer-blonde mop of hair windblown into a mess. As soon as he spots me, he stands tall with his hands on his hips and says, "Hey, Kid!"

"Zack!"

Tears that threatened earlier start flooding down my cheeks. My mother snaps something about not making a messy scene and Vera barks at her to back off, but I don't care. I'm too busy stumbling down the stairs and plowing into my big goofy stepbrother like a bulldozer. He absorbs the impact with ease, enfolding me in a bear hug.

"Heard a rumor you're coming home," he says in my ear. "Need a ride?"

AFTERWORD

Have you ever dropped a dollar in the jar to show appreciation for a street musician? Or attended a fundraiser to support "The Arts" in your community?

Don't worry, I'm *not* asking for money.

Honest reader reviews are the most important commodity in any fiction author's world. Positive reviews are more precious than platinum to a creative weirdo who makes up stories and sends them out into the universe.

I'd love to see your honest review on Amazon:

www.amazon.com/dp/B0794SY22X

It doesn't have to be a long, thoughtful essay (unless that's what you *want* to write). Forget those painful, horrible, awful book reports from school days. Just two sentences, or even two thoughtful words, would be greatly appreciated!

Also, this is not the end of Asha's story. It's more like her origin story. Because this girl is a superhero ... even if she doesn't wear spandex, a mask or a cape. In *Unhaunted*, Asha discovered that which makes her weird, also makes her powerful. Will she escape the shadow of her mother's lies and claim her place in the light? Find out in *Unbroken*, to be released in 2019.

Keep reading for a free preview.

Would you like to learn more about the mysterious Quinn family, experience more bewildering messages from beyond the grave, discover strange inheritances, and dive into new White Crow Mysteries ... including what happens to Asha, Xia, and Zack when they return to the magical town of Moonville, Ohio?

- Sign up to receive exclusive ghost stories, White Crow updates, and free eBooks at www.trishaslay.com
- Follow me on Facebook (www.facebook.com/TrishaSlayAuthor) to learn about upcoming releases, events and promotions.

Happy Hauntings,
Trisha Slay

SNEAK PREVIEW

Unbroken

By Trisha Slay

Lucy Sloan isn't afraid of ghosts. It's dealing with the living that gives her nightmares.

Coming Soon

PREVIEW - CHAPTER 1

Annabelle - Moonville, Ohio 1996

"Come on outside, Lucy Lulu. Come play with me in the moonlight."

Her whispers would echo from the shadow of our dogwood trees, and I would go. Every time I would go. Even though it was forbidden ... and so dangerous. Still, I'd sneak out of the house in the dark of night to skip through the woods with my ghostly friend, her laughter stirring the leaves around us.

She'd weave violets in my hair or teach me wild, frenetic dances with names like "Black Bottom" or "Snake Hips" until we collapsed on the grass giggling. On the hottest summer nights we'd splash in the lazy current of Queer Creek by the light of the moon. Sometimes we'd tiptoe across the black asphalt of the state highway to play hide and seek among the crumbling brick furnaces. Even after Grandmother caught me with my feet in the kitchen sink washing away the telltale grass stains and Grandpa Max padlocked the cellar door, even then, I still found new ways to escape.

The first visit came on a heavy, heat-soaked night in the summer of 1996. I remember that first night vividly, though our later adventures get twisted and tangled up in my mind. Grandpa Max had taken me to the Moonville Drive-In to see *Dragonheart* for the third time, and my brain wouldn't stop boiling with visions of friendly dragons and sword fights. After the echoes of *The Tonight Show* ended and my grandparents shut their bedroom door, I crept out of bed to search the night sky for signs of spaceships from other worlds.

"Hey, little Lucy! Why don't you come outside and play?"

That first time, I dropped down to the floor. My lungs wouldn't fill with air, and my ears were pulsing with the sound of my own heartbeat.

Don't look at the Shadows, Lucy. Don't ever talk to them.

"You hiding?" she asked. Her bubbling laughter filled the empty space around me.

Even though it was not the laughter of a living child, the sound was pure fun. Somehow her laughter made it possible to fill my lungs with breath. Fingers crossed, I stood up and walked to the window sill. At every step, I expected some horror to engulf me, but nothing happened.

Never, ever let them know you can hear their voices.

Climbing up on the window seat, I pressed my head against the aluminum screen and looked down on our back lawn. There she was, right below my window, a shade among shadows. In later years, she wouldn't come that close, but that first night she waited for me just outside the yellow puddle of light leaking from our kitchen window.

"There you are!" She started spinning in slow circles with her arms stretched out wide. "Now come on and play. I've got something to show you."

I'd seen her many times before that night, but I didn't know her name. Her blue-gray dress and beribboned braids were familiar to me, though I'd only seen them briefly when she skipped past me on the walking paths that wove through our woods, or when she balanced precariously on the railroad trestle over the creek.

Ignore the Shadows, or they will suck you in.

"Can you hear me?" I whispered to her.

She stopped circling long enough to plant both hands on her hips. "I hear lots of things," she answered, tilting her chin to look up at me.

They ruin everyone and everything they touch.

"I can't come out and play with you," I explained, the regret in my voice very real.

"Oh, yes you can," she answered, pointing to the cellar door that led to our basement, "if you really want to." Having issued her dare, she stretched out her arms again and started circling the other way.

For a few moments, I was frozen in place as the idea she'd planted grew and blossomed into something wild and wonderful.

Your mother refused to ignore the Shadows. Look what happened.

"Come on then," the shadow girl chimed, still circling. "Come out or I'll go away and find some other friend to play."

There might be worse threats to unleash on a six-year-old orphan, but the thought of being left behind seemed like the worst possible thing she could do to me.

"All right," I whispered urgently. "I'll try."

As I carefully inched open my bedroom door, she continued singing her challenge out on the lawn.

"Try, try, try to come out and play. Try really hard or I'll go away, away, away."

Once I had eased my bedroom door open wide enough to slip through, I tip-toed the ten or twelve feet to the back kitchen stairs. My eyes remained glued to my grandparents' bedroom door, looming ominously at the opposite end of the second floor hallway, as I squatted on the top step. Slowly and carefully, balancing my heels and palms on the edges, I lowered myself step by step down toward the kitchen. The ordinary groan of the fourth step seemed so loud that I pressed my right palm to my lips and waited for the sound of footsteps rushing down the hall. When none came, I continued down with a little more confidence.

Once in the kitchen, my buoyancy grew even more and I didn't bother to tip-toe across the black and white checker-board floor to the basement door tucked beside our massive humming Frigidaire. Stretching up, I slid back the iron industrial bolt with the tips of my fingers and the door obliged by swinging inward smoothly, without a sound. From there it was ridiculously easy to creep down a second set of stairs, through the swinging door that separated the laundry room from the rest of the basement, then up the bare wooden steps to press both hands upward against the cellar door.

It took every scrap of my strength to lift that door high over my head, step onto the grass, then twist around to lower it back into place. And I was more than a little peeved that the other girl, now standing in the shadow of our cherry tree, only watched me struggle with it. But once the door was closed and I had scanned the windows above to be sure I had really escaped, the exhilaration was indescribable.

A prisoner walking away from a life sentence could not

have felt giddier. First I threw my arms out and tried a few spinning circles in a revved up imitation of the other girl. When I got dizzy, I kept my arms wide and ran in crazy loops through the yard. My new playmate's intoxicating laughter rang out loud and clear, but I still didn't dare to make any noise of my own. I knew all too well how easily my Grandmother could hear me from the house. So, instead of noise, I threw myself into leaping arabesque movements in my best imitation of an Olympic gymnast.

The other girl clapped, then pointed to a spot between two sugar maple trees at the edge of my grandmother's garden before running ahead of me to lead the way. Without a second of hesitation, drunk on all this unfamiliar freedom, I followed her right into those woods.

Although the trees closed in around us, the full moonlight was so powerful that it found its way through the leafy canopy overhead to illuminate everything in a greenish silver glow. The shelter of the woods gave me enough security to talk.

"So where are we going?" I asked.

The girl, ahead of me on the path, twisted around and pressed a finger to her lips.

"Is someone here?" I whispered, swiveling my head around to look at the darkened woods.

All I could see were the silver outlines of the surrounding trees. The woods were alive with a cacophony of sounds—crickets, cicadas, frogs and so many other creatures I couldn't name—though none of it sounded human.

The girl just tapped her finger to her lips repeatedly until I nodded my head. Then we moved on. We walked in silence, single file, along the smooth dirt path. Although the trail was well-worn, my feet were bare so I kept my eyes focused on where I was stepping.

It seemed we walked on and on that first night, going deeper and deeper into the woods. In reality it wasn't so terribly far. As the trees grew thicker, the trail became a bit rougher with rocks and weeds so I really needed to concentrate on my feet. I was startled when the girl in front of me stopped suddenly.

We had reached the summit of a small hill. From here, the path descended at a gentle decline before opening into a wide, grassy clearing next to Queer Creek. What I saw in the clearing made me gasp in delight.

Here the moonlight glistened wildly on the water, creating a river of tiny stars. While the surrounding trees remained outlines etched in silver, the open grass took on a deep green hue that glowed. And everywhere I looked the air was alive with fireflies.

The other girl skipped in circles, gently stirring the fireflies along her path. Me, I couldn't figure out where to focus or what to do. Stepping forward like a sleepwalker, I let my feet carry me to our ordinary muddy creek, magically transformed into a dazzling spectacle. The water was singing a song to me, reaching out to touch me. I think I said something like, "I wanna swim," and peeled my sweaty cotton nightgown over my head before dropping it on the grass.

Before I could reach the water's edge, my new playmate suddenly appeared in front of me, hands on hips.

"I'm Annabelle," she declared, pressing her right palm to the middle of her chest. "This is my place. Listen to me. Do what I tell you to do. I'll teach you to walk safely among the shadows."

I nodded and a wide devilish smile spread across her face.

"Atta girl! Life hiding from shadows ain't no kind of life.

What you have is a gift. Don't you let your grandmother smother your light under her fear."

With Annabelle standing guard, I took the first of many late night swims that night; the cool water thrilling against my bare skin. Then we both lay in the grass watching the lights of the fireflies flashing all around.

"They're telling insect secrets with those lights, you know?" Annabelle's voice sounded far away as my eyes grew heavy. "Uh oh, sleepy time. Time to go."

I followed her back along the forest trail, my feet stumbling with exhaustion. When we got to the cellar door, she turned to me and held out a pinky. I imitated the gesture and felt a surprisingly icy tug as she linked her pinky with mine.

"Remember. Listen to me. Do what I tell you to do. Don't do anything I tell you not to do. Learn the shadow and the light. Peel back the secrets. I'll do everything I can to help you. Deal?"

"Deal," I agreed, suddenly wide-awake.

"All right. Be careful and stay safe." Then she disappeared, my pinky was hooked around nothing but night air.

Over the years, she came back many times; always at night. She couldn't do anything to get me out of the house or back into it undetected, but once I entered her woods, we were always safe. And free. I'd never felt such exquisite freedom before and never have since. Usually we played together in the heat of summer, but she also loved jumping through autumn leaves and the sparkling enchantment of new fallen snow. We collected bugs and watched moonflowers bloom. We sang silly songs I'd never heard before, picked wildflowers I'd never seen before, and played games I'd never played before. She taught me how to make perfect snow angels, how to turn a cartwheel and how to braid my hair ... but she never taught me one single fact about the life she lived before she died. I knew her name was Annabelle, but I didn't know her last name. She never mentioned a parent or a sibling. She never told me how she ended up among the shadows of Moonville. On bad days, when the memories of Annabelle threaten to engulf me and my chest aches under the weight of the stupid mistakes I made, I can't help wondering if knowing Annabelle's story might have made a difference.

If she would have shared just a hint of her own personal tragedy, perhaps my whole life would be different now.

Lucy

When the sound of "Dirty Deeds Done Dirt Cheap" started ripping out of my phone at five in the morning, I jumped out of bed like my sheets were on fire and nearly cracked the touchscreen fumbling to answer.

Instead of hello, I mumbled, "Wha-izit?"

"Ahhh ... Lucy? Don't be mad, okay?"

Already there were three strikes against this call. First, the hour. Second, any conversation that started like that was almost certainly going to be ridiculous. And third, I didn't recognize the voice and was forced to squint at the screen for a hint.

When my eyes finally focused, the name still didn't make much sense to me. Elton Kidwell. My grandmother's next door neighbor for over forty years. Elton and I did not chat on the phone, had not seen each other, or spoken a single word for nearly six years. His number must have remained in my contacts list as some ancient relic from the first cell phone I'd ever owned. The same cell phone Ona

Kidwell had given me as high school graduation gift and programmed full of every "important" number in Moonville, Ohio. I thought I'd purged my contacts list of any Moonville memories. Damn it.

I pressed the phone back to my ear. Elton was chattering away like it was high noon and we were besties.

"Just thinkin' I better call and give you some warning—"

"I'm sorry," I cut in, my voice like rusty water leaking out of my mouth. "Why are you calling? Is this about my grandmother?"

"This is Elton. Elton Kidwell," he shouted. "Can you hear me?"

"I can hear you perfectly fine. Please stop shouting." I paused briefly between each word. "Are you calling to tell me there's something wrong with my grandmother?"

"No. Why do you ask?"

This was absolutely surreal.

"Elton? Are you sure you meant to call me?" I asked. "This is Lucy Sloan. Irene's granddaughter."

"Well, I know who you are. I called you didn't I?"

I closed my eyes and pictured the Elton from my happier childhood memories. I remembered summer afternoons on his front porch with orange soda floats. I remember how he endured endless games of Monopoly on Halloween night to keep me entertained while every other child in the county was out trick-or-treating. I remember him circling the back-yard in his riding mower and whistling "You Are My Sunshine" loud enough to be heard over the growl of his John Deere. Most of all, I remember the winter I turned fourteen. Other neighbors brought baked hams and soupy casseroles to the house after we buried Grandpa Max. Elton brought his antique chess set and a box of art supplies.

So I really did try to pour every ounce of tolerance I

could muster into my voice at five in the morning with the residue of sleep sticking to my mouth when I answered him.

"Yes, Elton. Yes, you did. Now why would I be mad at you? Did you run over someone with your lawn mower?"

"No way," he replied. "I'm not drinking right now."

"You mean you haven't cracked one open yet this morning?" I laughed. It was rare to see Elton without a can of Pabst Blue Ribbon clutched in his left hand.

"No way," Elton continued without any sign of offense. "I've got to stay in tiptop condition for this job. Even without the complications, it's a really big job. Got to be fit as a fiddle."

"You're working on a project, Elton? That's great!" I didn't need to fake the enthusiasm in my voice. "You know my grandfather used to say you're the DaVinci of landscapers."

"Oh, well, that Max was always one of those people full of words. Me, I'm not so good with words. They all seem to get backwards on me," he said. "Guess I better get to the point of why I'm calling you." He immediately fell silent.

"Go ahead, Elton. I'm listening," I assured him, yawning over the last word.

Well, hell, if I was going to be trapped in a weird pre-dawn telephone conversation with a voice from my past, I might as well get some caffeine in my system. Sliding my feet into the oversized furry slippers I'd kicked into the corner just four hours earlier, I shuffled the ten steps from my bed to the tiny galley kitchen and popped the magic button on my coffee maker, the central feature on my three feet of counter space. Still no word from the other end of the line.

"Elton, there really can't be any reason for me to be mad at you, can there?"

Dead silence continued to speak volumes from the other end of the line. I leaned my back against the counter and surveyed my tiny garage studio apartment. Jars and tubes of acrylic colors and gel medium littered every horizontal surface, giving evidence of the previous night's work. In the middle of it all, the canvas that had kept me from sleep stood on my battered easel, finally finished. Now I needed to get the image online as another teaser for my crowd funding campaign.

"Elton?"

"I'm still here, Lucy," he answered. "I'm just stuck for the best way to get at this thing. The job ain't been going so well."

"I'm sorry to hear that, but—"

"Look, it ain't right, Lucy! I know you say they're harmless, and I ain't got anything against any kind of kids. You know that, right? But you can't even have normal kids running around a site. Everyone knows that. Thing is, it ain't only a matter of keeping them safe. Normal kids, I mean. It's about keeping the workmen safe, too. And see that there is the problem."

A terrible suspicion was starting to loom in the back of my mind, chasing away any sense of calm I'd manage to recover since the phone woke me from a deep sleep.

"There's a problem with an unattended child at the house you're working on, Elton?"

Even as I said it, I knew that was the wrong explanation, but I still had a glimmer of hope I wasn't reading this conversation correctly. "Can't you talk to a parent or—?"

Elton burst out in a fit of laughter that sounded like a cat spitting up a hairball. "How am I supposed to find a parent, Lucy? That's why I'm calling you. Maybe you can find 'em or at least figure out what the little one wants."

"Elton, please tell me the child you're talking about isn't dead."

Silence.

"Oh, shit, Elton! You can't be serious. What is this job? You aren't working for those imbeciles who are ruining Quinn Mansion, aren't you?"

Again, his silence did the talking.

"Oh no. No, sir," I sputtered, unable to swallow my anger. "Leave me out of this."

"It's not that anyone working on the project is stupid," Elton said slowly, "more like ... not very smart about ... you know, the nitty-gritty practical stuff."

"Okay, fine. I'm not going to argue with you about what constitutes stupidity. But every single person who has the misfortune of dealing with Xia Celeste agrees—she is a rude, loud, condescending, and absolutely miserable human being."

"She can get nasty," Elton agreed. I imagined him bobbing his head up and down in huge, exaggerated nods. "Sure can! She made my son's life miserable for a few years. But she is the mother of my grand baby. Anyway, Xia is not the problem I'm calling about. It's this kid a poppin' up wherever I least expect. You could fix that."

"No, Elton."

"I almost put a nail through my foot first time the little bugger crept up on me. Day before yesterday, I nearly fell off the porch roof. You got to talk to this girl, Lucy. Least ways I think it's a little girl, but I can't really get my eyes fastened on her, you know? You got to help her to find rest, or peace, or whatever."

"I said no, Elton." A sudden realization hit me. "And what were you doing on the roof? You're a landscaper. There's no rooftop gardens at Quinn Mansion."

"Had to get up on the roof to tarp it. Contractor can't keep people on the job. They all run off like a bunch of teenagers in a cemetery. Can't leave a big old gaping hole with the rain coming. Lucy, I can't afford to get laid up in the hospital with a broken leg ... or worse. You know my Daisy beagle won't eat one piece of solid food unless I'm there to fix it nice. Besides, you don't want the Quinn place to stay empty and rot to pieces, do ya? These California people can't afford to keep hiring workers only to have them all run off the property."

I took a deep breath to calm the rising surge of anger pulsing through my skull. "Answer me this – how exactly did the great Xia treat you when you told her that a ghost was ruining her renovations?"

Another long pause. "You know how she is," Elton muttered. "Said something about that bein' the draw of the property."

"Exactly. They are shooting a ridiculous reality TV show about turning Quinn Mansion into some kind of resort for ghost hunters. It's all over the internet. They wanted a haunted house. They convinced the Quinn Trustees to give them free reign over that house. If they can't handle the haunt, that's not my problem. I'm not going to play amateur ghost whisperer for Xia Celeste, and she doesn't want me there stealing her screen time."

"Dang it," Elton said with uncharacteristic force. "This isn't just about Xia and her ways. My granddaughter is embroiled in this mess. I was so sure you'd come and help us out."

I took another deep breath and tried to come at this from another angle. "Listen, Elton, maybe you can find someone else to help you. Try looking up paranormal investigators on the internet."

"You want me to talk to a stranger about ... about this stuff?" The last three words were spoken in a whisper.

"There are people out there who do this sort of thing all the time. Get out there and look for them. I can't get involved. That place is like ... it's like my own personal kryptonite. You know what I mean?"

"No. You always loved that place. We could never keep you off the property."

I walked back to my bed and sat on the edge, left arm folded across my body. "Yes, and it caused me all kinds of trouble. Big trouble. Legal trouble, Elton. I ended up in front of a judge who told me I was never, ever allowed to step foot on that property again. Never. Not for any reason." I paused, waiting.

"Which judge did you get?" he asked.

"That doesn't matter, the point is—"

"I don't think any judge can make you stay away from a place if the property's custodian invites you there. Sounds like a pretty dumb judge. Was it Mickleburg?"

"No, it was Harrison, but you're missing—"

"Harrison? You're talking about juvenile court?" he asked, and started up on a long fit of his hairball laughter. "You're twenty-four now, girl. Harrison retired and that juvie file is sealed anyways."

"Elton!" I yelled, unable to find even an ounce of patience. "Forget the judge. I thought you might listen to me if I brought up the law. I can't help you with this. In case you haven't noticed, and judging by this conversation you have not, I don't live in Moonville. I have not stepped foot in Moonville for over five years. I do not speak to my grandmother. I haven't spoken to her in over five years. I want nothing to do with either Irene Sloan or Moonville. That means I can't swing by to chat with you and your little girl ghost up at Quinn Mansion."

"I could have sworn she said you were coming," Elton said softly.

"Who told you I was coming?"

"The little one. Seems like she might know you."

Silence returned as my anger drained away into a puddle of shame. *Coward!* my inner demons raged. *Quinn Mansion is being pillaged and stripped of everything that was magical and wonderful. Why am I pretending this isn't the end of my world?* I thrust my fingers through the hair at the base of my skull and tugged sharply to keep myself from screaming.

On the other end of the line, Elton was backing down, full of apologies. Fighting the sting of unshed tears, I only caught bits and pieces of what he was saying.

"... really stupid of me ... internet at the library ... just ask the librarian for some help finding some paranoid investigators. Sorry, Lucy."

"Paranormal investigators," I corrected him. "I'll spell it, you write it down."

After I got off the phone with Elton Kidwell, sleep was impossible. Any constructive activity was impossible. I poured a cup of coffee and simply sat on the floor, knees tucked under my chin. The inky sky outside my windows brightened to pearly morning twilight. The first glaring sunbeam found me sitting in exactly the same position, staring at a tepid mug of untouched coffee on the floor in front of me. The unbearable brightness in the room finally prodded me to move. Instead of heading for the shower though, I shuffled my way down the stairs to the garage below my apartment.

Two walls of the garage were covered with floor-to-ceiling storage shelves. I had yet to develop any reliable filing system to quickly locate a certain piece among all my completed canvases, but it wasn't hard to spot the canvas I was looking for. It was the only one wrapped in black fabric and tied with blue ribbon.

Hugging the bundle to my chest, I ascended back to my apartment and replaced last night's completed work with the wrapped piece, but I couldn't make myself unwrap it immediately. First, I dumped my cold coffee down the drain and poured a fresh cup. Then I circled the room, sipping and staring at the bundle from every possible angle. I'd wrapped it in black velvety material years before and had refused to look at it since. Now it seemed to be buzzing with something that made my skin tingle. Finally, I swallowed a huge intake of breath, set down my coffee, and forced myself to walk up to the easel. One careful slice with a mat knife, and the ribbon fell away.

When I originally created this canvas, during my senior year of high school, I called it *Thou Shalt Not*. Although it was originally intended to be part of my portfolio submission to art school, the work evolved into my own twisted version of therapy at a time when I was drowning in a rancid pool of self-pity. The end result was the one piece I'd never hung on a wall or shared with another living soul.

The central feature—a mosaic of black and white images cut up and arranged to re-create my mother's tombstone—was bad enough. *Helena Sloan. Born September 3, 1965. Died October 20th, 1993. Beloved Daughter.* Down the left side, torn pieces of newspaper articles about her murder were pieced together with ripped family photos to form a border of thorny roses. An antique Ouija board etched on transparent film overlay the entire canvas; an afterthought intended to soften the harsh visual impact. But the element that riveted my attention that morning, the image I'd shuffled down to the garage to retrieve, was an inked sketch depicting the peaked roof, arched windows, and turreted tower of a gothic Victorian mansion along the right side of the canvas.

Someone unfamiliar with Quinn Mansion might not recognize the architectural elements, but they were as familiar to me as my own childhood home. Much to my own amazement, the sight didn't bring a surge of anxiety or tighten my throat with dread. I poked at my own memories, looking for any remnant of the raw shame that the house had once symbolized. All I seemed to feel was a weird, muted ache of longing.

When I finally pulled myself away from admiring my own emotional garbage, I walked into the shower cushioned by a bubble of detachment. Not my problem. That's what I'd told Elton. And for a few brief, lovely hours I was able to maintain that illusion.

ABOUT THE AUTHOR

Trisha Slay grew up in a haunted house located near the heart of the Buckeye State. She currently lives in the North Georgia Mountains where she divides her time between ensuring everyone on the planet has the opportunity to pause for refreshment every day, hunting down true ghost stories, and dreaming up new White Crow Mysteries. When she's not hunched over a computer, she enjoys hiking in the national forest with her husband and rescue dogs. She also loves exploring all aspects of Star Wars geekery, visiting historic cemeteries, photographing wildflowers, helping homeless pets, and sampling red wine. However, she's learned the hard way that writing about restless spirits while drinking Zinfandel can result in wicked nightmares.

Connect with Trisha:
www.trishaslay.com

facebook.com/TrishaSlayAuthor

twitter.com/SlaytheWriter

instagram.com/slaythewriter

pinterest.com/slayzak

goodreads.com/Trisha_Slay

amazon.com/author/trishaslay

ALSO BY TRISHA SLAY

White Crow Short Fiction:

Haunting Las Vegas

Mystique

Grimm Beaker

Note: All White Crow short fiction stories are available as FREE ebooks to my email subscribers. Go to www.trishaslay.com/subscribe to claim your free books.

Novels:

Unbroken (White Crow Book 2 - Coming in 2019)

Not So Long Ago, Not So Far Away